It's not just a book about love; it also tackles the importance of family ties and Kim's relationship with the people around her. The story was a rollercoaster ride, and I really enjoyed reading this book. Very satisfying ending.

-Gee Arra, *Goodreads*


I absolutely love this book. This is truly an artwork. I was so into it that I finished reading it in two days.

-Miriya Little, *Goodreads*


A Hundred Weddings by Jessica Schreave is an effervescent, pick me-up romantic novel. With a pinch of humour, whirlwind of emotions and exciting drama, the author made the book hundred times worth reading it! The plot and strong writing make this novel memorable.

-Shreya, *Goodreads*


A book which I thoroughly enjoyed reading. Jessica has woven the story in an amazing way.

-Simmi Samantara, *Goodreads*

**Typewriter Pub**, an imprint of Blvnp Incorporated
A Nevada Corporation
1887 Whitney Mesa DR #2002
Henderson, NV 89014
www.typewriterpub.com/info@typewriterpub.com

ISBN: **978-1-64434-029-5**

**DISCLAIMER**

This book is a work of fiction. The characters, incidents, and dialogue are drawn from the author's imagination and are not to be construed as real. While references might be made to actual historical events or existing locations, the names, characters, places, and incidents are either products of the author's imagination or are used fictitiously, and any resemblance to actual persons living or dead, business establishments, events or locales is entirely coincidental.

# A HUNDRED WEDDINGS

JESSICA SHCREAVE

*For my very supportive parents, Gemma and Romeo, I love you both so much!*

# FREE DOWNLOAD

Get these freebies and more when you sign up for
the author's mailing list!

*jessica-schreave.awesomeauthors.org*

# PART I: THE ENGAGEMENT
## Chapter I

KIM

"You failed your exam, *again.*"

Mr. Jeremy Bradshaw, my math teacher, glares across the desk and furiously slides my test paper towards me, almost sending it flying if it weren't for my quick hands slamming it back on the desk. I cautiously eye the paper and notice the big red F on the right side.

I sigh, return my gaze to him, and merely shrug.

"I'm sorry, but I just don't think we'd be using Calculus in real life, so why bother putting much effort to it?" It was a lame response. Honestly, I was just too busy stalking boy bands on their Instagram profiles the night before the exam.

He pinches the bridge of his nose. "This is your third time taking this test, and you still haven't passed it, Ms. Roberts." He scoots forward and stares directly at me with his intense sea green eyes. "And this is the third time I've told you this: Please. Take. This. Seriously." He emphasizes each word with a firm pause.

"Maybe a thousand dollars will make you change that F to at least a C minus?"

My math teacher glowers at me as if I've just uttered the stupidest thing he's ever heard.

I've never really been good at math, but I also never failed that subject. I lived off with Bs in grade school, and I'm pretty satisfied with that. But high school teachers decided that it would

1

be fantastic to mix various symbols with numbers, and I learned to accept Cs since freshman year.

But just when I think it's my last year to endure math, this arrogant twelfth-grade math teacher thinks he can change the world by giving out difficult pop quizzes and exams.

"How many times do I have to tell you that I don't need your money?" He crosses his arms, making me notice the visible lines of his chest through his thin white V-neck shirt. "Do you want me to call your dad?"

"Tattletale," I mumble.

He scoffs. "Oh, I'm so going to call your dad, young lady."

I raise an eyebrow. "Do it. I don't really care."

My dad is always in various business meetings, hence his phone is turned off almost all the time. If there's an emergency, I just have to call his secretary, which I'm a hundred percent sure this teacher has no knowledge of.

His jaw clenches. "You're getting a math tutor."

"I won't pay for it." Money isn't really an issue for me, but I refuse to be taught by someone who's probably just a suck up to teachers so they could ace a subject.

"You don't have to. I'm going to pay for her tutoring services." I roll my eyes. "As your teacher, I'm saddened that I'm failing to educate you well, so I'm doing the best I can to rectify this situation."

I want to pull my hair out. Can he not really get it? I hate Senior Math because we won't even use Calculus in real life unless someone wants to be an engineer or something. I don't think anyone can help me ignore the insignificance of this subject.

"Fine. Do whatever you want. Can I go now?" I just want to leave his office before my frustration gets ahold of me and I do something stupid like break my teacher's nose or pull out all his teeth. Or probably both.

"Yes," he answers, and I'm about to stand up when he unexpectedly adds, "I'll talk to Hailey next week about your tutoring schedule so you can both start within this month."

I sit back on the chair and gape at him. "The hell you are!"

"Miss Hailey West is an excellent student, and I'm sure she can help you with your…issues. My decision is final. You can go now."

"We'll kill each other before you can even blink!" I hate that girl as much as Mr. Krabs despises Plankton, and Mr. Bradshaw knows this. "You're punishing me, aren't you?"

He does not retract. "I said you can leave now, Ms. Roberts." The tension thickens, and I give him one last dirty look before standing up and heading towards the door, slamming it loudly behind me.

Ugh. Who does he even think he is? It's not my fault I can't understand a single thing that comes out of his mouth that has been blabbering nonsense about numbers for the past two months.

The only good thing about him is that he's handsome and maybe a little hot with his chiseled arms and all. But I'm not going to let him know that. That'll only inflate his already gigantic ego.

My best friend, Ella, is waiting for me outside the wooden door. "Everything okay, I hope?" She's wearing the usual school uniform: a black coat with the school logo on the left, an above-the-knee black skirt, and white socks that reach her knees; a Gucci bag strapped around her body as her arms press books close to her chest.

Ella and I met in second grade when she was still a new student in Weatherford Elementary. And like any typical new student, she had no idea how to make friends, so I did it for her and sat beside her during lunch break with my peanut butter and jelly sandwich and talked nonsense with her. We've been inseparable since then.

"Yeah, I just failed my exam. Nothing unusual," I say with a forced smile.

"Aw, that's okay. I'm sure you did your best with that test, and that's what matters." She's such an optimist. "Oh, I know! Let's have a Leonardo DiCaprio marathon at my place. Just let me put these in my locker." I let her pull me through the hallway until she suddenly stops in a corner, causing me to stumble on my feet.

"He's here," she mumbles.

"Who?"

"You know who."

I gasp. "Voldemort?"

She glares at me. "No, you idiot."

Ella cocks her head to the right, and I follow her gaze.

Oh.

"Kyle." I put my palms over my cheeks to hide the reddening of my face. He's so hot.

"He's just standing there beside our lockers," she murmurs then changes her tone immediately. "Oh my gosh! What if he's waiting for you?"

The dashing, the ever charming Kyle Wilson. He's everyone's typical good-looking boy-next-door with his copper brown hair that rightly frames his attractive face, perfectly sculpted nose, and plush kissable lips. He's also sweet, caring, and funny, which makes more girls swoon all over him. Including me.

But of course, if he asks me if I love him, I'd lie.

Kyle and I were once close friends back in grade school, together with Ella and a few kids. Then high school happened, and everything changed. He became part of the popular group, since he's our school quarterback, while Ella and I are stuck as wimpy teenagers.

"Oh shoot, there's The Leech," Ella says in disgust.

Hailey, also known to us as "The Leech," saunters towards Kyle and wraps her arms around his neck. Hailey West is our stereotypical campus queen bee with long dark hair, a pretty face, a curvy figure, and long tanned legs, which have been wrapped around countless men. But one thing that's not stereotypical about her is that she's a straight-A student. "Beauty and Brains" is what they call her.

She is a mixture of black and white American, which makes her more attractive in the eyes of everyone in this whitewashed

4

school. But we don't hate her because she's beautiful and we're a duo of insecure bleached-looking girls. There are also several students here of different races, and they're all nice. We dislike Hailey because she is dating the best guy on campus while also seeing other boys, and that's just so wrong.

We try to ignore them as we reach our lockers.

"It sucks that we have different classes. I missed you," Hailey says as she slowly puts her finger on his face. I try not to grimace.

"Yeah?" he replies huskily before planting his lips on hers. Instead of being more irritated, I suppress a smile when I notice Ella's repulsed face.

"Some people just don't realize the difference between a hallway and a room," Ella says as she continues to arrange her stuff.

Hailey rolls her eyes at us. "Fine. I heard the janitor just left his closet."

Kyle clears his throat and carefully pushes her away. "Uh...I'm not in the mood today."

"What? Why?" Hailey pouts, wrapping her arms around his waist. Ella then slams her locker shut and faces them with an aggressive expression.

Oh no.

"Because you're a walking leech," Ella says with a forced smile that takes us all by surprise.

With no hesitation, I clutch her elbow and drag her away from them. I know if she utters another foul word, they'll both end up in the office or in the hospital, whichever comes first.

"Kyle can do much better than her," Ella comments once we're a few feet away from them.

"Let's just go," I tell her as I grip the straps of my bag on my shoulders. We make our way to the parking lot and climb inside my Porsche since Ella's cousin is borrowing her car.

I am about to start the engine when my iPhone buzzes on the dashboard. The text is from my dad telling me to come home early because he has important news for me. I sigh and tell my best friend to postpone our Friday tradition. She takes the news with a childish pout.

I drop her off in front of their wide metal gates, and she waves me goodbye with a sad smile. We were really looking forward to that Leonardo DiCaprio movie marathon with barbecue-flavored Lays and Cheetos in our stomachs.

*Really bad timing, Dad.*

Once I arrive home, I see my dad sitting on the couch with a laptop. I kiss him on his left cheek then sit beside him, curious about what he is doing.

"How was your day, sweetheart?" he asks as he turns to kiss me on my forehead.

"It was alright," I answer nonchalantly.

"That's good." He then closes his laptop and places it on the coffee table in front of us. "Baby, we need to talk." And with that statement, random images about all the things I've done in the past days flash in my mind.

Oh no, what did I do now?

"Uh, why?"

"Kim, I—"

But I interrupt before he even reprimands me.

"Dad if this is about failing my math test again, I'm really sorry, but please don't take away my phone for a week again," I say, almost out of breath.

"What?" He sounds genuinely surprised. Oops. I guess it's not what he wants to talk about.

I shake my head quickly. "Nothing, Dad." I show him an innocent smile. "You were saying?" I really hope whatever he has in mind right now would make him ignore what I just said.

He heavily sighs. "Okay, um, how should I say this?" He tightly closes his eyes like he is thinking of the right words to say then opens them again. "For the past few months, our company's revenue has been decreasing drastically." I notice an obvious disappointment on his face.

"I'm so sorry, Daddy. If there's anything you want me to do, then don't hesitate to tell me." I hate seeing my dad this disappointed. He's been in so much pain and stress, and it hurts me to see him like this.

He squeezes my hand. "Well, there's one thing you could do."

My heart heavily pounds in my chest. "What is it, Dad?"

Why do I feel like I won't like what he'll be saying next? I hold my breath as he purses his lips and hesitantly replies to my question.

"Marry the Lincoln Corporation's heir."

# Chapter 2

My mom was killed in a car crash.

It was a peaceful Sunday morning, December 12, 2004, in Los Angeles, and I was in my dad's office at home playing with my dolls when the phone rang. My dad automatically pressed the loudspeaker as he worked on his laptop, thinking it was merely a business call.

At the age of four, I still didn't know what the words *passed away* meant, but the sadness in the nurse's tone made me stop combing my Barbie's hair. I confusedly glanced at my dad whose voice cracked when he told the nurse he'll be on his way.

Everything was pretty much a blur after the call. But the image of my dad falling on his knees as he pulled me in a tight embrace, crying in agony, is still perfectly encrypted in my mind. My four-year-old self wanted to ask what happened, but perhaps my heart knew it already. We cried together. I told my dad it'll be okay although I wasn't really sure what was happening.

My fifth birthday was the next day, December 13, and instead of blowing a pink candle on a chocolate cake, I lighted a big white candle for my mom's funeral. Instead of wearing a blue ball gown, I chose to wear a black dress, since I saw people wearing it too. And instead of guests singing me "Happy Birthday," we played all my mom's favorite tunes in the audio player.

I cried myself to sleep on my birthday because a sudden realization kicked in—my mommy wouldn't be kissing me goodnight anymore.

We buried her five days later on my parents' wedding anniversary.

Apparently, my mom was on her way to her ob-gyn because approximately two hours before the accident, three pregnancy sticks showed her positive results, and she immediately scheduled for a doctor's appointment. She did arrive at the hospital, although sadly, for a different reason. Her gynecologist told us that my mom was so excited on the phone. She was planning to surprise my dad on their wedding anniversary once her second pregnancy was confirmed. As it turned out, she was indeed, which broke my dad's heart even more.

The man who was driving the vehicle that killed my mom was the younger brother of the current president of the Lincoln Corporation. Although the said brother was immediately put behind bars, they used their money to reduce his sentence to three years. They must have bribed the judge or something; no one really knows for sure. All I know is that the Lincoln family is a bunch of selfish pricks with no souls. My dad and I couldn't do anything because they're obviously more powerful than us. I wanted to curse the world for its unfairness.

Lincoln Corporation and Golden Shovel Properties were once sister companies. Our forefathers were family friends, helping each other as they developed lands throughout America. But after the accident and the obvious bribery, my dad broke off the friendship and competed with them instead. For thirteen years, we contended to be the best land developer in America.

So, no one can really blame me for my aversion towards this arrangement.

Because he's got to be kidding, right?

"What?" I screech, shooting my dad one of my death glares. "But they're your rivals! They're like Apple and we're Samsung!" My mind fumbles around various possible reasons as I process what he's trying to imply. This has to be a joke. It has to be.

"I know, but they heard of our quandary, and they're willing to help." Wrinkles on his face become more evident as he tries to persuade his daughter, and part of me wants to give in to his request just so I can take away his strain. But I remain in my stance.

"With a catch, of course," I frantically mutter. "Why in the world would they want me to marry their son in the first place?"

"Because it will strengthen the security of our partnership with them."

"That doesn't make sense at all. But, Dad, you can't just give me away to some stranger."

"I'll never do that without your consent." Why do I feel like there's more to this than he lets on?

"We've never even met this heir of theirs."

"I'm sure he's a nice guy." He stares at me with his powerful, convincing eyes. I stand up from my seat and gape at him incredulously.

"Are you serious right now, Dad?" This is absolutely ridiculous, for Pete's sake!

My dad tries to reach for my hand, but I back away. His face falls from my reaction. "I'm not forcing you to marry anyone. I'm only asking if you're willing to help the company by marrying someone."

"I'm barely eighteen. I haven't even finished high school yet." I glower at him.

"You're gonna be eighteen soon," he replies. "Just think about it, okay?"

I pause and shake my head. "Don't get your hopes up, Dad."

I go straight to my room to find my peace of mind.

~

Five days have passed, but I never relented to my dad's ridiculous request although he kept bringing it up whenever he had the chance—like while I was watching TV in the living room last Saturday morning. He brought three bags of Cheetos then asked me if I have thought about it yet. I said no.

Also, during our dinner last Monday when he let our chef cook all of my favorite food. He even bribed me with the latest model of Porsche. I almost said yes.

But I did agree on meeting the Lincoln family for a Friday dinner. Dad said it'll only be for us to get to know each other more. No need to make any final decision just yet. It'll be a simple dinner meeting with our former close family friend who became our rivals.

And like I said, my dad shouldn't get his hopes up, since I'm never going to get married this soon. I'm still pining over the same guy I've had a crush on since kindergarten.

"What are you doing with your hotdog?" Ella scolds me, forcing me to look down on my plate and see the little pieces of beef meat strewn all over it.

Oh. I didn't realize I was already butchering the hotdog, since I was too busy looking at the wicked witch of the west, aka Hailey West, sitting in the far end table with the basketball team. Is she cheating on *my* Kyle?

How dare she! I really want to drag her by the hair out of this room right now. If she can't stay loyal to Kyle, then she better just break up with him, instead of publicly showing how he's not enough for her.

"It's an animal graveyard on your plate." Ella reprimands me as she stares at the fried chicken and chopped hotdog in front of me. Ella is a vegetarian, so, there's that. "I'm so sorry for your death," she whispers to them.

"The hotdog is already dead. It has no feelings anymore." I jeer at her.

"Just be ready for the hotdog ghosts that will take their revenge on the people who killed and ate them."

I grin for a second. Ella can be really childish sometimes.

"Hi, Kim. May I sit beside you?"

Ella and I immediately freeze when we hear *his* voice.

*Please, oh please, tell me I'm not dreaming.*

We both turn our heads in slow-motion to look at the guy who just spoke. I secretly pinch my arm to wake me up and check if this is just one of my daydreams again.

Ouch! Yup, this is all real.

"Uh, sure." I beam at Kyle as I scoot to my left side, giving him enough space to sit and enough space for me to breathe. I think my heart is going to explode any minute now.

I feel my knees shaking, stomach churning, and palms soaking with sweat. I want to face-palm myself.

*You're so embarrassing, Kim! Can't you act normal just this once?*

"Thanks." He places his tray on the table, sighing. "Sorry to disturb you though. I just don't want to be a loner at a lunch table." He grants me his charming smile, making me catch my breath. "The guys are currently training."

I'm busy staring at his tantalizing hazel eyes, so Ella is the one who asks, "Why aren't you training with them?" I'm so lucky that my best friend can also be my spokesperson.

"I'm just not in the mood. Hailey and I had a fight last Saturday," Kyle responds and sighs. "She just can't stop hanging out with random guys. But I guess I just have to live with it, right?" He looks at me and gives me another one of his heart-warming smiles, but I know it's a forced one.

This is what I was talking about earlier.

Every time Hailey hangs out with different guys, Kyle is always the one who is left alone and dejected, all because he's too nice and sweet to cheat on her for revenge. I think he'd rather be alone in a corner than be unfaithful to his girlfriend.

"Is she cheating on you?" I know it's a rude question, but I need to know if he's aware of his girlfriend's true nature.

"She told me she's not."

"And you believe her?" Ella scoffs. "I mean, look at her laughing with those guys as if you're not here."

He shrugs. "Sometimes I don't know what to believe in anymore."

I quirk an eyebrow. "But why are you still with her if you have your suspicions?"

"Because we're perfect for each other. Well, that's what everyone is telling us. The charming quarterback and the sexy straight-A student. We belong together, they say."

*You belong with me*, I want to tell him.

But instead, I say, "Oh, that's just stupid."

Quoting a song is probably not the best idea to confess my unrequited feelings for him. I'll only look more pathetic than I already am.

After a few minutes of chatting and teasing and a few heart-stopping moments, the bell finally rings.

"See you later, girls. It's really nice talking to you both again," Kyle says as he hauls himself up. I want to convince him to stay longer, but I immediately disregard that thought and just wave him goodbye.

"You do realize that you were such a helpless phony for the last twenty minutes, right?" Ella chuckles. I know that. She doesn't have to rub it in my face.

"He's just so hot." I search for the lip-gloss inside my bag. I take out all my books with frustration and surprisingly find it at the bottom. "Aha!"

"Small things like that shouldn't really be in the books compartment." She chuckles. "You do know your bag has a front pocket, right?"

I ignore her as I apply the pink gloss on my lips. Kyle and I might not be in the same class today, but there's a possibility I might run into him again.

"Let's just go. We still need to—" I give a panicky glance at the clock on the cafeteria wall.

"We only have two minutes left before class starts!" Ella shrieks. I simply put some books inside and carry the thin ones, since it will probably take too much time to put them all in. We hurriedly stand up from our seats and dash in the hallway like kids being chased by angry dogs.

"Ouch!" I accidentally bump my head against someone's chin.

My books fly out of my arms and onto the floor.

"Ms. Roberts, Ms. Summers, what are you still doing here? Class starts in a minute," Mr. Bradshaw, our math teacher, asks as he rubs his chin. I don't answer and decide to just pick up my books from the floor.

After I'm sure I picked them all up, Ella and I run down the hallway again. "Ms. Roberts! Your—" he shouts, but I don't bother to look back.

I'll just deal with whatever I left there later. I don't want to be late for history class, the only subject I enjoy because of that funny teacher—unlike that grouchy math teacher.

# Chapter 3

"Mr. Bradshaw is becoming more handsome every day, don't you think?" Ella giggles under her breath from her seat. I scowl at her and give her a 'shut up' look. "Oh c'mon, everybody's talking about him, too" she adds.

I look at our teacher who is busy discussing numbers on the board. My eyes trace his tall, broad body: from his unruly, dirty blond hair down to his glossy black shoes. His eyes are warm and serious.

Nope, nothing new about him. I glance back to my friend who is already busy daydreaming of our teacher. "Stop ogling over him, or you'll have your own drool all over your desk," I say in a low voice.

Yeah, I know he's handsome and tall and smart and almost perfect, but that doesn't mean people should swoon all over him all day.

"I'm not ogling. I'm just admiring. I wonder if he already has a girlfriend or maybe a wife. I'm sure she's so lucky."

I squirm. I definitely doubt that.

"Whoever that girl is, I'm pretty darn sure she is so unlucky."

"Ms. Roberts and Ms. Summers, would you mind sharing your conversation with the class?" Mr. Bradshaw unexpectedly chimes in. We just gape at him in embarrassment for a good ten seconds. "I guess not. Kimberly Roberts, in my office after class."

My jaw drops. What the heck is wrong with him?

"But, Mr. Bradshaw!" This is so unfair.

15

"Mr. Bradshaw, I was talking too." Ella protests.

*You go, girl! We will endure this like sisters.*

"No buts." Mr. Bradshaw turns his back to us.

If looks could kill, the one I just shot him would probably have him six feet underground.

~

Wow, I never thought Mr. Bradshaw's office doorknob would look so shiny. And no, I am not using this beautiful doorknob as an excuse to not enter his office. Nothing's wrong with admiring objects, right?

*Yeah, keep telling yourself that.*

*Why am I even talking to myself? Ugh, I'm so pathetic.*

I knock three times on the wooden door.

*Please don't be inside. Please don't be inside. Please don't be inside,* I chant inside my head with each knock.

"Come in," he answers.

Oh well, there goes my prayer.

I slowly open the door and peek inside, checking if it's safe to enter. Who knows what this egotistical jerk is capable of.

"Take a seat, Ms. Roberts." He gestures to the chair in front of his desk, so I do.

"Mr. Bradshaw, before you could say anything else, I would like to clarify to you that we were talking about the lecture you were discussing." Yeah, I'm a complete liar. "And besides, Ella was talking too. Why didn't you call her name?"

He's just looking at the familiar notebook he's holding, scanning the pages warily. Great. Just great.

"Sir, I really need to go home." I grip the edge of his desk, trying to get his attention.

"Here." He slides a notebook on his table towards me.

Wait…what in the world? How did my diary get in here?

"You left that on the floor when we bumped at each other yesterday."

This is so bad. This is really, really bad. Like end-of-my-world bad.

"D-di-did y-you…did you read it?" I reach out for my diary. My legs start to tremble that I'm sure there would be pee all over the floor any minute now.

*Please say no.*

"Well, I just scanned the pages, but I didn't read it…much," he answers, and I gulp. "But one page caught my attention. That's why I read everything on it. I saw my name."

And instantly, my breath hitches again.

"And you read about what, sir?" I ask anxiously.

"I think it was something about having a crush on me on the first day of class?" He leans closer, grinning.

*Kill me now, please.*

I can still remember how I described him in my diary.

> *Dear diary,*
>
> *OMG! I just met that hot teacher everyone was talking about! His name is Jeremy Bradshaw and he's just so bae! And he glanced at me! I swear, he glanced at me! For like two seconds, we had sparks. OMFG I want to marry him and have his beautiful babies, maybe 3 insanely attractive babies. I hope we have twins. That'll be so cute because he's just so damn gorgeous and hot! Did I mention he's hot? Like, <u>super-hot</u>! Ugh. His jaws. Ugh. And his arms. His arms look so strong. I hope he finds me pretty. And I really wish I'd get to hug him before I graduate. Good luck to me!*
>
> *Love, Kim*
> *P.S. Do you think he's single?*

I just want to repeatedly hit my head on the desk. My redundant use of the word *hot* to describe him that time makes me want to die in humiliation.

Two months ago, I was charmed by this teacher's good looks. Now, all five and six inches of me hates this bigheaded nutjob who always embarrasses me in front of the class.

"It was all just a joke." I deny, embracing my diary close to my chest. I really need to secure this thing.

Water. I need water. I need water to drown myself.

"Hmm, sure. Whatever you say." He pushes back in his seat and humorously stares at me.

He really finds this amusing, huh?

"Is that all, Mr. Bradshaw?"

So, he just called me to his office just to give my diary back?

"Yes. Unless you have something else in mind?" He smirks. "Maybe confess your undying love to your *bae*?"

My ears instantly heat up, and I just want to dig my own grave right now.

"Shut up." I stand up from my seat and dash towards the door, but before I could even reach for the knob, he speaks again.

"And Ms. Roberts?"

I turn to him with a glare. "What?"

"I'm very much single." He goads me, humor evident in his eyes as he stifles laughter.

*Swallow me now, Earth. Just swallow me and never bring me back.*

I slam his door behind me and cover my face. Greek gods in Olympus, why?

Maybe I should just drop out, move to a foreign land, change my name and never return.

Gah! I hate two-months-ago Kimberly.

Once I regain a bit of calm by internally screaming , I rush towards the corridors that are currently trafficked with students huddling around their lockers, getting ready to leave school. Thankfully, I instantly spot the girl I love the most walking with a bag hanging on her shoulder, looking down at her cell phone. I scurry to catch her, but someone clutches my elbow, bringing me to a complete halt.

"Whoa! Hello there, sunshine." Hailey greets me, a hateful smile on her lips.

"What do you want?"

She tightens her grip around my arm, making me flinch.

"Stay away from Kyle. He's mine."

18

I raise an eyebrow at her. She was the one who was busy flirting with the basketball team, and now she's accusing me of flirting with Kyle? She is one crazy girl.

"I wasn't flirting with him."

"Oh please, everyone knows you have a crush on my boyfriend."

I instantly pull my arm away from her hold.

"Accuse me with whatever you want, Hailey. At least I don't cheat on my boyfriend like you always do."

Because I've never had one.

I walk away from her and saunter towards my best friend, who is probably standing beside my locker by now, waiting for me.

"Hey," I call out once I'm in her earshot. Her head instantly looks up, and her eyes show she wants to find out what happened. I enter the code to my locker, which then clicks unbolted. Inside sits my pouch and a few books, undisturbed and in the same position as I left them this morning. I bring out the two books I need to study tonight.

"So, what happened in the office? I'm really sorry if—" I don't let her finish and give her my diary instead. "Why are you giving me your diary?"

"Remember when we ran into Mr. Bradshaw yesterday and I dropped my books on the floor? Well, guess what? Of all the books that I could've forgotten to pick up, why does it have to be my diary?" I angrily close my locker door, leaving a loud bang behind it.

"Calm down, Kim. Maybe Mr. Bradshaw respected your privacy and he..." I shoot her an annoyed look, and she instantly knows what I mean. "He read your diary, didn't he?"

"Yes! Like, who does that? He didn't respect my privacy! He already knew that it was my diary. He shouldn't have opened it!"

Before I can whine any further, I feel something vibrating in my pocket. I dig for my phone as I groan.

Dad: *We have a meeting with the Lincoln family tonight. I sent our family driver there to make sure you come home early. I'll have another driver get your car later.*

Oh, I almost forgot about our dinner tonight.

"I need to go. My dad's waiting for me," I tell Ella. She nods and smiles at me then gets back to her phone.

I wonder whom she's been texting these past few days.

I scamper out the campus and to the parking lot where my driver is waiting for me outside. He politely opens the car door for me, and I unhappily climb in.

# Chapter 4

I check myself in the mirror, making sure I look decent but not desirable. The last thing I want is for the Lincoln heir to have a crush on me. Although, admittedly, I'm one of those girls who look like a homeless person when not wearing BB cream or lip-gloss. I'm not pulling myself down. I just know the truth that my natural face isn't attention-worthy.

So, with less makeup, the better chance I have of him not gaining any interest in me. And my outfit: a simple long sleeves gray knitted dress that reaches my knees, paired with black doll shoes, no jewelry. I'm not even wearing any colored lipstick. I merely applied a Chapstick earlier so my lips won't feel dry. That heir is so going to find me boring.

"Sweets, are you all set?" Dad asks after closing the door behind him.

"Maybe," I say, still looking at my face in the mirror. I snatch the face powder on my desk and place it inside my purse. I glance at my dad, and he's looking at me worriedly. "Is there something wrong, Dad?"

"Nothing. I'm just glad you agreed to meet him," he says. He looks bothered.

"I guess this is the least I can do for our company." I give him a warm hug and rest my head on his shoulder. "This is just a meeting, right? I'm not agreeing to be engaged to him yet," I tell him warily, and he nods. I can sense his uneasiness.

We both leave my room and head outside to our car.

Ten minutes later, we reach our destination.

The place looks amazing. Colorful lights wrap around the bushes and trees. There are flowers by cemented paths leading to the restaurant's entrance. A waiter stands by the clear glass door. We enter the restaurant, and a stunning brunette young woman welcomes us. We tell them our names, and she cheerfully brings us to a private room.

"Adrian Roberts, we're so delighted you came. It's been so long." A guy with brown hair, wearing a dark suit and tie greets Dad. A blonde-haired woman in a beige dress is standing beside him. They're both good-looking and elegant. I presume they are Mr. and Mrs. Lincoln.

So, where's their son?

"Jay would be here any minute," Mr. Lincoln says as if answering the question in my head.

"That's great. My daughter and I are both excited to meet your son." Dad glances at me, and I force myself to smile, a very distressed smile like I'm about to do a number two.

Excited? Yeah right, more like terrified.

~

I just finished listening to the 1989 album on my iPod, and Jay still hasn't shown himself. They're still talking about business stuff and their old acquaintances that are too boring for my liking, so I just continue scrolling through my second playlist when our attention is caught by Mr. Lincoln's buzzing phone.

"Oh, it's Jay. Excuse me for a second." He immediately leaves the room.

"I'm really sorry, Kim, that my son is making you wait." Mrs. Lincoln reaches for my hand.

"It's alright." It's not a complete lie because it's actually fine with me if ever he doesn't show up. "Although I'm curious because when I Googled Jay Lincoln, nothing much showed up."

Mrs. Lincoln smiles at me. "Well, he's really the shy type, unlike his sister who is busy in her modeling career. He doesn't want anyone to recognize him as the heir of Lincoln Corporation. The last time he was publicly seen was when he was still a six-year-old boy, then he never showed himself to the cameras again. He's even using a different name for the public. Jay is really humble and sweet, so I'm sure you two will get along in no time." Her smile is so warm, like an ember in this chilly room.

I really should've brought my jacket.

"Mr. Roberts, my son will be here any minute now," Mr. Lincoln says when he returns. "He got off late from school, and he needed time to clean up a bit."

From school? So, I guess he's about my age then.

"I'll just go to the restroom." I stand up from my seat and make a beeline for the door. I just need to get out of this place and get some fresh air. I'm tired of hearing discussions about business plans and negotiations, especially when it involves me.

I am about to touch the knob when the door suddenly opens, revealing the last person I am expecting to see tonight.

"Kyle?"

# Chapter 5

I smile. If I had known Kyle is my supposed fiancé, I would've dragged him to a priest myself and shared our wedding vows whether he liked it or not.

I'm going to be married to my childhood crush. I want to jump and scream in glee.

"Kim?" His eyes find mine.

And being the lovesick girl I am, I tuck a hair behind my ear. "Hey, Kyle."

He reluctantly raises a hand and says, "Hey," too. But his muddled eyes search the room. "I don't think Hailey's in here." Then he backs away slowly, and I think my heart stops when he says, "Wrong room. Sorry."

He embarrassingly waves goodbye and leaves me standing there, completely dumbfounded.

What the actual hell? Did that really just happen?

I think my dad asked me something, but I'm still mortified and immobile, so I'm not sure if he really did. The door is still wide open when another guy appears, his attention on the phone in his hand.

I take two steps backward at the sight of him.

"No way," I mumble under my breath. He must have heard me because he looks up and his face immediately becomes pale as a white sheet.

"Sweet mother of Zeus," the guy mutters in disbelief.

"Jay, I'm so glad you're finally here!" His mom walks towards us and gives him a kiss on the cheek, yet his eyes remain on me, and mine on him. "Why do you both look so surprised?"

I finally find my voice. "He's my teacher."

"You're a student at Weatherford High?"

I merely manage to nod in response because my mind is shouting, *The gods are punishing you, Kim. You literally died from too much embarrassment earlier, and this is your hell.*

Everyone is quiet until Mr. Lincoln breaks the silence. "Why don't we all take a seat first." I am about to sit in the same place where I sat, but they insist that it's better if Mr. Bradshaw and I sit together. What's good with that?

"Mom, Dad—" Mr. Bradshaw starts. "I know this is only just a simple meeting, but I've already made my decision. Kim cannot be my fiancée. She's my student."

Five seconds of more silence.

Three pairs of eyes stare at us as if they're thinking of the next move.

"Leave your job then." Mrs. Lincoln unexpectedly suggests. "I don't really like you being a teacher anyway."

"What?" Mr. Bradshaw stares at her mother with incredulity. "No! Why would I leave my job to be with this…spoiled brat?"

I clench my hands. "Well, you're a damn useless teacher anyway!"

He opens his mouth to fire another angry remark when my dad slams his palm over the table, making us flinch and fall into silence.

"Watch your words, Kimberly Adriana." My father used my full name, which means either I shut up or there will be ass whooping later. Like what happened in fourth grade when I stole a hundred dollars from his pocket and secretly went swimming with Kyle and our friends in a private resort.

Mr. Lincoln stares directly at his son. "I'm sorry, Jay, but the moment you agreed last night, we immediately called everyone who can help prepare the wedding. It would be embarrassing to cancel them all. I'd *hate* to cancel them all."

His words slowly_rattle in my brain, reverberating around the empty space in there. They already finalized everything?

I immediately look at my dad. "You said this dinner is just something to help us decide whether to continue the engagement or not!"

He falls silent for a while. "I'm sorry, princess."

"Dad!" I think I'm going to explode. "You promised me you won't do anything against my will."

"Unbelievable." Mr. Bradshaw stands up and leaves the room.

"Kim." Dad tries to reach for my hand, but I retreat. I can't believe he would break such a promise. "We just want what's best for both of you."

"Best for us or best for your businesses?" I retort and scurry away.

When I leave the room, tears quickly rush down my cheeks. I love my dad, but right now, I have all the right to be angry at him. He promised me! He promised he won't do anything unless I agreed to it. I merely agreed to have dinner with the Lincoln family, and now I find out that all wedding plans have already been made?

I storm off the restaurant and notice Jeremy out in the garden, looking down at the grass under his feet, his arms crossed over his chest. I think he noticed my shadow because he immediately looks up to face me.

"What are you doing here?" he says angrily.

I wipe away my tears before speaking. "I'm sorry for what I said a while ago. You're an excellent teacher, and I'm in awe of you. It's me who has a problem, not you."

"It's alright," he coldly replies. "I'm sorry too. I didn't mean to call you a spoiled brat. I was just surprised that my mom asked me to quit my job just for the sake of our wedding. They know how much I enjoy being a teacher."

A few seconds of silence hovers us until I speak again, "Are they serious about the wedding plans being finalized?"

His jaw clenches. "My parents are always serious about everything. So, yeah, I guess we're really getting married."

"Can't we do anything about it?"

He turns to look me, showing his frustration. "I don't know. But if my dad wants something to happen, he will do everything in his power to make it happen."

I sulk in defeat. "I just don't see why they're dying to get us married. I see different companies partnering without giving away their children. It's like I'm in some sick cliché book where some stupid writer thinks it's cool to have this as a plot."

He laughs softly. "I think our parents want the perfect match for both of us. My parents know how much a control freak I am. I want everything in place, unblemished, and organized. Then there's you: irresponsible and rebellious. Perhaps they think opposites are the ideal combination and we'll be a good balance for their business. It's just a theory though."

"I'm going to forget the insults you just said."

He shrugs. "Hey, I'm just stating a fact."

I roll my eyes at him. "So, why are you even a teacher if you're already the next CEO of the Lincoln Corporation? Don't get me wrong, being a teacher is such an honorable job, but you're an heir to a billion-dollar company, so why even bother teaching?"

His body suddenly becomes rigid. I can sense his apprehension by the way his jaw ticks and his knuckles form into fists. I attempt to say, *Never mind*, but he still replies, "I've always wanted to be a teacher when I was a kid. And my youngest sister hates this profession."

His answer is so soft and brief, I almost didn't hear it. That doesn't really make any sense, but still, I nod and decide to change the topic instead.

"So, about this forced engagement, what are we going to do now?"

A smile slowly creeps onto his face as he turns to me, then clutches my wrists and pulls me closer to him, making me gasp.

"Let's make three beautiful babies." He quotes from my diary then eases forward until our faces are mere inches away. "Hopefully, we'll have twins." He winks.

"Wha…"

I'm still speechless when he suddenly laughs.

"You're blushing."

This guy is going to be the death of me.

My hands instinctively cover my cheeks. "No, I'm not."

He shakes his head, still chuckling. "Don't let that get into that big head of yours. I was just teasing." He grips my elbow. "Let's go back inside. It's cold out here."

I walk confusedly behind him as he leads us back to the room.

"So…" Mrs. Lincoln glances at Jeremy's hand on my elbow. "I hope everything's alright now?"

Mr. Bradshaw immediately pulls his hand away and thrusts it in his side pockets.

"It's not like we can do anything about it anyway," he replies with a shrug.

"Great! Does a February wedding next year sound good? Yeah?"

# Chapter 6

"Hey wake up." Someone commands and pokes my cheek, making me grumble out a curse.

"Five minutes." I lift my blanket and place it over my head, covering my whole body from head to toe. I roll to the other side of the bed, facing away from him. There is nothing you can do to separate me from my cozy bed, mister—whoever you are.

"Wake up, come on now." He starts poking my arm lightly. Six more pokes and I give up before my skin forms a bruise. I get rid of my soft blanket and open my eyes at a snail's pace and see a very handsome guy with a beautifully pointed nose. He is sitting on the edge of my bed. I blink my eyes again before I'm able to focus my vision.

"What are you doing here?" I sit up and tug the blanket to my chest.

Did he do something to me? I'm so going to kill him if he did.

"Your dad allowed me in your room to wake you up. I didn't do anything to you." Mr. Bradshaw sneers at me. "You have a body of a fourteen-year-old. I'm not even tempted."

I try not to be offended.

"Why are you here anyway?" I ask, still holding on to my blanket. "I don't have anything under my PJs, okay?"

He stands up and forcefully pulls the blanket off me.

"Just get ready. We're going to meet someone."

"But, Mr. Brad—"

But he has already closed the door behind him. Well, that was just rude.

Considering our circumstance, can I just call him by his first name, Jeremy, like what a normal fiancée will do? Or do I have to continue calling him Mr. Bradshaw, since he's still my teacher?

I dash to my bathroom and take a thirty-minute shower. I usually take an hour or so, but, of course, I don't want it to be a setback in his so-called outing. I step out of the steamy shower and out of the bathroom only in my towel. I'm about to take the thing off when the doorknob clicks and Jeremy's head pokes in.

"You're taking so long." His eyes immediately widen. "Definitely not a fourteen-year-old body," he mumbles and smirks.

My mouth hangs open. I blush furiously as my stomach makes a quick flip and I feel an insane urge to run back to the bathroom and vomit everything I have inside me.

"Oh my gosh! Get out! Get out!" I angrily hurl my pillows at him. "You pervert! Get out!"

"You're the one who didn't lock the door!" He raises his hands in mock defeat then closes the door again.

That pervert! First, my diary, and now, my body? He really doesn't know what privacy means, does he? I sigh and quickly change into decent clothes: an outfit that isn't too revealing nor too shabby, just enough for me to move freely. A pair of denim jeans and a Swiftie Forever tank top is the perfect combo.

"Let's go," I tell Jeremy as I step out of my room. He glances down at me. I really want to strangle him and wipe that stupid smirk off his face.

My dad is sitting on the couch, quietly reading a newspaper. He looks at us.

"Good morning, Kim," my father says. He turns his gaze to my teacher. "Please take care of my princess. She can be clumsy sometimes."

"I will, sir." Jeremy clutches my elbow to drag me out of our house and push me inside his car.

30

"You're such a gentleman, you know that?" I scoff, rolling my eyes at him. He just glowers.

The car engine roars. I rest my head and find myself dozing off.

~

"Kim, for the love of Zeus, wake up!"

I open my eyes.

*Where am I?*

I turn my head to take a glimpse of the guy right next to me.

*Jeremy? Why is my math teacher here?*

I close my eyes again, trying to remember what happened.

*Oh yeah, we're meeting someone.*

When he's convinced that I'm already fully conscious, he climbs out of the car. I follow him out. He locks the vehicle with the mini remote in his hand. I look up to see the tall building before us.

We're in a mall that's probably miles from home since I haven't visited this place before. He scampers towards the building, leaving me sprinting behind him.

Why can't he walk a little slower?

"Hey, wait up!" I shout. Good thing I'm wearing flat doll shoes, or else I'd be on the ground in no time.

"Turtle," he grumbles as he grips my hand and tugs me with him.

We end up in front of a small fancy restaurant in the mall. He keeps turning, looking for someone.

"Jay!"

We both turn to the woman who called out his name.

My jaw drops to the floor because wow, she's so stunning. And I'm not making a mountain out of a molehill.

Her dark blonde hair flows like a wave. She has a glowing, cream complexion, a straightly sculpted nose, soft pink lips, faintly elevated cheekbones, and full breasts. Her dress perfectly fits her

31

slender curves. Her eyes are bright, hazel-green, gleaming with delight.

She strides towards us, and I glance at Jeremy and see him smiling. I've never seen him smile like that, a smile full of longing. This girl must be really special to him.

Releasing my wrist from his grasp, he wraps his arms around the woman for a hug.

"I missed you so much, Jay!" the girl says with glee.

"I missed you too, Jade." Jeremy kisses her left cheek. And that's it. That's the final straw.

I turn away from these lovebirds.

Unbelievable. So, he woke me up early in the morning just to rub it in my face that he already has a girlfriend? Okay, fine, whatever. As if I'm interested in that stupid wedding anyway.

"Kim, where are you going?" Jeremy shouts behind me, but I don't bother turning back to him. I quicken my pace, but he immediately catches up to me and seizes my arm.

"I'm leaving!" I yell, pulling my arm from his grasp. Damn, he's strong.

"Stop being a brat."

I narrow my eyes at him, but he quickly drags me back to the spot where his girlfriend is standing, looking inquisitively at us.

"Hello." She greets me, her smile reaching her eyes.

Life is so unfair! Why can't I be as beautiful as her? And why do I have a feeling that I've seen her before? I don't know if I saw her personally before or if it was on television.

"Let's go," Jeremy says and takes the girl's hand.

You're one hell of a player, mister. You brought your fiancée to meet your girlfriend. Now, you have two beautiful ladies walking next to you. Nice, very nice.

We find a table in the fancy restaurant and order our meals. They keep chatting and telling each other stories while eating whereas I'm here, all alone, chewing.

*It's just you and me, Mister Beef,* I tell the tender steak on my plate.

By the looks on how they're bonding, there's no doubt that they're really close, like they've known each other for years, or even a lifetime.

"So…" The girl wipes her stained lips with a table napkin. "Who's this girl?"

*Thank goodness! After talking for fifteen minutes, you finally notice me.*

"She's my student," Jeremy answers her.

*Fine, deny me as your fiancée. I don't care.*

"Ah, I see." She smiles at me and holds out her hand. "My name's Tennizia Jade, but you can call me Jade. What's yours?"

Gosh, even her name sounds beautiful.

"I'm Kim." I lightly shake her soft hands.

"I'm really sorry if we almost ignored you a while ago. I just really missed this sweet, cutie boy so much." She pinches Jeremy's cheeks, making him glower at her. "It's been two years since I last saw him."

Wow, two years? That's so long. No wonder why Jeremy is always down in the dumps. His girlfriend was away from him. But now that she's here, maybe he'll go back to his original self—this sweet and affectionate Jade described him as.

Jade turns to Jeremy. "So, why did you bring your student here? Are you tutoring her for the weekend?"

Now that she has mentioned it, I'm back to wondering why indeed—other than the obvious reason that he wanted me to meet his girlfriend.

"Dad told me to bring her here. He said we need some time together to bond." He lifts his fingers midair, air-quoting the word *bond*.

She stares at him for a moment, thinking about his statement. "Is there something I should know here?"

Yup, there is.

"Um, yes." He clearly doesn't know how to tell his precious girlfriend that our parents are forcing us to get married.

33

I take my glass of juice and try to have a small sip, looking curiously at Jeremy, wondering how he will announce our unexpected engagement.

"Jeremy Bradshaw Lincoln, you know how much I hate it every time you keep secrets from your sister." Jade pouts.

I nearly choke on my fruit drink. The liquid goes down the wrong pipe as soon as I hear the last word Jade says.

"You're his sister?" I ask between coughs, wiping my wet chin and nose.

*You're so embarrassing, Kim.*

"You okay, dear?" Jade asks.

"You're Jay's sister?"

"Hmm…well, the last time I checked, we still have the same parents. So, yeah, I'm his sister. Why'd you ask?" She stares at me for a moment like she's reading my thoughts.

"Wait, did you think that I am his girlfriend?" She prods, and I nod, ashamed of myself right now.

"You're kidding, right?" Jeremy says in disgust.

"I'm sorry." This is so humiliating.

"Honey, I went to Paris two years ago to pursue my modeling career, and we've never seen each other since then, so I really missed my baby brother.

"So back to my question, is there something you two are hiding from me?"

"She's my fiancée," Jeremy declares.

Jade drops her fork on her plate. "What? But you're her teacher! Can't you wait until she graduates first? Do you really love her that much that you're willing to risk both of your reputations for the sake of your relationship?"

I feel like hiding behind a wall.

"I understand Kim because she's still young, but you're the older one here, so you must know what's right from wrong!"

She is about to say another word when Jeremy surprisingly shoves the table napkin into her mouth to silence her.

"Jeez! One hour of being with you and I'm already wishing you're back in Paris," Jeremy says. "Our parents arranged us to be married to secure the partnership of our companies."

Jade removes the cloth from her mouth and playfully throws it at his face, making him grimace.

"Why would they do that?" she asks.

"Because we're puppets of our own parents," Jeremy grumbles, forcefully stabbing the beef with his fork.

I couldn't agree more to that.

# Chapter 7

After we explain the surprise engagement to Jade, she and I continue to talk more about Paris and how gorgeous French men are—which made Jeremy feel so uncomfortable.

Jade is, apparently, three years older than Jeremy, so basically, she's twenty-eight while Jeremy is twenty-five. She also tells me about the different commercials she made and her other international projects where she endorses different kinds of clothes, shoes, makeup, etc. So that's why she looks familiar!

Once we finish our lunch, Jade and I head to boutiques while Jeremy chooses to stay in the bookstore. He's such a geek.

While deciding which perfume to buy, Jade suddenly approaches me, her eyes full of sincerity.

"Kim, I love my brother so much, and I know you don't have any feelings for him yet, but sooner or later, you might. I'm saying this based on my own experience.

"I went to Paris to get away from a heartbreak. Our parents also set me up with someone. Eventually, I told that guy I loved him. He said he loved me too, yet he still cheated on me, Kim, and it broke me." She then turns her attention to the perfume she is holding.

"I don't want that to happen to Jay. So please, Kim, if the day comes when he tells you he loves you—I know he will—let him know exactly what you really feel. Don't pretend to have the same feelings for him when you're obviously interested in someone else just because you don't want to hurt him. Please, Kim, never lie to my brother. Could you do that for me?"

"Of course," I answer. She smiles at me before going back to the lipstick aisle.

I feel a sudden wave of uneasiness after our conversation "Uh, I'm just going to check the clothes over there."

She simply nods.

I practically dash towards the women's clothing section to get away from her. I'm not really scared of her, just a little intimidated. And maybe a bit guilty.

"I kinda like this one, baby." I hear a very familiar voice. I instantly look up and see the one and only Hailey West.

I hide behind the rack of clothes and notice she's with a guy.

Is that Kyle? But his build is so different, and it doesn't help that she's blocking the man's face, so I really can't see his face.

I sprint to another shelf of garments to take a closer look, and my eyes almost bulge out when I realize Hailey's obviously cheating on Kyle—with our history teacher.

As if my nose couldn't pick a better time to feel itchy, I sneeze. Which instantly gets Hailey's attention. I try to duck, but she has already noticed me.

"Kim?" she asks and walks toward me.

This is so awkward.

My head is currently between two blouses in the rack as if I'm some stalker. I close my eyes and curse at how slowly I reacted. I don't want her to think she's so famous and interesting that I've dedicated my time to stalk her like some crazy fan.

Then someone suddenly grasps my waist, forcing me to leave my embarrassing position. I look up, and Jeremy suddenly drapes his arm around my shoulders.

"You owe me for this one," he mumbles under his breath.

Our history teacher narrows his eyes at us.

"Good day, Mr. Gregory Campbell." Jeremy casually greets the other man as if this is completely normal.

Mr. Campbell nods and puts a hand around Hailey's waist. "You too, Mr. Jeremy Bradshaw."

I've always known that our history teacher is pretty hot, but he's already in his early thirties and stands five feet eight. He is too old and short for my liking. Unlike Jeremy who's only twenty-five years old and stands six feet and two inches. But I guess Hailey doesn't really have a type as long as the guy is breathing.

Hailey remains quiet, so I initiate the conversation. "So, you're dating our history teacher."

Jeremy's grip on my shoulder tightens.

"Well, aren't you a pot calling the kettle black." She rolls her eyes. "Who knew you had it in you to date our math teacher? At least I don't pretend to be a good girl."

I scoff and cross my arms over my chest. "At least I'm not a two-timing snake." My eyes search for Mr. Campbell's shocked reaction, but his face shows that he already knows about it.

Wow.

"Does Kyle know about this?"

Jeremy suddenly interrupts. "Look, can we just forget this ever happened?" I look up to see the expression on my fiancé's face.

Mr. Campbell shrugs. "Sure. Works for me."

I quickly remember something. "Aren't you married to Mrs. Katrina? Our music teacher?"

Jeremy glowers at me, but I ignore him.

Mr. Campbell clears his throat. "That's none of your business."

"We're leaving now," Jeremy sternly states. "You didn't see us. We didn't see you. Have a great day ahead." He pulls me to the other direction.

I just can't help but comment on Hailey, so I tell her, "Have fun ruining a marriage!"

She scowls. Jeremy grips my wrist tighter and leads me away from them. We end up in the children's clothing section.

"Why can't you keep your mouth shut?" Jeremy asks. "I was trying to keep the situation friendly, yet you can't even zip that big mouth of yours!"

"She's cheating on Kyle! And he's cheating on his wife!"

"I don't care about that petty crush of yours." He points a finger at me. "You have no idea how conniving Gregory is. He's capable of doing the unthinkable," he says in a lower voice.

I gasp exits. "But he's our funny history teacher."

"He may look and sound delightful at school, but underneath that façade is a despicable man," he says. "Sometimes, please know how to take a fuc—" he pauses and glances at the glaring mother with a male toddler nearby "—a fudging hint."

"Sorry," I mumble.

Something buzzes in his pocket. He fishes out his phone and reads a text while I continue to ponder what just happened.

"Jade needs to go since she still has a photo shoot in an hour." He grips my arm and is about to drag me to leave, but I pull away.

"I want to do some shopping first."

"Seriously?" he asks as if I've just begged him to give me a dinosaur.

"This is my first time in this mall, and I want to explore it."

He groans. "Fine, let's go shopping." Then he drags me again. I'm starting to worry that my arm will fall off if he continues this all day.

~

It's already 8:30 in the evening and the mall is about to close. I'm carrying five shopping bags, and my so-called fiancé doesn't even bother to help me. I expect him to be walking behind me, but when I turn around, he isn't there, so I decide to head to the parking lot.

Maybe he got tired and decided to rest in his car instead of escorting me in my shopping.

What a gentleman. Not.

Only the tall street lights are illuminating my way now, and I completely forget where we parked.

"Kim Roberts, right?"

I gasp when Mr. Campbell approaches me from the dark. I instinctively stop in my tracks, and he's now in front of me. "You should've taken your boyfriend's hint though." His dark cobalt eyes taunt me, and I want to cower.

"I swear, I won't tell anyone about you and Hailey." Dread rises in my chest, and I contemplate running away.

He touches my hair and tucks a few strands behind my ear. "Good girl."

I wish on my lucky stars that someone would come to rescue me from this man.

"Is everything alright in here?" a guy suddenly speaks, causing Mr. Campbell to spin around. "Do you know this guy?" the stranger asks me. He has a thick British accent.

He's wearing a black hoodie and a pair of round Harry-Potter-like glasses.

"Everything's alright," my history teacher answers and turns to me. "Goodnight, Ms. Roberts." Then he saunters away from us and into his vehicle where Hailey is smiling from the shotgun seat as if she's entertained by my horrified state.

I watch them drive away.

"Are you alright?" the guy asks.

I just nod.

"You know him?"

I hesitate. "Yeah, he's just telling me to go home, since it's getting late."

He gazes at me as if he knows I'm lying but chooses not to press further.

He holds out his hand. "I'm Tyler."

I try to think of a different name since he's still a stranger. "Chloe. My name's Chloe." I take his hand, and he suddenly brings it close to his lips.

*Whoa there, pretty boy.*

I immediately pull my hand away, and he mumbles an insincere apology. I know he's cute, but he can't just kiss my hand like I'm some kind of queen. We should know each other more first, then he can kiss me like a queen.

40

I take a step back just in case he's more of a villain in this situation.

"Ms. Roberts!"

I turn and see my second least favorite person—Jeremy.

"This is going to be fun," the guy beside me amusedly murmurs.

Jeremy angrily walks toward us and glowers at Tyler. "Who the hell are you?" His eyes are so full of resentment; I'm quite scared he's going to bite the boy.

"Jeremy, calm down," I tell him as if I'm reprimanding a petulant child.

Tyler gives him a boyish grin. "Name's Tyler, but you can call me *babe*." He winks playfully.

Wait, is he swinging the other way?

"What?" Jeremy asks.

"I'm just helping your friend, mate. I didn't do anything wrong."

They both stare at each other. Jeremy is obviously studying Tyler while Tyler is nonchalant.

"Let's just go." I pull Jeremy away from the scene, irritated by his over-protectiveness.

"Who was that and why did he kiss your hand?" Jeremy asks once we're both in the car.

I ignore him.

"Why did you let him kiss your hand?" he asks in a more arduous tone.

I raise an eyebrow at him. "Are you jealous?"

He makes a grumbling sound and ignores my comment. "Why were you with him?"

I rub my sweaty palms on my jeans. "He practically saved me from Mr. Campbell." Damn it, I remember his face close to mine again, and I just want to erase it all.

He scoots forward and leans closer, searching me for any injuries or bruises. "What did Gregory do to you?"

41

I purse my lips. "I'm fine. I think he was just trying to warn me."

He pinches the bridge of his nose. "This is what I've been telling you earlier. Greg is a sly man. Just don't do anything stupid again and you'll be fine."

Don't do anything stupid.

Alright, I should start choosing my funeral dress then.

# Chapter 8

It's Monday again.

Laziness is yanking me down and tempting me to curl on the floor and sleep. Do students really need to go to school this early? That should be against the law! Kids like us need sleep—plenty of sleep. Anti-early school hours should really be implemented in this country.

As I walk languidly down the school hallway, I see a horde of students, mostly girls, gathering around the bulletin board.

What's all the commotion about?

Our principal never posts anything on the bulletin board unless it's really important like class suspensions, holidays, etc. I don't remember hearing news about any of those, so I'm really curious about what are they thrilled about.

My best friend has her attention on the board, too. I call her from afar, not wanting to squeeze into the crowd. Luckily, she glances in my direction. I wave at her and shoot her a 'what is going on?' look. She hurriedly runs toward me, and I see in her eyes that she's really excited about something.

She gasps for air. "Hot…hot guy…hot guy alert!" She pulls me along with her.

Ugh. I called her so that I don't have to join this massive pile of squealing students, but I guess she hasn't thought of that.

"Excuse me! Move!" She vigorously pushes anyone that is blocking our way. "Look!" she points at the large banner on the board.

*WELCOME, LANCE KNIGHT*
*From: Weatherford High school*

There's a picture of a handsome, brown-haired guy below it.

"Lance Knight. Sounds familiar. Who is he?" I whisper to Ella, but I think some girls beside me heard my question because they start joining the conversation.

"OMG! Do you even live on this planet?"

"Are you even in this generation?"

Wow, I never thought not knowing certain celebrities can make me an alien and prehistoric. And the last time I checked, I was asking my friend, not them. Jeez.

"Are you serious, Kim? You really don't know him?" Ella asks.

"Well, I wouldn't be asking you if I did." I roll my eyes at her.

"Lance Knight, the newest male singer from London. So basically, he sings with a sexy British accent!" She shakes my shoulders.

"So why are we welcoming him?"

"According to the news, he'll be staying here in California for about a year or two, and now he's going to study in *our* school." She jumps like some lunatic. There's no doubt that she really is a fan of this boy.

We hear the bell ring, signaling the start of class.

As we enter the classroom, I have a glimpse of Jeremy sitting quietly on his chair while reading a book. My stomach suddenly flips.

What was that? I'm sure I went to the bathroom this morning before going to school. Must be too much milk from last night.

After a few minutes, he starts to discuss that day's lesson, which I don't and will never understand. I just stare at him, particularly on his very handsome face, admiring his manly features.

*Divide this from that, then multiply the sum of this and that, then blah blah blah blah blah...*

No matter how hard I try, I still don't get the lesson, so I just continue gawking at my very good-looking fiancé.

Suddenly, we hear a knock. Everyone pays turns to the door. All the girls start chatting excitedly.

Jeremy opens the door, and the chatter gets louder. Since I'm sitting in the front right corner of the room with the door blocking my view, I can't see the visitor's face.

"Sorry if I'm late. I was in the office getting my schedule."

Jeremy tenses up. "You're the new student, right?" He sidesteps, allowing the student to enter.

Oh. My. Gosh.

The new guy really is handsome, and these girls aren't exaggerating at all. Why on Earth haven't I known of this new male singer?

"Ah! I love you, Lance!"

"Will you marry me?"

"Lance, I will give you my soul!"

I turn to Ella and watch her press her hands on her chest as if she's having an asthma attack. But I know she's not because her face shows how excited she is to see Lance.

We are all shocked when Jeremy suddenly slams a book on his desk, making the whole class fall into silence. "Class, don't show your terrible behavior in front of our new student."

Finally!

"Now, kindly introduce yourself to everyone." Jeremy gestures from Lance to the class.

"Hey, I'm Lance. I hope we'll all be friends here." Lance is already wearing the male school uniform on his first day.

And his accent. That very familiar British accent.

I lean closer to have a better look. My eyes widen once I recognize him. He was the gentleman who I met at the mall's parking lot! Tyler!

Why didn't he tell me he's a singer?

I think Jeremy recognizes him too because the man is glowering at him. My only prayer is that Lance won't recognize either of us because if he does, that will only cause a lot of trouble.

"There are a few available seats over there, Lance. You may sit wherever you want."

Lance glances to where Jeremy is pointing. I then remember that there is a vacant chair behind me. He flashes a smile once he spots me.

Oh no.

He approaches me and says, "Hi."

But I try not to pay any attention to him. I take out my notebook and copy the notes on the board instead, pretending to look busy.

Out of the blue, a phone rings and momentarily interrupts the class. I look up and see Jeremy take his phone out from his pocket. "It's the principal. I'll be back in a sec." He leaves the room.

"So, you're ignoring me now?" Lance whispers behind me. I turn around to face him. His face is only a few inches away from mine.

"I'm not ignoring you. I'm just busy." I fake a smile then return my concentration to my notebook that is covered with a bunch of incomprehensible numbers.

"You're dating our teacher, huh?" He teases, and I feel my stomach flip. Of course, he recognized Jeremy.

"We just met up with her sister. Our families are close friends." This is not completely a lie because our parents really know each other.

"Sure," he says, sarcastically. "So…do you have a boyfriend?"

"I don't." But I do have a fiancé, and, of course, I'm not going to tell him that.

"So, is it okay if I ask you out?"

"I thought you were gay?" I simply answer, still not looking at him.

He chuckles. "No, I'm not. I was just kidding that time." Huh, I guess he was only playing with Jeremy's head then. "So, can I take you out on a date?"

"Dude, we've only just met."

"So? You said you're single." Hey, I never said I'm single.

"Because you're weird," I retort. A few girls near me gasp. "And I don't know you yet."

"I am not weird." He laughs. "And that's the purpose of our date, to get to know each other."

"Still no."

"Please?"

"No." I face him again.

"Please?"

I roll my eyes at him. "Ugh! Fine!"

I just want him to stop talking.

"I promise you won't regret this." Then he quickly kisses me...on my chin.

He smiles at me, showing two dimples on each cheek while I'm still dumbfounded.

What just happened?

"Ms. Roberts, Mr. Knight!" I turn and see Jeremy glaring at both of us.

Did he see that kiss?

"In my office right after this class."

Yup, he did.

~

"We do not tolerate such inappropriate behavior in this school, Mr. Knight." Jeremy's penetrating sea-green eyes travel to mine. "And you should've known better, Ms. Roberts."

I want to roll my eyes but refrain from doing it. He's being so irrational right now. It's not like Lance and I were found doing the nasties in the classroom full of students. It was a simple peck on the chin—which completely took me off guard, might I add—yet he's acting like we murdered innocent babies a few minutes ago.

47

"In my defense, I only found her adorable, so I kissed her," is Lance's stupid response.

"On the freakin' chin!" I emphasize, nonetheless.

Our math teacher continues to glare at us. "I don't care if it's on the chin, nose, lips, or any part of her body. It was still an intimate gesture inside the classroom, and that is strictly prohibited."

Is he really serious right now?

I move my hands in exasperation. "Oh, heavens no! We made an intimate gesture! Such transgression we have committed! Whatever shall we do?"

Lance puts his hand on his chest. "I'm the one who sinned. I should solely repent."

"Are you both making fun of me?" Jeremy asks.

My lips curve into a fake smile. "What do you think?"

He sneers.

Lance adjusts himself on the chair so he can be more comfortable. "I'm sorry, but don't you think you're overreacting over a simple kiss that is not even on the lips?"

I pitch in. "It was a simple peck on the chin, nothing more!"

"But—" Jeremy starts, but I interrupt him before he says something illogical again.

"But nothing." I pull Lance up from his seat. "Let's go, Lance. We're wasting our time here." We both leave our infuriating teacher's office. I'm sure he'll text me saying I'm being immature again for walking out on him, but I don't care. He's being insufferable right now, and I just can't stand that kind of unreasonable pride anymore.

Once we're outside his office, Lance sniggers. I give him a questioning look, and he shakes his head while smiling as if what happened completely amuses him.

"What's so funny?" I ask while we head to our class. Surprisingly, we both have the same class schedule today.

"Are you sure you're not dating that teacher?" Lance probes.

My face flushes. "I already told you, we're not dating."

He shrugs. "He sure was acting like a jealous boyfriend back there."

More like a jealous fiancé.

"So, Tyler, huh?" I tease, remembering his fake name last Saturday night.

He rolls his eyes. "Tyler is my second name. What about you, Chloe?"

"Chloe is just a name I usually give to strangers." I grin at him. "And I've always wanted my name to be Chloe. Sadly, I'm stuck with Kimberly."

"Maybe you can name your daughter Chloe then."

"We'll see."

Lance and I reach the room for our English class, and, as expected, about half of the girls in the room start fangirling over him. One girl even jumps off from her seat and jumps on Lance, making them both land on the floor.

"I love you so much, Lance!" she squeals while covering every inch of his face with kisses.

Lance's scared eyes find mine. "Help."

I laugh as I try to pull her off him. She keeps swatting me away but eventually stops harassing the poor guy once Lance promises a coffee date with her tomorrow. The redheaded chick gives him one long kiss on the lips before standing up and going back to her chair, leaving Lance exhausted on the floor.

I offer a hand and help him stand up. "You should really have a bodyguard."

"I'll tell my manager about it," he says seriously while fixing his uniform.

*You shouldn't even be here*, I want to add but remain silent instead.

# Chapter 9

By 3:00 PM sharp, the bell rings.

Almost everyone excitedly swarms around us since Lance is seated near me again. My chair almost tips over when three girls try to climb on it just to be closer to him. I could've died right there if it wasn't for Ella's quick hands that steadied me.

Okay, maybe *died* is too much of a stretch. But the fact remains that these girls will do anything just to get a picture or an autograph from their beloved Lance Knight.

It takes Ella and me five minutes—five most traumatizing minutes of our lives—to free ourselves from the crazy crowd and out of the classroom. One would think this isn't a private school with the way those girls are acting. I think I heard Lance shout to wait up, but I ignore him and choose to survive instead.

Survive first, cute boy later.

"Shouldn't celebrities like him be homeschooled?" I ask Ella while unbolting my locker.

Ella shrugs. "I guess. But I'm not complaining...sort of. I don't mind having *the* Lance Knight in our school." She stares into space as if imagining a scenario with him.

"I watched his YouTube videos last night, and he isn't even that good."

Ella gasps and glowers at me. "How dare you! Lance Knight is freakin' perfect!"

I simply shrug as I arrange the mess in my locker. "He's not even half as good as Ed."

She puts her hands on her waists and chastises me like a small kid. "He's not like Ed Sheeran because he is the one and only Lance Knight, and, before you know it, he'll be extremely popular, and I'd be proud to say I've been his fan before he even hit full stardom."

I'm about to make another remark just to play with my best friend's head, but the sound of heels clicking on the marble floor interrupts us, and, suddenly, we feel the presence of The Leech.

Hailey walks towards us with her glittery red lips smirking.

Ugh. What does she want now?

"He's here because of a girl," she says smugly.

Ella arches an eyebrow. "And how would you know that?"

She crosses her arms over her stuffy boobs. "Let's just say I have connections."

I couldn't help myself but comment about the last time we saw each other. What can I say? She brings out the worst in me. "Connections with our history teacher?"

Ella's hands instantly grab my arm as if telling me she wants to know everything. Yet Hailey remains composed as if she has been expecting that jab.

"From our math teacher, actually," she answers with her sultry voice as if hinting that there's something more. I give her a judging look, and she merely simpers.

"From Mr. Bradshaw?" Ella asks, completely puzzled.

Hailey wets her lips. "He's so good. No wonder Kim is dating him." Then she walks away, her hips swaying.

I hate her so much.

~

I tell my best friend everything: from the day my dad announced my engagement to our math teacher up to the night I met Lance at the mall's parking lot where I also saw Hailey with our history teacher, Mr. Campbell.

Now it's 6:00 PM and it's starting to get cold outside. Ella and I are sitting on my bed. She is gaping at me as if I've just told her I discovered the secrets to immortality.

"Say something." I snap my fingers at her.

She blinks, closes her mouth, then opens it again to speak. "So, you're telling me you're currently engaged to our extremely hot teacher and you became friends with a British singer you just met in a parking lot?" She shakes my shoulders. "Kim, I want your life!"

I roll my eyes. "Trust me, if I can trade my life with yours, I will."

Then she unexpectedly slaps me hard.

"Shut up. You have two hot guys wrapped around your finger! What's not to like?"

I slap her back. "One, Mr. Bradshaw hates me because of my poor performance in his class, and I don't like him very much either. Two, Lance is probably just a playboy who treats every girl he finds interesting as special, then throws them away once he's done with them."

Ella massages her aching cheek, but I would not dare apologize. We hurt each other physically sometimes. Okay, fine, all the time, but that just proves how deep and real our friendship is. We're not one of those friends who will compliment you on simple things then stab you in the back while smiling at you. We won't hold back on telling the truth to each other despite how emotionally or physically hurtful it is.

If the other one has bad breath, we immediately comment something like, *"Did you just eat a used diaper?"* and that's us still being nice. And if the other one refuses to believe how positive something is about her, we literally slap the truth to the other's face. That's just how we sincerely love each other. True friendship right there.

"At least give me Lance, since you're already engaged to Mr. Bradshaw."

I pause to think about it. "Actually, if I had to choose between those two, I'd have to choose Lance, since we're the same age. I don't like to be tied down to some cranky, old man like Mr. Bradshaw."

I fluff my pillow and rest my head on it. Ella props herself on her elbows, looking at me with her questioning eyes.

"Why? Mr. Bradshaw will die of old age, and that would leave you a rich widow."

Now that she's mentioned it...

"You're probably right. Okay. I choose Jeremy then."

"You're such a gold digger." She laughs and lies flat on my bed.

I jab a finger to her ribs. "I'm already a rich gold digger."

We binge-watch *Supernatural* for five hours straight until Ella's mom calls her to bring her ass back home. My best friend asks for an hour more, but Mrs. Summers threatens to lock the gates if she's still not home in ten minutes.

I think Ella is giving The Flash a run for his money by how quick she dashes out of my room without even saying goodbye. The drive to her house is about twenty minutes, and I have no idea how she'll be able to reach it in ten. But given her speed a while ago, I think she might actually make it. Good thing she brought her car this time, or else she'll have to wait for an Uber outside.

I check the time on my watch, and it tells me that it's already 12:30 PM. I still can't sleep, so I grab my iPhone. When I'm about to watch a funny video of puppies, an unknown number appears on the screen. I reluctantly swipe to answer the call and wait for the caller to speak first, but all I can hear are some whispers of cussing and a bit of shuffling.

Finally, the caller speaks, "Kim?"

I know that voice.

"Mr. Bradshaw? Hey." Why in the world is he calling me at this hour?

I hear more shuffling of papers from his end. "Have you read our suggested marriage contract already?"

"Dad hasn't given it to me yet. Why?" Now I'm more curious.

He cusses again then breathes out. "Well, you should ask for it. I don't think you'll like it either."

Why is he acting like a nervous douchebag right now?

I roll my eyes although he can't see me. "It's just a marriage contract. I'll read it once my dad lets me."

"It's a weird marriage contract." He's probably just being overly dramatic again.

"Weird in what way?" For all I know, the contract possibly just contains how long or, perhaps, how short we'll have to stay married.

"For instance, one clause says that we can't file for divorce. Ever. Or else we'll have to give up more than half of our inheritance from our parents."

I almost drop my phone. "No way!"

"I know! Also, one clause states that we can't have kids until you're twenty-five," he adds. "I'll be thirty-two by that time, and I want kids before I hit thirty."

This time, I really drop my phone on the bed as if it has an infectious disease. I turn on the loudspeaker just so I won't put my phone close to my ear.

"Mr. Bradshaw, are you high?" I genuinely ask because what other reason would there be for him to say a stupid comment like that?

He scoffs. "I'm just being practical. The least they can do is change it. Maybe after your college graduation?"

Okay. Wow. Just wow.

"Okay, hold up just a second there." I place my hands on my hips because I can't believe what I'm hearing right now. "First, you're against not having the right to file for divorce, which implies that you're actually planning to divorce me anytime soon. And now you're complaining that you can't have kids before you're thirty?" If only I can strangle him right now. "So basically, you want to have kids, and you want a divorce. So, what, like, you're gonna leave the kids for me to raise on my own then?"

"I never said I'm planning to leave you. It's not something people normally plan, Kim. But my point is, what if we can't stand each other more than we can't right now?"

This is ridiculous. "You *are* planning to leave me with the kids."

He groans. "You're not getting my point. I'm just thinking of the possibilities here."

I sarcastically laugh. "We're still not married, and you're already thinking of the possibilities of getting a divorce."

Can he hear how nonsensical he sounds right now?

"You're childish for not being able to see my point," he says bitterly.

I clench my hands, and I want to reach inside my phone and punch him. "And you're a potato for not realizing how absurd your point is."

He pauses.

"What does a potato have to do with this?"

I am speechless for a while because honestly, I don't have any idea either. But it sounded harsh in my head before I said it. Now that I've thought about, it does sound absurd.

"Goodbye, Mr. Bradshaw." I hang up.

Un—freaking—believable.

Am I really going to marry that conceited nincompoop?

What have I ever done to deserve the ire of the universe? I was simply living my life as a seventeen-year-old senior student who fangirls over boybands.

I don't do drugs or alcohol. I don't even do occasional smoking. I'm a decent daughter, to say the least, yet now I'm suddenly plunged in this idiocy that will surely take away my sanity, especially with a fiancé as uncaring as Jeremy Lincoln.

Oh, well, at least he'll die first.

# Chapter 10

I start my Tuesday morning with a frown.

Before I slept last night, I received a text from that devil-sent math teacher, informing me that Hailey will be tutoring me every Wednesday.

The hell she is!

Wasn't annoying me about our marriage contract not enough? Now he just had to remind me that I have a tutoring session with that witch he slept with. Ugh.

My best friend isn't even around to cheer me up because she has a doctor's appointment for her leg that she broke when she was younger. She still has no idea how she broke it. It's practically healed now anyway, but the doctor still wants to check it once every six months.

So now I'm stuck alone with a chicken sandwich in the lunch table because Lance is eating at some fancy café since he promised someone a date. It royally sucks that I only have one best friend and one newly found friend who can't even eat with me during lunch.

And as if the universe enjoys me in a bad mood, Hailey takes a seat in front of me. Her ebony hair is tied in a messy bun, but she still looks stunning. Why can't I be as gorgeous as her? Whenever I try that messy bun thing on my hair, I look like a hobo who hasn't showered for years.

"So, you suck at math, huh?" She smirks. I take a big bite of my sandwich and tear the chicken forcefully with my teeth, imagining it's her head. I simply scowl at her as I exaggeratingly chew my bread. "Mr. Bradshaw emailed me yesterday about tutoring you."

I swallow and take a sip from my apple juice box, still not giving her an answer.

She giggles. "Sweetie, don't be shy. Although, you should be mortified because you're the only one who failed that math test."

"Don't you have boys to flirt with? Stop wasting your time talking to me," I say.

"But I enjoy talking to you." She tries to take my hand, but I pull away. "I think we might be great friends, don't you think?"

I shudder in disgust. "I don't befriend sluts. Sorry."

She chuckles. "That's rich coming from you, dear. Dating the Math teacher doesn't make you a saint either."

I could tell her we're not really dating, but why would I even defend myself to this depraved wench? "Get lost, Hailey. Please."

She puts her hand on her chest. "Aw, you said *please*." She pushes the chair backward to stand up. "See you. Can't wait to see how you make a fool of your self tomorrow." Then she saunters away.

My chicken sandwich almost crumbles to pieces with how much I'm clenching it with my hands. I groan and just quickly finish eating. Even with the fact that I have a history class later at 1:00 PM and I'll be seeing that psycho teacher again, I won't waste perfectly delicious food just because I'm in a bad mood. That's blasphemy.

Once I'm done drinking my apple juice, I grab my bag, stand up from my seat, and march towards the teachers' hall. I enter Jeremy's office without knocking and find him sitting by his desk with an open mouth and a fork of an appetizing piece of beef steak raised midair.

He scowls at me then brings the fork down. I situate myself on the chair that I've been so used to sitting on and cross my arms over my chest.

"I was eating, Miss Roberts," he says, frowning. "What do you want?"

"I don't want to be tutored by that leech."

He raises an eyebrow. "Hailey West?"

I scoff. "Glad to hear you know which leech I am referring to."

"What about her then?" He takes a drink from his water bottle.

"I don't need a tutor. What I need is a decent teacher who's good at teaching me math, not some chick you've slept with."

He gags. And without warning, I feel water all over my face. I shout a few incoherent words, grab a tissue from the box, and wipe his spit off my face.

"I'm sorry," Jeremy says frantically as he wipes the water off his desk too. "But are you implying that I've slept with Hailey? Where in the world did you get that?"

I throw the used tissue at him. "Hailey is a cheater and a liar. You slept with someone who's known for the things that she does on the mattress. This is why we can't have nice things, Jeremy."

He stares at me as if I've gone mad. "Did you just Taylor Swift me?"

"Did you just use Taylor Swift as a verb?"

"Never mind." Jeremy waves me off. "I know that. That's why I've never slept with Hailey."

I roll my eyes. "Yeah, right."

"I've never even slept with anyone. Where did you even get that rumor?"

I put my leg over the other and glare at him. "I don't care if...wait, what?" Did I really hear him right? "You've never slept with anyone?"

His lips form a thin line, and a deep red color slowly creeps up to his face. He's blushing. Jeremy Lincoln is blushing!

"That's none of your business." He takes a long swig from his water bottle while I'm gaping at him as if he just told me that he's Santa Claus.

"But aren't you, like, twenty-five?" I press further. I just have to know more.

"I said that's none of your business."

A wide grin spreads across my face. "You're still a virgin at twenty-five? Oh my gosh, this is gold. This is really gold." I cover my mouth with my hand to suppress myself from laughing.

"Kimberly Roberts, if you can't stop acting like a child, get out of my office."

"Are you gay?" I really hope not because I don't want to be married to someone who's not even slightly interested in me.

"No, I just have high standards. And that's still none of your damn business. Now get out of my office. Your next class starts in ten minutes."

I shake my head while still giggling. "You do realize someone might be hunting for you so they can sacrifice your twenty-five-year-old virgin blood to the gods, right?"

"Stop being immature, Kim."

"Oh my gosh! What if your old virgin blood is the answer to world peace? You can save world hunger!"

Childish, I know. I didn't realize twenty-five-year-old virgins still exist in this day and age.

He puts his elbows on his desk and covers his face with his hands. Jeremy Lincoln is embarrassed, and I'm enjoying every second of it.

"Kim, for the love of everything that is good, please get out of my office."

His phone rings, and my eyes find the screen where an unknown number is flashing.

"Aren't you going to answer that?" I ask him.

He looks at his phone on the desk. "Not until you get out."

I simply give him a wicked smirk and refuse to leave. Let's see who's tougher.

After a few more seconds, the phone finally stops ringing.

"I don't even want to go to my history class. Mr. Campbell is in there," I state, and he just nods although I can sense that he's already irritated of my presence.

"Well, you can't stay here either. I have a class to teach in a few minutes."

His phone vibrates again, but this time, only a message appears.

I take a quick glance and read it. I get goosebumps.

*I'm coming for you, Jay.*

Is he being stalked?

Despite the weirdness, I still manage to say, "Virgin blood, I tell you."

I leave his office. If he is being hunted because of his unique virgin blood, I don't want to be in the room with him and be dragged to some abandoned village full of witches. I think I'd rather torment myself with Gregory's company. Thank you very much.

As I make my way towards my history class, I receive a text from Ella. She says she'll be attending her afternoon classes since her doctor only did a few tests on her leg this morning, but she'll be a little late.

I enter the classroom and see the psycho teacher busy adjusting the AC. I guess I'm in luck since I don't want to make any eye contact with him today, or any day for that matter. I take a seat at the back of the class despite the possibility that someone might get mad at me for taking their seat. I'll probably just bribe whoever that person is with a lot of money.

Three more minutes before the class officially starts and Lance comes in with a redheaded girl hanging by his arm, the same redhead who jumped on him yesterday. She gives him a quick kiss on the cheek then leaves. Lance smiles when he spots me, then strides my way and sits on the chair next to me.

The girls don't attack him much anymore. They just throw a few glances and batting of eyelashes his way. Although some still try to take a picture with him, they aren't that wild compared to yesterday. I guess they're done worshiping him now since this is his second day.

"Hey, stranger. You look like someone killed your cat. What's up?"

"That math teacher again." So, I tell him the summarized version of how Jeremy is forcing me to be tutored by Hailey who is a mean girl but also a smart student.

"A nerd who sleeps around. Cool. I don't hear that every day."

Really? That's all he got from my ranting?

We notice Mr. Campbell standing in the middle of the classroom, which means that students should settle down now because his lecture is about to start. When everyone is finally facing the front, he presses his hands together and makes a dad joke. He always does before starting the class.

"Okay, so I found this on the internet and credits to whoever thought of this," our history teacher says excitedly while rubbing his palms. "What did the cell say to his sister when she stepped on his toe?"

The whole class answers, "What?"

Silence. Anticipation.

Mr. Campbell grins. "Mitosis."

A moment of realization...Then everyone sniggers and giggles.

Except me.

Everyone knows dad jokes are supposed to be so bad that you can't help but laugh at how cringey they are. But I still can't bring myself to even smile now that I know his real personality.

He starts discussing more about the Cold War, and I listen intently because despite how uncomfortable I am right now, I still have to pass this subject.

I glance at my phone's screen to check the time. Twenty minutes after one and Ella isn't here yet. I know she said she's going to be late. I just was not expecting her to be this late. She probably won't even be allowed to come inside the classroom now, since we have zero tolerance for tardiness in this school.

Mr. Campbell has asked us to answer the questions he has written on the board. The questions are easy, and I'm sure I can answer pretty much all of them if my stomach isn't aching right now. This is definitely a number two.

Darn it, this is for not chewing my chicken sandwich thoroughly.

I raise my hand, and Mr. Campbell gestures towards me.

"Yes, Ms. Roberts. Care to answer one of these questions?"

I clench my hands over my stomach. "The first one is Russia. I need to go to the bathroom."

"That's wrong, but alright." He takes out the hall pass from his drawer, and I quickly run toward him to get it. I mutter a *thank you* and dash out the classroom.

I slam the bathroom door open because the call of nature is that intense. Only I almost forget what I am about to do when I find Ella pressed against the wall, arms tightly wrapped around a guy as he kisses her savagely.

They immediately pull away from each other once they realize they're not alone. I stand motionless as I try to grasp what is happening—my crush and my best friend.

The gods must really hate me today.

# Chapter 11

I've known Kyle longer than I've known Ella.

We met in kindergarten, and Kyle Wilson was that cute and funny boy with beautiful hazel eyes that every kid wanted to play with. Even at the age of five, every girl or boy already wanted to hang out with him in the sandbox. He was that charismatic.

Yet I never had the courage to approach him or make the first move. I was a blonde girl with freckles on my cheeks and nose. I thought that he'd be appalled of my face.

Except he wasn't because three days in the kindergarten class, he asked me if I could color his drawing with him. And at that moment, I told myself that he would be my Prince Charming and we would live happily ever after. Typical five-year-old fantasy. Pathetic, I know.

We weren't exactly best friends, but we were still close.

Then in second grade, this shy new student came into class with a limp leg and striking eyes—Daniella Summers. She had light brown hair that flowed down to her waist, and I was amazed at how silky and soft it looked.

Ella Summers was simply lovely.

I was eating with Kyle and a few friends of ours when I noticed her alone on a bench, not even touching the food in front of her. I didn't hesitate to sit beside her and share a meal with her.

She said she was homeschooled all her years because of an accident until her mom allowed her to go to a regular school once she could walk without anyone's help. There was grave sadness in her voice as I listened. I could tell that just by the way she talked to me despite her smile.

I introduced her to my friends, and Kyle was the first one to greet her.

One week later, Ella and I became close, and I finally told her of my undying love for Kyle. She giggled at my silliness because who already uses the word *love* at our age, right? But I told her I was and that I was going to marry Kyle someday. She merely nodded and supported my infatuation with him.

Ella knew my feelings for Kyle for years. How can she do this to me?

I can't really start a scene or something since Kyle isn't my boyfriend in the first place. But I still feel betrayed. Ella just broke the best friend code.

"Hey, Kim." Kyle greets me with embarrassment. I glance up to him and offer a forced smile.

"Hey." I awkwardly wave because, despite this hellish situation, my body can never deny my attraction to him.

He puts his hand behind his neck. "We thought everyone was in class."

I clear my throat. "I have to use the bathroom."

Now I'm wondering who's going to acknowledge the elephant in the room.

Apparently, Ella does. "Kyle broke up with Hailey yesterday."

I simply nod because that's really all she can say right now especially in front of Kyle. She can't really start explaining herself why she was making out with the guy I've always liked. No, she can't. Not in front of Kyle, at least.

"Okay, so…" I point my thumb behind me. "Can you, like, leave? I need to use one of the toilets, and it would be awkward if you're both here."

Kyle chuckles. "Oh, of course." Then he grabs Ella's hand, and they exit the bathroom together. I think my heart just cracked.

Ella even tries to catch my eye, but I am having none of it. I simply get inside one of the cubicles and cry while doing my business. I use the tissue to wipe my tears. I hate this right now.

After I'm done, I opt not to return to history or even attend my last class that day. My chest is too painful for me to even concentrate anyway, so I just sulk in the music workroom that I'm sure no one is going to use until tomorrow.

Damn it. Why am I even hurting like this? He's not even mine, to begin with! Why am I acting like I've just caught my boyfriend cheating on me with my best friend when he clearly isn't mine. Seriously, this is stupid! I am acting stupid.

*Stop being stupid, Kim.*

But it still hurts despite my reasoning. Probably because of the fact that my very own best friend knows I've been pining for Kyle all my life and yet she still made out with him. The least she could do was tell me.

I take out my phone and text her.

*How long have u been together?*

It doesn't take long before she responds.

*About 2 months. I'm really sorry, Kimmy*

Two months? But she said Kyle and Hailey had only broken up yesterday, and I'm pretty sure they were still dating a few months ago. Does this mean...

Me: *ur Kyle's side chick?*
Ella: *Hailey is cheating on him too. Kim, where are u? Let me explain everything.*

I cannot believe my best friend is even capable of doing this.

Me: *Wow. I didn't know u'd stoop this low*
Ella: *u dont understand. Pls, Kim. Where are u?*

I roll my eyes and choose not to respond.

She tries calling me multiple times, but I always press ignore. She even leaves a voice message, telling me how really sorry she is and that she was planning on telling me soon but didn't know how to. It only makes me more upset. Why can't she understand that as shallow my reason is, what she did still offends me?

For two months they've been seeing each other, and she has never dared to mention it to me? I would understand if she just confessed it to me sooner. But instead, I was smacked in the face with the reality that Kyle chose her and not me.

I can and will forgive Ella, but not today. She should just let me wallow in my misery for at least two days, then we can talk without me bawling out my eyes. I'm not really mad at her, just disappointed. Seriously disappointed.

I also got a text from Lance earlier, asking me where I was, and I just told him I wasn't feeling well, so I left school early. I really don't want to talk to anyone right now.

The bell rings outside, but I do not leave the music room. I might bump into Ella or Kyle, or worse, Hailey, and I'm not ready to face any of them yet. I wait an hour more just to be sure that everyone has left before I cautiously open the door to exit the room when someone pushes the door open from outside.

"Oh, hello," the girl says with a sweet smile. "I didn't know someone would be inside."

"I was just...having a girl moment," I reply. I tuck strands of hair behind my ear. She smiles at me and nods.

"I see. I once had a girl moment too back in high school." She gestures with her right hand. "May I come inside?"

"Sure. Of course. Sorry." I open the door wider and give her enough space to let herself in. She slightly bows her head in gratitude, something like Korean people do, but she doesn't appear Asian at all. In fact, she looks like a mixture of Latina and White.

The woman saunters towards the front of the classroom where the choristers usually stand then roams her eyes around.

When I think she's done scrutinizing how big the room is, she approaches the grand piano then plays a few keys.

She's quite tall, probably five feet and nine inches. Her long brown hair falls down to her elbows. Her small eyes are fairly brown with a hint of gray, and her cute pouty lips shimmer in pink lip-gloss. She's so beautiful.

I think I'll start my lesbian phase now.

Kidding.

"Are you a new student?" I ask her.

She smiles and shakes her head. "I'm going to be the new music teacher here."

But she looks so young.

My eyebrows furrow. "What about Mrs. Katrina?" I hope nothing bad had happened to her. She's so nice.

"She just discovered she's pregnant and wants to take her maternity leave next month." Okay, that's good news for her, I guess. Deep inside, I still feel bad for Mrs. Katrina; she's carrying a baby with a cheating husband, Mr. Campbell.

"That's great for her," I simply say. "So, I guess you'll be our temporary music teacher?"

Really, Kim? As if she didn't just say that ten seconds ago?

"Not until December though." She walks towards me and cheerfully takes my hand. "I'm Jewel Riggs, by the way." Her smile is so infectious.

"Kimberly Roberts." I can't help but smile back at her. "But you can just call me Kim."

"Kim. That's a really cute name."

"And yours is so…exquisite."

"Wow, I have my parents to thank for my *exquisite* name, I guess." She lets go of my hand and goes to the door. "I'll be leaving now. I just wanted to have a look at the music room so I'll be more familiar with it when I get back next month. They just hired me a while ago."

"Oh, I'll be leaving too. I'm done with my girl moment now." We both share a soft laugh.

I close the door behind me, and we walk side by side through the hallways.

I've only met this young lady less than five minutes ago, and I already feel so comfortable with her. I really hope we'll be great friends despite her being a new teacher in this school.

We're both about to exit through the main door until we hear someone cuss loudly.

We glance to our right and find Jeremy standing a few feet away from us. His expression is clearly dumbfounded, his knuckles almost white from gripping his laptop bag.

"I told you I'm coming, didn't I?" Jewel tells him.

# Chapter 12

Our new music teacher beams at me.

"You go right ahead. I have catching up to do with my boyfriend," she says it so cheerily that I just nod as she saunters towards my fiancé.

I try to catch Jeremy's gaze, but his eyes are glued to her as if he can't believe she's really standing in front of him.

His girlfriend.

Wow. Okay. Totally not expecting that.

Jewel puts her hands behind his neck and pulls him down for a kiss. I glance away and hurriedly push the door to leave the building, my feet taking big steps as I make my way towards the parking lot. Once I'm inside my car, I simply stare at the steering wheel.

My fiancé has a girlfriend.

My fiancé has a beautiful Latina girlfriend with curvy hips and sexy thighs.

Am I jealous? No. Insecure? Maybe.

And I know for a fact that I'm not mistaking that girl as his sister again because I'm pretty sure siblings don't kiss.

Will he break up with Jewel once we're married or will he continue his relationship with her? Part of me wants to think that I'm fine whether he has a mistress or not since we never really wanted to be together anyway. But will I really be okay with the fact that I'm sharing my husband with someone obviously more gorgeous than I am?

No decent wife would really want that, married by love or not.

I guess I just have to talk to him about this tomorrow. Or maybe I can talk to dad tonight and tell him about Jeremy's girlfriend and that I'm not willing to marry a man who is in a relationship.

Once I get home, I go straight to my dad's office, expecting him to be sitting by his desk, working on his laptop. Except he isn't. I ask one of the housekeepers if she knows where he is, and she simply replies a no. I check his room, but he isn't there either. But when I hear the shower running from his bathroom, I take a seat on his bed and decide to wait for him to finish.

I glance at the picture of him and Mom on the side table. In the picture, my mom has her arms wrapped around my dad's neck while her head is resting on his shoulder. My dad's hand grips her arm. They both look so young in the photo. I wouldn't really be surprised since they started dating during their freshman year in high school. They're one of those lucky high school sweethearts that end up marrying each other.

Sadly, their happy married lives didn't last long because of that horrible accident.

Now I'm more curious on why, of all people, Dad had to ask help from the Lincoln family? One of them killed my mom. It also doesn't help that they obviously did something to reduce the sentence. I know there's something more about our sudden engagement, but why is he trying to hide it from me? Perhaps I just have to ask him for the marriage contract, just in case, the real reason is indicated there.

I sigh and lie on my parents' bed. I preoccupy myself with *Riverdale* on my phone as I wait until I realize that my dad has been in the shower for almost an hour now.

Weird.

I stand up and knock on the bathroom door. "Dad?"

No one answers.

My heart starts to beat fast. "Dad, you okay in there?" I twist the doorknob, but it's locked. "Dad, open up. It's me, Kim."

70

My knees are feeling weak by the second. I repeatedly hit my palm against the door.

"Dad! Open up!"

Damn it, he's still not answering. I run outside his bedroom and call for help. One of the workers fetches the key and hurriedly returns to my dad's room. Tears are welling up in my eyes as the worker unlocks the door with unsteady hands. One maid is rubbing my arms to comfort me, but I'm still shaking.

The door slams open.

*No. Please, gods, no.*

I see my dad's body slumped on the tiled floor.

Blood. So much blood.

No. No. No. This is not happening.

The worker carries my dad up. He's unconscious, and his head is bleeding.

The house staff holds me tighter as I shout and cry, begging my dad to wake up.

Three more men enter the room and lift his unconscious body down the stairs.

I come down with them and see Jeremy at the door, gaping at the scene before him. He immediately helps the men carry my dad to our van, and I follow them inside. His cold hands pull me in a tight embrace. I grip his shirt and let myself cry on his chest.

I have no idea how long it took us to reach the hospital. All I know is that a stretcher has already been prepared when we arrived. Nurses rush my dad into the emergency room. I want to follow them, but Jeremy stops me, telling me to just let them do their job and save my dad.

I cry more.

He helps me walk toward the waiting room, and we sit together on the waiting bench. He's still holding me close, and I'm still weeping in his arms. I can't stop crying. My head hurts. My chest hurts.

I feel so weak. So scared.

My dad can't die. He just can't.

~

My fiancé hasn't said anything. He's not even whispering comforting words. Probably because he doesn't know what will happen to my dad either. He refuses to give me false hope, so I just wrap my arms around him and hold him tighter.

An hour has gone by, and I'm still enveloped in Jeremy's arms. I have stopped crying now, but my chest still hurts. I'm still terrified for my dad. One nurse informed us that he had a heart attack and hit his head with the fall. He's breathing but still not stable, and they're doing the best they can to make sure he'll live. She returned to the emergency room. That was thirty minutes ago. My fear increases by every passing minute.

"Do you want something to drink?" Jeremy asks, his chin on top of my head.

"No." My voice sounds cracked and weak. I slightly pull away from his embrace and look up to him. "Why are you here?"

He couldn't possibly have known what was happening to my dad before he got to our house, could he?

He sighs. "I wanted to explain myself to you about Jewel. You were out the door before I could even talk to you. I didn't want Jewel to suspect about us, so I just let you leave."

I sit up straight. "You don't have to explain about your girlfriend. It's fine."

"Ex-girlfriend. We broke up seven years ago."

"Oh." But he still let her kiss him.

"I saw hurt in your eyes when she tried to kiss me. I couldn't do that to you." Tried? "Just so you know, I pushed her way before our lips could even touch."

Somehow that makes me feel less bad about this situation "There wasn't hurt in my eyes. Get over yourself."

He just nods and amusedly says, "Sure." Which means he doesn't believe me.

Jerk.

"Why did you break up?" I need to talk about something else to calm myself. Thinking about my dad's imminent death only

72

makes me want to cry, and I don't think my body could take another hour of crying.

Jeremy is hesitant at first. "We shouldn't have gotten together in the first place."

"Why? She's really beautiful though."

He shakes his head. "It's complicated."

"Did you love her?" Why can't I stop putting salt to the wound?

He tucks strands of hair behind my ear. "I thought I did, but…I couldn't have possibly loved someone like her."

Now I'm more curious. "Why?"

It's evident in his eyes that he doesn't want to answer that question. Fortunately for him, another nurse exits the emergency room.

"Mr. Adrian Roberts is stable now, but we're still not certain when he'll regain consciousness." That makes me feel a little better.

"When can we see him?" Jeremy asks.

"We'll be sending him to a private room in a few minutes. You can see him by then."

"Thank you," I tell her, and she goes to the other direction with a reassuring smile.

About ten minutes later, we stand up as they release my dad from the ER on a stretcher, an oxygen mask attached to his face, layers of gauze covering a quarter of his head. He's unconscious but breathing, unlike an hour ago when we barely felt a pulse on his wrist.

Jeremy kisses the top of my head. "He's going to be okay."

The doctor informs us that they'll be bringing him to the best private suite on the top floor since our trusted house staff have already worked on the needed hospital documents for my dad. I'm just glad I'm clearly not alone in this.

Once my dad is already settled in his room, I can't help but cry again, not out of sadness but of relief. In spite of his unconscious state, the doctors assured us that he'll wake up within this month. Jeremy holds me as I cry with a small smile.

Two hours later, everyone has dispersed and returned to our house. Jeremy left to buy a McDonalds meal for us. It's only 8:45 in the evening and I'm already sleepy, possibly because I've shed so many tears today. One of the house staff offered to watch for my dad so I can go home where I can rest, but I refused. I'm his daughter, and I should be the one to look after him.

The door opens, but instead of Jeremy with a takeout bag, a good-looking blond man in a business suit enters the room. He is probably in his late thirties. He holds a suitcase in his right hand and a thick book in his left.

I stand up from the couch as he cautiously approaches me. "Marc Eaton, your dad's lawyer." He offers his hand in front of me, and I shake it with uncertainty.

"Kimberly Roberts."

"Your dad has told me a lot about you." He smiles. "Should we take a seat?"

We both do. He opens his suitcase on his lap. I watch him warily as he scans the papers.

What is he doing here?

I'm not really comfortable sitting beside a stranger right now. I've heard his name countless times. He's my dad's most trusted lawyer, and I know I should trust him too, but this is my first time meeting him in person, so I'm still a little guarded.

I exhale in relief when Jeremy enters the room with our dinner. He eyes Marc curiously, and I just shrug.

"He's Marc Eaton, my dad's lawyer," I tell him. Marc gives him a small smile and returns his attention to the papers.

"Ah, here it is," he says then hands me a small white envelope. I simply stare at it.

Jeremy sits beside me. "What's that?"

"This is Adrian Roberts's last will and testament…sort of. It's a letter for Kim."

I can't help but scowl at him. "My dad is still alive, Mr. Eaton."

The lawyer chuckles. "I know. But your dad specifically told me to give you this letter the moment a near-death experience happens to him. I'm just following orders, Kim." He's still offering the envelope to me, so I just take it.

"Have you read this?" I ask him.

He shakes his head. "I haven't. It's perfectly sealed. But your dad informed me what that letter contains so I can help with any procedures if anything happens to him."

"Procedures? What do you mean by that?" Jeremy probes.

Marc merely stands up. "Let's just say that letter contains the reason why you ought to be married immediately." He takes out a card from his pocket and hands it to me. "Call me when you need more clarifications."

I cautiously take the calling card, and he leaves the room.

# Chapter 13

*My sweetest Kimberly,*

*If you're reading this, then that only means either of the two things: I almost died or I have died.*

*I wrote this letter the moment I told you of your upcoming engagement with the Lincoln's heir because I have a very weak heart and I know I'm going to die sooner than what I was hoping and I don't want to keep you in the dark for too long.*

*First, I want to tell you how much I love you, princess. I'm so proud of what you have become despite not having your mother with you; you grew up to be a wonderful young lady with a beautiful heart. I'm in awe of you, my love. Don't ever forget that.*

*Second, and I hope you won't hate me for this, the reason why I wanted you to marry Jeremy Lincoln because your mother has left you a large trust fund that we can use to save the company. She made it when you were only four. It was your late grandparents' money that she placed so I can't really open that trust fund until we follow at least one of her conditions indicated in the contract. The trust fund can only be managed once you're wedded to Jeremy Lincoln or you have your first child with anyone. She said the money was actually her gift to you.*

*I really have no idea why your mother had made those conditions. But princess, please don't hate me for using you to get that money. I only wanted what's best for us and marrying you off to Jeremy is the only way I could think of, unless you got pregnant at the age of 18 which I'm sure you won't agree to and I don't like that idea either.*

*The trust fund has never crossed my mind for years. Until I saw how much money we were already losing and I remembered your mom's supposed gift for you. It was a difficult decision and I pondered it for months but it was really the quickest way to save our company.*

*If you're reading this because I'm dead then don't worry about the company just yet. I have a few reliable people, including your grandma, who will manage it until you're ready. But if you're reading this and I'm still alive, I hope you'd find it in your heart to forgive me someday, princess.*

*I love you always.*

*Your dad, Adrian Roberts*

I stare at the letter in utter shock.

A trust fund that can only be opened if I marry Jeremy or I have my first child.

Wow.

Was my mom high on drugs when she made that condition? Seriously, why in the world would she want me to marry Jeremy in the first place? She's definitely on to something.

I close the letter and put it back inside the envelope. I'm now sitting beside my dad in his hospital bed. Now that I know all of these, I can't really hate him for pushing me to marry that guy. My dad only wanted to save the company, and I'm the only one who can help save it.

"You're done reading it?" Jeremy says across the room. He's sitting on the couch I was on earlier, currently eating a burger and fries.

I just nod because I'm still a little speechless.

"Mind sharing why we're forced to get married?"

"No." I shake my head, and he narrows his eyes.

"Fine. Then you're not getting any of these." He closes the McDonalds paper bag as he frowns at me. Wow, that was so childish.

"I'll tell you later. Just, not now. I'm still trying to absorb all the words."

"May I read it?"

I scowl at him. "No. This is personal."

"Fine." Then he continues eating his fries.

Even though he really wants to know what the letter contains and I refuse to tell him yet, he still doesn't leave me with my dad. I tell him multiple times that I can manage on my own, but he still wants to make sure I won't break down crying again tonight.

Fortunately, the private room has two extra single beds, so that is where we settle ourselves in an hour later. The beds are two feet away from each other too, so that's a plus.

Jeremy is facing the ceiling with his arm over his forehead while I'm on my side, looking at him. Is he asleep? His eyes are closed, so I stare at his facial features, hoping to find sleep any minute now. He licks his lips, and I gasp when he turns his head to me with a smirk.

"I can feel you watching me." I force my eyes to close, and I hear him snicker. "It's okay to be obsessed with me, Kim."

I open my eyes and glare at him. "Shut up."

"Are you really not going to tell me what's in the letter?" He's so persistent.

"I'll tell you tomorrow."

"Will you go to school tomorrow?"

I don't hesitate to answer no.

"Okay. Good night, Kim."

~

I wake up with the smell of chocolate and pancakes.

The curtains are drawn together, but I know it's already morning. I glance to my left to check my dad, and he's still asleep in his bed. I really hope he'll wake up soon.

My phone vibrates beneath my pillow, so I retrieve it and find two missed calls from Ella and one message from Lance, asking me how my dad is.

How did he know?

So, I texted back:

I rub my hands over my face to wipe the sleep off my eyes. I can hear someone preparing food in the small kitchen located at the far left of the private room, so I follow the smell of pancakes and find Jeremy placing plates on the small round table with three chairs. He looks up to me with a boyish grin.

"I made breakfast."

I eye him curiously. "It's nine in the morning. Why aren't you at school?"

"I told the school that we had a family emergency. They have substitute teachers anyway, so no worries."

"You didn't have to." I rub my palm over my arm. "I'm fine, really."

He ignores my comment and proceeds to put the pancakes on the two plates.

"Let's eat." He pushes a chair backward, and I take a seat on it. The pancake looks delicious, but my mind refuses to acknowledge that I'm hungry. Jeremy occupies the chair beside me and notices something is wrong. "You don't like pancakes?"

"They're actually my favorite. I'm just not hungry."

"You didn't eat your burger or anything last night, so I don't believe you're not hungry."

I roll my eyes. "I think I'd know when I'm hungry."

He takes my knife and fork on the table and cuts a small slice then raises it close to my mouth. "Say aah."

This is ridiculous.

"Dude, I'm not a child."

"Well, you're acting like one." The tip of the pancake touches my lips, and I can smell its pleasant aroma. Automatically, my stomach rumbles. "See? You're hungry." He laughs.

I take the fork from him and eat the food myself, glowering at him while he's looking at me with a satisfied smirk.

After I swallow, I arch an eyebrow. "Happy?"

"Very."

For a few minutes, we eat in silence until his mouth opens to speak again. "So, about that letter. Mind telling it to me now?"

I exhale heavily. He'll find out about it anyway. "Both our parents want us to get married."

"I think we've already established that."

"I mean, my mom also wanted us to get married."

He gawks at me curiously. "How? I'm sorry, but I don't believe in ghosts."

I take a gulp of my hot chocolate before answering him. "There was this trust fund that my mom made when I was four years old. It can only be used if one of the two conditions is met. Either I marry you or I have my first child."

"Was your mom high on something when she made that?" he asks, and I slap his arm. Although it doesn't really sound farfetched.

"I don't know, but…that's what she wanted, and my dad needs to take hold of that trust fund so he can use it to save our company."

He plays with the fork on his lips, and I can't help but stare at it. "But my parents also wanted me to marry you. Do they know about your mother's trust fund?"

I shrug while still staring at his lips. "Maybe you can ask your parents" Will his lips taste just as good as his pancakes?

*Whoa. Danger zone. Snap out of it, Kim.*

"I'll ask them later." He nods then eats his pancake again.

Once we are done eating, I offer to wash the dishes, but Jeremy fights for it and commands me to sit on the couch and watch some TV instead. We argue for about two minutes until I give up and huff outside the mini kitchen.

I approach my dad and place a soft kiss on his hand that has no tubes before relaxing on the couch. Good thing the TV is compatible with Netflix, so I put my account in and watch *Stranger Things*. I'm halfway through the episode when my phone vibrates for an incoming call.

It's Ella.

My mind contemplates whether I should answer it or not. I decide for the former. I swipe the screen to accept the call.

"Finally! Oh my gosh, I'm so sorry, Kim! I'm so sorry." She's crying, and my heart breaks just hearing her sound this upset. "I heard about your dad, and I want to visit him, but I don't know if you'll throw me out or something."

I blow out a hefty breath. "You can visit if you want. You know I won't throw you out."

"Oh my gosh, really?"

"Yeah, just promise you won't make any loud sounds." Then someone knocks. "Hold on. Someone is at the door." I open it, and Ella instantly lunges and envelopes me in a tight hug.

"I missed you so much, Kim. I'm really sorry. I'm so sorry. I'm sorry, Kim." She cries on my shoulder. "Please don't hate me. I'm nothing without you."

I return her embrace. Why would I even think I could resist this girl?

My hand gently pats her back. "Hey, it's fine. I'm not mad at you."

She holds me in arm's length, her eyes puffy from probably crying too much. "I ended it with Kyle. I'm really sorry for being so selfish."

I hit her arm. "Why'd you do that?"

She hits me back. "Because you're mad at me and I don't want to lose you."

Gah! And this is why I love this girl so much. No matter how much she has hurt me for not telling about her and Kyle, she still tries to rectify it, despite how stupid she was for doing it.

I pull her in for another tight squeeze. "You know I'd never hate you. But I'm disappointed, so you have a lot of explaining to do."

"I know, I know." Then she gasps and releases me from her hold. "Hot guy!"

I spin around and stagger backward. Jeremy's naked torso is on display as he looks at us blankly, his obviously wet shirt hanging on his shoulder.

My eyes won't leave his six pack. Ella and I are both drooling while my dad is still comatose in his bed.

Why, oh, why would he do something like this?

"Why aren't you in class, Ms. Summers?" he asks as if there's nothing wrong with being half naked in front of two high school girls.

Ella gulps. "I wanted to see my best friend."

"Why aren't you wearing a shirt?" I ask him.

Jeremy grimaces. "Obviously, my shirt is soaked. Blame the spoon."

He strides towards his black bag on the bed, takes out a new white T-shirt, and wears it over his head while Ella and I ogle him. He spreads his wet gray shirt on the back of the chair and returns his gaze to us and says, "I'll be reading in the kitchen if you need me."

Ella clutches my arm and whispers, "Our math teacher is so hot."

A smile forms on my lips. "I know."

# Chapter 14

"We only make out whenever he breaks up with Hailey," Ella says, and I gawk at her incredulously. Her face shows a mixture of pride and humiliation. I don't know if I should smack her on the head or cheer for her.

"That still makes you the side-chick, the mistress in their relationship." I chastise her.

"Technically, no." Ella denies. "I'm more of Kyle's rebound whenever they break up. You know they're in an on-and-off relationship, right?"

"And you're fine being the rebound?" I can't believe my best friend agrees with that kind of arrangement. I would never be okay with that.

She just shrugs "Yeah. Kyle is cute and a great kisser. I don't really have genuine feelings for him. It's more of a physical attraction."

I shake her shoulders. "You've slept with him?"

Ella coughs awkwardly. "No?" I flick her nose because she's definitely lying. "Ouch, okay, sort of." What does that even mean? I flick her forehead. "Hey! That was hard!"

"Well, because you're lying to me!"

She groans. "We haven't done anything yet, but we've already slept together, *literally*, with our clothes on after watching *Game of Thrones*. Nothing happened at all. Is that truthful enough for you?"

I narrow my eyes at her, still suspicious. "And when was this?"

"Last Friday, the night they broke up again."

"You hoe!"

Her head drops to her hands. "I know!"

I pull her in for a hug. "There, there. I'll still love you even if you become a stripper."

"Really?" she says with puppy eyes.

"Or even a prostitute." I kiss her forehead. "I'll accept you no matter what."

Jeremy exits the kitchen and eyes us apprehensively on the couch. I can't really blame him since Ella and I have had weirder talks before. We're loud people, and we've also had people almost calling 911 on us for spouting out disturbing sentences.

"Should I be worried?" he asks, and we shake our heads. He slowly nods, still uneasy. "Are you not attending your afternoon class, Ms. Summers?"

Ella glances at the wall clock on top of my dad's bed. It's already 12:00 PM. She turns her attention to him. "Are you not teaching for your afternoon class?"

"Family emergency." He winks at me. "That man over there is going to be my father-in-law soon, so I need to be here with my future wife."

And now my stomach is filled with pesky pests.

Ella rolls her eyes. "Fine, I'm leaving." We both walk towards the door. "Uncle Adrian may be unconscious, but that doesn't mean you two can do dirty stuff in this room. That's just wrong on so many levels."

I glare at my friend and push her out the door while she controls her laughter.

"You have a weird friend," Jeremy says behind me.

"But if you really want to, be quiet!" Elle shouts from the other side of the door, and I cover my face in embarrassment.

Yeah, I really have a weird friend whom I'd murder soon.

"We will!" Jeremy shouts back, and I instinctively glare at him.

How dare he entertains my best friend's craziness?

"Don't forget to share the details, alright?" Ella says, and I open the door again to hit her with my flip-flops, but she's already running away from me. She glances back and waves me goodbye before entering the elevator. I close the door, groaning.

Jeremy laughs. "I like your friend."

"Shut up."

~

When night falls, Jeremy finally decides to take a shower. The bathroom is located in front of our beds, and I am lying on mine while writing an English essay that is due tomorrow. The door opens, and Jeremy comes out with only a towel around his waist. I literally drop the pen I am holding when I notice the droplets of water running down his chest. My eyes follow him as he walks barefoot towards his bed without a care in the world.

Staring at my teacher's V outline on his waist makes me blush.

Jeremy unzips his bag, takes out clean clothes, then peers up to me. I think I'm drooling when he sees me because he winks before saying, "Mind turning around?"

I instantaneously whip my head to the other direction and close my eyes. "You know you could've just changed your clothes in the bathroom, right?"

"Nah, you like it this way." He chuckles, and I throw a pillow behind me, hoping it hits him even though I'm not looking. "I'm taking off my towel now, try not to peek. But you're still welcome to do so if you really want to."

I grumble and cover my face with my hands. "Stop being a pervert!" The sound of the wet towel hitting the marble floor makes the situation more awkward.

Although he is more than two feet away from me and I'm facing the opposite direction, the thought of a completely naked man in the room with me burns my face, for Pete's sake. I can hear more shuffling behind me and I know he's wearing his clothes now, but my mind can't help but imagine him doing so, and I hate my stupid brain for doing that. Now, my face becomes hotter by each passing minute.

At last, he says, "It's safe now."

I slowly move my head and only open one eye. He's only wearing a pair of gray boxers and a white T-shirt, so I close my eyes again. "You're not wearing pants!"

This idiot.

"I don't wear pants to bed."

"You wore pants last night."

"And I was really uncomfortable. "Stop being a prude." The sound of the blanket covering his body make me assume he's under them. so I open my eyes to glare at him.

"Wear some pants. My dad is in here," I tell him.

"He's asleep. Now stop talking, or I'll remove my boxers too." That instantly shuts me up.

About four hours later, I am finally done with my English essay. I remember that I threw my pillow at him a while ago, so now I'm without a pillow. I glance at Jeremy on my right, and he's sound asleep while hugging my supposed head cushion.

I stand up from my bed and approach his, making sure I won't make any sound. Then I carefully pull out the pillow away from his grasp, but he clutches it tighter to him. I gently remove his arms instead, which makes him grumble.

"Go to sleep, Kim."

"I need my pillow," I whisper.

"Sssshhh."

I roll my eyes. "I can't sleep without a pillow."

He grudgingly opens his eyes. "I said sssshh!"

I sit on his bed and try to pull the pillow from him, but he's holding it tighter, and he's obviously stronger than me. "Damn it, Jay. Stop being a child."

Unexpectedly, he pushes the pillow on the floor and forces me to lie down next to him by pulling my wrist. He's not hugging me like in the movies, but he's still gripping my arm between us, our faces only a few inches away.

"I hate it when someone wakes me up in the middle of the night," he states, frowning.

"And I hate it when someone doesn't want to give my pillow back."

"You're the one who threw it to me."

"Because you were making dirty jokes!" I instantly blush at the memory.

He suddenly smirks. "You're blushing again." His hand releases my wrist to flick my nose. "I knew it. You enjoyed seeing me in my towel, you naughty girl!"

I shove him backward. "Eew. Shut up." I immediately sit up to get away from him, but he snakes his arm around my waist and pulls me back, making me squeal.

He places a quick kiss on my nose before releasing me. "That's for waking me up."

I grab my pillow from the floor and hit him with it. He grabs my wrist again and sits up so he can kiss the corner of my lips.

I gasp. "Dude!"

"Well, stop bothering my sleep!" he yells. I am about to hit him again with the pillow, but he instantly kneels on his bed and cups my face. "Hit me with the pillow one more time, and I'll drag you in this bed and sleep on top of you."

I scoff. "You're just all bark but no bite."

He smirks wickedly as he yanks me down to his bed. I'm not really sure how he actually did it, but I suddenly find myself underneath him, my head facing sideways, a pillow over my cheek while his head rests on the other side of the pillow.

I struggle beneath him. "You're so heavy." Although a pillow is separating our faces, I can sense him smiling. "I can't breathe!" I pull my knee up, but he pushes it back down.

"Yes, you can." He laughs then shifts his body on top of mine so he can be more comfortable in our position while I'm obviously not.

I pinch his arm. "Get off me!"

"Let's do twenty questions first." Seriously? "Alright…okay, who was your first kiss?"

"We're not having this conversation." I push his chest, and he rolls to the other side. I remove the pillow from my face and glower at him.

"Come on, I'm curious. Who's your first kiss?" he asks with a playful smirk.

"Some girl named Shayne in freshman year."

He stifles a snort. "Really? A girl? I didn't know you swing that way."

I slap his arm. "I'm straight, and it was just on the corner of my lips because she admitted she liked me, then tried to kiss me, so I instinctively moved my head to the side, but it was too late, and I felt a quarter of her lips on mine."

He laughs. "Alright, some girl to girl action then. But it's still not considered a kiss, though. What about a real kiss?"

"It's a close one." I shrug. Why are we having this conversation in the middle of the night again? "Alright, I'm going to sleep," I tell him, but, out of nowhere, he pushes me down on my back and presses his lips on mine. The kiss is brief and feels almost like a whisper.

It doesn't take long before he pulls away and winks down at me. "There, you're welcome." He pulls me up and gives my lips another quick peck. "That should serve as a lesson not to wake me up again."

I punch his chest. "I wanted Harry Styles to be my first kiss!"

He scrunches his nose. "Well, I wanted to marry Scarlet Johansson, but I'm engaged to you. We can't always have what we want, pookie bear."

"Don't call me that." I try to hit him again with the pillow, but he smacks it down.

"Do you want me to kiss you again? A French one this time?"

I pinch his hand.

"Oh! You really want to be French kissed, young lady."

I show him a heart sign, then immediately flip him off with my middle finger.

He cups my jaws, and I think he is going to pull my face toward him again. However, we hear a soft whimper. We both glance to my sleeping dad as he makes another grousing sound.

"I'm going to call a nurse," Jeremy says, and I quickly head for my dad's bed.

"Dad?" I squeeze his hand. "Are you going to wake up now?"

He blinks. "Kim?"

Jeremy comes with a male nurse who checks my dad's vital signs.

"Yes, Daddy?" I bring his hand to my lips.

"Kim...don't..." He squeezes back, and I almost cry. He's really waking up.

Jeremy and I put our ears closer to his mouth so we can hear him better.

"Don't what, Daddy?" I ask him.

"Don't...French...kiss."

My dad closes his eyes again and sleeps for two more weeks.

# Chapter 15

November has finally ended, and now it's Christmas month.

What I hate about living in California is the lack of snow during this time of the year. Usually, my dad and I would fly to my grandma's villa in New York where there is snow just so I can enjoy white Christmas. Nevertheless, the doctors didn't allow my dad to travel anywhere for another three months because of his ill condition. But that is absolutely fine with me.

For the two weeks that my dad was in the hospital, Jeremy and I would go to school together while one of our house staff took care of my dad. He would just drop me off two blocks away from school so we won't raise any suspicions. Then once school is over, either we'd return to our house to get more stuff, or we'd go straight to the hospital again.

For two weeks, he slept in the private room with me and Dad, prepared breakfast, lunch, and dinner. Sometimes when he's tired from work, we'd just order a takeout, which probably only happened four times, since he believes that fast food is seriously unhealthy. We also spent Thanksgiving together with a bucket of fried chicken.

Lance visited on the first week, but he only stayed for half an hour because Jeremy kept glaring at him from across the room even though he's eating the glazed donuts Lance brought for us. When I hugged my friend goodbye, Jeremy wasn't in the mood to cook, so I ordered pizza instead. Lance didn't make another visit, so we just resorted to texting and calling. Jeremy would always get out whenever I was on the phone with Lance. I guess he wanted us to have some privacy.

I wouldn't say my fiancé and I played house while Dad was comatose for two weeks, but we kind of did. He'd make our meal for the day, and he eventually agreed to let me wash the dishes. Our house help offered to stay, but I told them I'd like to feel independent just for a few days.

And I really liked having my future husband solely for my eyes to feast on whenever he came out of the shower. He said the steam of the hot water made him sweat. But I know he enjoyed seeing me blush just as much.

That jerk.

Unlike Jeremy, I chose to change my clothes inside the bathroom whenever I was done in the shower. I didn't mind the heat. I think I'd rather sweat a little because of the steam than sweat like a pig because Jeremy was in the room while I was trying to put some clothes on. Closed eyes or not, that's just uncomfortable for my liking.

Then when my dad woke up, permanently this time, Jeremy held me while I cried happy tears. Dad couldn't remember what he said the first time he woke up about two weeks ago, and I'm glad he couldn't because that would be awkward all over again.

They discharged him two days ago, and now he's resting in his bedroom with one female and one male nurse to accompany him. He also has two personal maids by his side.

My dad can walk, but he needs plenty of rest and a lot less stress.

I don't like to sound grateful of my dad's near-death experience, but I'd like to see it as a simple blessing in disguise because Jeremy and I have become closer in the two weeks we spent together in the hospital. My dad noticed it too when Jeremy drove us both home, and he's glad we no longer argue every minute like we used to.

Only every hour.

Like right now.

"I refuse to have a math tutor!" I stomp my foot on his office floor.

"But it's not Hailey anymore!"

I roll my eyes. "I. Don't. Want. A. Math. Tutor."

"Stop being so childish, Kim."

"You already taught me during our time at the hospital. I think I can answer the test now."

Every night, when he didn't have something important to do and I didn't have homework, he would sit beside me on the couch, open a textbook, and teach me math.

"But what about your midterms tomorrow? I didn't cover much of that while we're at the hospital."

"I think…I can pass that too." Fingers crossed.

"What if you can't?"

"What if I can?" I cross my arms over my chest, challenging him.

He runs his hand through his hair in frustration. "Fine. I'll just give you more books then." He stands up and turns to his right where his bookshelf is. He takes out two books and hands it to me. "These contain a few tips and tricks in calculus. Read and study these, Ms. Roberts."

Ouch. We're back with surnames again. I thought we're at least friends now.

I scoff as I take the books. "Fine, Mr. Jeremy Lincoln, I mean, Mr. Jeremy Bradshaw."

He perceives the disdain in my tone as he sits back down. "What now?"

"Ms. Roberts is such a mouthful. You know you can just call me Kim, right?"

"You don't mind when I call you Ms. Roberts in the classroom."

He really doesn't get it, does he? "Yeah, but we're alone now."

Jeremy's face reveals an irritated expression. "Fine. Kim. Are you happy now?"

I tap my finger on my chin as if thinking further. "Try Queen Kim?"

He shakes his head in amusement. "I mean it, *Queen* Kim. You need to take this seriously. This is your senior year, and if you fail at least one subject, especially math, you can't graduate on time. You need to be a role model for our future babies."

Future what?

"What?" My eyes almost bulge out of my sockets.

"Nothing. I didn't say anything." He covers his face with a book.

"I'm pretty sure you said something." He's so adorable when he's embarrassed.

"Shut up," he mumbles. "Just study those books."

"Okay, so that I can be a role model for our future babies, right?" I tease him.

He lowers down the paperback, narrowing his eyes at me.

"Are you mocking me, Ms. Roberts?"

"No, no." I wave both my hands in front of him. "I'm just saying that I must really study hard so when we already have our future babies, I can be an inspiration to them. That's what you were implying right?"

"Oh, so you are mocking me." He stands up from his seat and walks around his desk so now he's standing before me while I'm looking up since he's a few inches taller.

"Maybe I am." I slightly tilt my head to the right.

"Is that an invitation, Kim?" A smirk appears on his tempting lips. He leans forward until his head reaches the side of my face, his warm breath tickling my ear. I try to step back, but my legs just hit the chair behind me, preventing me from moving away.

"What are you doing, Jay?" I grasp his arm as he places a soft kiss below my ear.

"Accepting the invitation." The vibration of his voice sends chills through my spine.

My breath hitches when he grabs my waist and pulls me closer to him. He plants another kiss on my jawline.

"I will kick your nuts." I'm not even joking.

Jeremy lifts his head from my neck and gazes at me amusedly. "I dare you."

I lift my leg and attempt to knee his crotch when he suddenly closes the distance between our lips. I gasp.

My wide eyes gawk at his closed ones. He cups my cheeks and tries to deepen the kiss, but I do not return it. Instead, I twist his nipple with two fingers through his shirt.

"Crap!" he shouts and stops kissing me.

Then we hear the doorknob twist open, and we immediately pull apart. Jeremy sits on top of his desk while I take a seat on the chair behind me.

The door slowly opens, revealing Jewel beaming radiantly at us. Her personality is so unique and charming. She's obviously a lovable person.

"What are you doing here, Jewel?" Jeremy snaps.

The lovely lady playfully pouts. "They said this is your office. Did I interrupt anything?"

Even when pouting, she looks absolutely adorable.

"No." I stand up from my seat and offer her a smile. "I'll be leaving anyway."

"No, don't. We're not done *talking* yet," Jeremy says, but I ignore what he said and leave his office without bothering to say goodbye.

"I missed you, Jay," is the last thing I hear from Jewel before I close the door.

I find Lance leaning against the wall outside Jeremy's office, scrolling through his phone. He looks up when he notices me and grins, showing his perfectly white teeth.

"Hey." He greets me. "I was waiting for you."

"You were?"

Lance wraps his arm around my shoulder. "Didn't you say last week that we'd go on that date you promised me the first time I came here?"

"I did?"

He slightly pinches my nose. "When I called and you said we'd go on a date after class once your dad is released from the hospital. Well, your dad is fine, and it's Monday, so…"

Okay, now I remember. "Oh. Yeah. Alright."

He presses me closer to him and hugs me with one arm. "Ah, finally!"

I laugh and push him gently. "This is just a friendly date."

"If you say so." He winks.

We walk through the hallways, his arm still draped on my shoulders. Random girls glare at me, so I snake my arm around his waist just to annoy them more. They're practically killing me with their eyes.

Once we're out of the building, Lance turns to me. "You sure Mr. Bradshaw won't mind?"

"Why would he? I told you, that teacher and I aren't dating. We're just close because our families have been friends for years."

He makes a skeptical face. "He stayed with you in the hospital with your dad."

"Again, he's just a family friend who cares for my dad."

"And he kept scowling at me when I visited you."

"He's just being overprotective." I raise an eyebrow at him. "Do you still want to go out or not?"

He grins. "Of course, I do."

Lance brings me to his car, a black Bugatti, and opens the door for me, bowing his head in respect. I laugh at how silly he is. Once we're both inside, he plays a song on the music player and starts the engine. The voice of the singer sounds very familiar.

"Do you seriously listen to your songs in your car?" I amusedly ask him.

"Nah, just wanted you to hear how awesome I am," he says, laughter evident in his eyes.

"You sound like a cat." Actually, it's sexy with a hint of cuteness.

He puts both of his hands under his chin, forming a V. "Am I a pretty cat?"

"A pretty cat who is being strangled under water."

He huffs. "You're so mean."

I laugh and pat his head. "Let's just go."

He starts to drive. "Where do you wanna eat? Please don't say anywhere, or I'll hate you."

I slap his arm and look straight through the windshield to think and notice Jeremy walking out of the building with Jewel. My eyes follow them as they walk casually side by side towards my fiancé's car. Where are they going? Why are they still together?

Lance notices them too. "Jewel is so obsessed with that guy."

I immediately look at him with inquisitive eyes. "You know her?"

He shrugs. "We dated for two months when I was in Korea last year for my promotions. It was a secret because she's older than me and I was a minor back then. But I really liked her."

"And how'd you know she's obsessed with Jeremy?"

"Why'd you think we didn't last long?" he mutters, his hand gripping the steering wheel tightly. "She kept telling stories about her and that Jeremy guy. She even showed me pictures of him. I was obviously just a rebound. She told me they just broke up a week before we dated, so I should've seen it coming, right?"

I'm speechless. Didn't Jeremy say that he and Jewel were done seven years ago?

# Chapter 16

We end up in Starbucks because I'm craving for their blueberry cheesecake.

Lance orders a hot brewed coffee while I order frappe with chocolate kisses. He looks at me funny when I ask for more chocolate syrup and whipped cream from the female barista.

Once seated, he says, "You can't even taste the coffee in that."

I take a sip from my delicious cold coffee. "What can I say? I like my cream with coffee."

He shakes his head in disgust. "You're an abomination to coffee lovers."

"Shut up." I slice the blueberry cheesecake and put it in my mouth. I close my eyes and moan at how delectable it tastes.

Lance makes a gagging sound. "Well, that was disturbing."

"Hey now, don't judge my love for cheesecake. I didn't judge you when you enrolled in our school." We've been friends for almost a month now, and he still refuses to tell me anything.

He brings the mug close to his lips and inhales the scent. "Oh, how much I love coffee."

I scowl at him as he watches me with teasing eyes while he drinks his black coffee.

"Come on. You promised that you'd tell me on our date."

When I was in the hospital, Lance called and asked how my dad was doing. I told him he was still unconscious but doing fine according to the doctors. Then he proceeded to ask me if I could go out with him once my dad has woken up since our supposed date was canceled last time. I was still hesitant because would it really be ideal to go on a date with him while I was engaged? He convinced me by promising he'll tell why he's in our school if we go out on a friendly date.

I've been asking him that for days, yet he remained secretive. So, I agreed, and now here we are, having our first date just so I can get that answer from him.

He chuckles as he places the mug on the table. "Alright, what do you want to know?"

I roll my eyes. "Why are you in our school when you're clearly a celebrity? Shouldn't you be homeschooled instead? Hailey said you're here because of a girl. Is that true?"

He shakes his head. "It's complicated."

"Then explain it to me."

Lance fidgets with the rim of his mug. "It's quite a long story."

I refrain from rolling my eyes. "I've got time, Lance."

"Well…" He pauses as if contemplating what to say next. "Let's start with my dad first. He had a wife and two kids, but he cheated on his wife with Carlisle Knight which is my mom. When she gave birth to me, he left his family to be with us. Anyway, when I was five, my dad proposed to my mom, and when his ex-wife found out about it, she drowned their son then killed herself after."

I gape at him, still in utter shock from what he just said.

What kind of mother does that to her own son?

Lance continues. "When my dad found out about it, he got drunk at his brother's house, and on his way home he, uh…he got into an accident and killed someone."

I couldn't even swallow my own saliva. "Killed, how?"

"He crashed his car with someone else's." He looks down on his coffee and sighs heavily. "My dad was put behind bars while my mom and I immediately flew off to her hometown in London to hide from the press. But seeing as my dad's family is quite well-off here in America, he was only sentenced in jail for three years, then he followed us in London to live a quiet life. He never married my mom, but he still stayed with us."

Lance was five years old when the accident happened. His dad was only put to jail for three years because of their powerful family. I can't move a muscle. My heart pounds in my chest as if shouting at me to tell Lance what I know, but my mouth feels like a desert.

Lance takes my silence as a hint to continue. "Then last month, my dad got a call from his brother that my cousin is getting married soon, so we flew back here to attend the wedding."

I find my voice to say, "And this cousin of yours is…"

"I know his name is Jay but I haven't met him yet. I think I did when I was younger. But he's older than me, so we didn't hang out much. I can't find him on social media either, so I don't really know for sure what he looks like today. My dad is the only one who visits their place since we got here, but maybe on my cousin's wedding, I'll finally get to meet Jay."

Should I tell him? But I don't know where to start, so instead, I say, "So, your family is staying here for good?"

He shrugs. "Maybe. I don't know. My dad said it's probably time for us to forget what happened in the past. It's been thirteen years anyway. But I still feel uncomfortable being here."

I look directly at him and ask, "Why?"

His eyes are full of guilt and so much self-loathing. "My dad killed a pregnant woman, Kim, and I might have only been eight years old when I found out about what he did to free himself, but I already knew that what he did was not fair to that woman's family. And now we're back here in America, and he's strolling around here like he did nothing wrong while all I've been wondering is, what if I meet that woman's bereaved family here? What would I tell them? Should I apologize for what my dad did?"

"What your dad did isn't your fault," I tell him.

"It kind of is. When my dad proposed to my mom, it was because I asked him to. If I didn't pressure him to marry her, his ex-wife wouldn't have gone crazy and killed her son, and my dad wouldn't be drunk and crash into that woman's car. Every month, I sent letters to my dad in jail, saying I hope he comes home soon because I miss him. And he did. He damn did."

My chest hurts so bad. I want to comfort him, yet I also need comforting myself. This date has gone from friendly to dramatic real quick.

"You shouldn't blame yourself for that. You were only a child." I'm surprised I still have the energy to speak.

He closes his eyes and takes a lungful of air. It takes several seconds before he opens them again, showing a boyish smile as if he didn't just tell me a very disheartening and appalling story. "So, that's my life. Pretty screwed up, right?"

I manage to force a smile. "It would've been better if you just said you're in America because of your cousin's wedding. That gloomy story only made me sad." He has no idea how much that information cracked me inside and opened a dam of emotions.

He takes another drink from his coffee. "Sorry, but I also wanted to just let all that frustration out. The guilt and shame have been feeding on me since I got here. Now I feel like that heavy load is a little lighter."

"Then I'm glad you told me." Sort of.

"And pretty girls fall for screwed up guys because they want to fix them." He winks at me, and I scoff jokingly.

I play with the straw on my cup before taking a sip. "What about your other sibling? You said your dad's ex-wife only killed your brother."

Lance remains quiet for a while. He then looks outside through the glass windows. "I heard the ex-wife had been abusing her kids since my dad left them. Fortunately for my sister, the ex-wife's friend stole her away from her before all hell happened, seeing as my sister is smaller and easier to sneak out."

I still can't believe their mother would do that to them.

"So, your sister is still out there? Alive and well?"

He returns his attention to me. "Hopefully. My dad decided that it would be better to just forget his past family and just

100

let my sister's aunt take care of her. I've never heard from my sister since the accident."

"But you've met her before?"

He nods. "We met once when we were about four. She's only a few months older than me. I don't remember her face much, but I can never forget how uniquely beautiful her eyes were. She had this condition where her eyes differ in color. One eye is mauve while the other one is gray. She was also really sweet and bubbly."

"What about her name? Did you even try to search her online?"

"Her name's Aiah. Aiah Lincoln. But her adoptive mother probably changed it already." He shrugs. "But I recently hired a private investigator just to know where she is. That's also the reason why I'm here. The one who adopted my sister, Jeanne Bricks, recently donated a large amount of money to Weatherford High."

"Okay," I say, stretching the O sound because just hearing him say that his sister's surname is Lincoln just solidifies my theory. I try to find my voice. "So, this Aiah, any suspicions who she is?"

He shakes his head in dismay. "I think I already have a feeling who she is. I just don't know for sure."

"Who?"

"I don't want to say anything yet because I might be disappointed."

"Oh, c'mon! Just tell me already." I press.

He seems reluctant but eventually answers, "You."

If I were drinking, I might've showered him with the coffee from my mouth.

"No." I slowly shake my head "No. That's impossible. Like, really, really impossible."

Is it? I mean, I could still remember my mom's death when I was barely five, and I'm pretty sure I can still remember a few things when I was a kid, and Lance was definitely not in those memories.

101

Unless I was brainwashed. Maybe Jeanne used hypnotism to place all those memories in my head. Maybe the mom I know is Jeanne Bricks and she only changed her name.

Wait, am I really considering this?

My heart starts pounding in my chest, and I probably look like a constipated orangutan while thinking of the possibility.

Then Lance cracks and laughs. "Damn, if you could only see your face right now." What? "Hey, I was kidding. Just wanted to see your reaction."

I throw my straw at him, and it hits him on his left cheek.

"That wasn't funny!" I can't believe I actually considered what he said. "Was all of that even true? Or did you just make all of that up just to make fun of me?"

He chuckles and shrugs. "Was it believable?"

My hands fly out in frustration. "Oh my gosh! You made me listen to all those lies?"

I feel so dumb right now. I want to choke him to death and feed him to the wolves.

He raises his hand in front of me. "Alright, jokes aside. Everything I said is all true except me considering you as Aiah."

"I don't know what to believe anymore." I narrow my eyes at him.

"I swear in my dog's life that everything I said is true. But I am considering someone else though."

"Who?"

He takes the straw from his lap and plays with it. "That chick, Hailey."

I scoff. "You said Aiah was sweet. Hailey has no sweet bone in her body. Trust me."

"But she has a scar on her chest."

Wait, what? "And how would you know that?"

He grins like an innocent boy. "I met Hailey a few weeks ago through a friend. I fooled around with her, and I noticed the long scar. I was thinking maybe she got it from her abusive mother years ago. I discovered she's also studying at Weatherford High. Hailey also has the same dark brown hair as my sister's."

Lance is officially a playboy in my list.

"What if Hailey is Aiah then? So, you basically fooled around with your sister?"

He awkwardly coughs, his ear brightening red. "We only made out, but yeah, it's still messed up. But I swear I only formed that theory a week after we first met." It's still disturbing. "Now I'm kind of hoping she's really not Aiah because of what we did, but part of me is also hoping she is."

"But what about the different eye colors? Hailey has both brown ones."

He bobs his head in understanding "Yeah, but it's the twenty-first century. She may have undergone some eye surgeries…or something. It's very possible though."

We continue chatting more about his life and mine that I almost forget my issue with Jeremy and his supposed ex-girlfriend, Jewel. I'm still planning to confront him about it though.

Then I hear my phone ringing in my bag, so I fish it out and see an incoming call from my friend, Ella. She wasn't in class today again because she's having one of those monthly girl problems.

I am about to accept her call when I realize something. Why am I so slow? Why didn't I think of this earlier?

I grip my phone and stare at the screen where Ella's name is flashing. I can't bring myself to answer it or even move for that matter.

This is ridiculous, but what if it's true?

I swipe the phone to accept the call and bring it close to my ear.

She greets with a loud "I hate being a girl! This hurts like hell! OMG! I need you to watch a movie with me so you can listen to me whine more."

"Ella?" I say, gazing straight at Lance who's curious why I'm suddenly apprehensive.

"What?"

I press the loudspeaker so Lance can hear her too.

"Your eyes have different eye colors, right?" I ask, and Lance immediately leans forward to listen more. I can't believe this is actually happening.

"Yeah, why?"

I smile at the guy in front of me. "And you refuse to have it changed because you want to feel unique, but you also wear contact lens so you won't look weird."

She laughs. "Why the sudden fascination with my eyes?"

Lance gapes at me incredulously and tries to grab the phone from my grasp, but I slap his hand away. He sits back and crosses his arms like a child who didn't get what he wanted.

"Quick question, your mom's middle name is Jeanne, right?"

"Bish, I'm dying from losing so much blood coming out of my vagina, and you want to know about my mother's middle name?"

I should've told her she's in loudspeaker and that everyone around could hear her. An old couple from across the table glower at us, and I merely give an apologetic smile.

Lance gapes at my phone as if it has some sort of disease.

"Just answer the question," I tell my friend.

She groans. "Ugh. Yeah, her full name is Micah Jeanne Summers."

I nod although she can't see me. "Does Jeanne Bricks sound familiar to you?"

"Yeah, that's like her pen name." She adds, "She also uses that whenever she wants to secretly donate."

"Did she recently donate to our school?"

Silence.

Lance and I wait for her to answer. I even check my phone again if she's still on the line.

"She did it to fund the physics lab because...um, I'm failing that class, and she wants me to pass. I hope you won't judge me. I just really need to graduate."

People say California is big. I beg to disagree.

"I'm with Lance, and we're on our way to your house. Is that okay with you?"

She giggles. "Yeah, I'll be wearing a short dress. Don't judge, m'kay?"

If only she knew.

# Chapter 17

In an average day, it takes fifteen minutes to drive to Ella's house from the coffee shop.

But Lance drove it in twelve. Possibly ten.

Throughout the drive, Lance bombards me with questions regarding Ella's life, so I tell him everything: from the first day I met her when we were in second grade, with her limp leg and beautifully unique eyes, up to her favorite food, music, and hobbies.

And everything seems to fit since he lost her when they were five and maybe she was just homeschooled for two years. What is still confusing to us is why Ella doesn't seem to remember anything from the accident because surely, she would've told me something as momentous as that. Or did she choose to keep it a secret from everyone?

I help Lance find my best friend's place by telling which corner to turn and which street to go straight on. Finally, we stop in front of Ella's giant, blue gate, and we notice her waving excitedly at us by the window from her room upstairs.

Then she disappears, and in a matter of seconds, she's out the door, welcoming us as we climb out of Lance's car. She tells their guard to open the gates, and she instantly leaps to hug me.

"You brought Lance Knight to my house. I love you so much," she whispers, and I embrace her back, contemplating between laughing or sighing deeply. I manage a giggle instead. She pulls away from me then turns to her attention to Lance who's eyeing her cautiously. "Let's get inside."

She takes Lance's arm while her right hand holds mine. She brings us to her lilac painted room. I have been in her room countless times, and nothing has changed. She has never brought a boy to hang out with us in her room, except her four-year-old cousin, Zain. Lance is obviously an exception.

Without second thoughts, she pushes Lance to sit on the edge of her bed while she rummages into her pile of CDs in the cabinet beside her curved LED television.

I take a seat beside him and whisper, "Should I ask her now?"

"But she looks so happy," Lance says in the same hushed tone as he gazes at my best friend.

"What are we doing here then?"

Lance blows out air in defeat. "I don't know."

I squeeze his arm. "Do you want me to ask her?"

My friend shakes his head. "I just want to see her as…Aiah."

Ella pulls out a disc from her pile and spins to face us. "*Inception* anyone?"

Lance quickly grins. "I love that movie. Put it in!" he tells her then pulls me towards the center of the bed so our backs are resting on the headboard.

"Yey!" Ella proceeds to insert the disc in the DVD player. Once the introduction starts on the screen, she grabs the remote and situates herself on Lance's right, squeezing him between us. With her enthusiastic mood right now, no one would think she was just wailing in agony about her PMS a few minutes ago.

I sense Lance turn his head to her. "So, Kim told me about your unique eyes."

Ella nods nervously. "Yeah. That's why I wear contacts. I don't want people to think I'm weird, but I don't want to have an eye surgery either since I like having unique eyes even though I don't want others to see it," she answers while her attention remains on the TV in front of us.

I notice her hands fidgetting on her lap, which means she's thrilled about being this close to Lance, yet she can't look at him in the eye since she'll most likely blush. If only she knew she's blushing for her brother.

That's so messed up.

"But you can still see clearly without them?"

She nods again. "Yeah. I just wear contacts to hide my different eye colors."

Suddenly, Lance puts his hand above hers, making her—and me—gasp. She immediately turns her head to him, then she glances at me, her eyes practically shouting, *WTF is happening?*

I think he's planning to tell her in a slow pace with no intention of upsetting her or hurting her head, and I'm glad he's considerate like that.

"Would you mind taking off your contacts for me?" Lance says.

Ella nods in confusion. "Um, okay." Then she rushes straight to the bathroom.

I pause the movie and ask Lance, "How are you planning to tell her?"

He shrugs. "I don't know, but I want her to be the one to tell *me*."

"And how would you do that?"

Lance isn't given the chance to answer because Ella just opens the door. Her mismatched eyes are so breathtaking to look at. Beguiling, even. She has the eyes of an enchantress.

Given the fact that I rarely see it, since she always hides them, it still amazes me how my best friend gets a thousand times prettier with her innate smoky eyes. One eye is mauve, and the other is gray, just like Lance's description of Aiah.

Coincidence? I think not.

"Tada?" Ella says as she approaches us. "Weird, right?"

"You're beautiful." Lance couldn't help it anymore and adds, "Aiah."

We're expecting a certain reaction from Ella, like a recognition after hearing her real name or a small gasp, implying her disbelief about how Lance has discovered it. But her eyebrows only furrow in confusion.

"Who?" And that's how we know she has no idea who she really is.

Maybe she forced herself to put her bad childhood memory at the back of her head. I can't blame her, seeing as she was abused by her mother. I probably would've done the same thing.

Lance shakes his head, disappointed. "Nothing. Let's go finish this movie."

He doesn't say another word until the film is over and he tells Ella he needs to go home to his flat, which I just discovered is the British term for an apartment.

It's evident that Ella is saddened that we're not going to stay longer. I'm surprised she didn't tie him up and lock him in her closet because I could totally imagine her doing that.

No, wait. Not *imagine*.

My best friend is definitely capable of doing just that. I know because back in fourth grade, she once hid her girl cousin's puppy inside her closet and took care of it from there for almost two weeks until one of their maids heard the puppy barking while Ella was in school. As expected, her cousin has stopped speaking to her, and the dog, luckily, is still alive and well.

Lance drives back to school since my car is still parked there. Unlike our drive en route to my best friend's house, he is eerily quiet this time, like he's really dismayed that we didn't get anything out from her. When I tell him that we should've just informed Ella of our theory before we left, he tells me he doesn't want to trouble her perfectly normal life. That would be selfish of him, he said.

I'm glad he's respectful of her feelings.

When he drops me off in front of my car, he forces a smile. "It was still a nice date, right?"

I smile back. "One of a kind."

Excitingly full of mystery, to be exact.

"See you tomorrow." He winks. "Drive safe. Thanks again for today."

"You too." I wave him goodbye as he drives off.

Footsteps on the pavement make me aware that I'm not alone tonight. I glance to my right and see Jeremy from a few feet away, walking toward me with his hands inside his pocket. The street light above him is like a spotlight.

I thought he already left with Jewel?

"So, you were in a date?" he asks once he stands in front of me. "I kept calling your phone, but you weren't answering."

Shoot. I literally slap my forehead. "Sorry. I forgot to charge it."

He continues to glower at me. "And why were you in a date with Mr. Knight? I thought this engagement involves exclusivity."

This hypocrite, seriously.

I cross my arms over my chest. "I saw you left with Jewel. Exclusivity my foot."

He rolls his eyes. "I simply drove her to her place. I came back here because I forgot to bring my files with me, then I noticed your car. I tried to call you, but you weren't answering." He runs his hand through his dirty blonde hair in frustration. "Do you have any idea how worried I was that someone might've had kidnapped you or something bad has happened to you?"

I almost cower in shame with how much genuine fear his voice has.

"Sorry, My phone was dead." I bite the inside of my cheek. "But why did you drive her home? Are you still dating? Are you back together? Or did you really break up?"

I sound like a jealous chick. Jeez. This is not good.

Jeremy sighs heavily. "I told you, Jewel and I are over. But she's still a family friend, and she needed a ride to her place since she's not feeling well."

Not feeling well? I'm pretty sure sick people don't smile like she did a few hours ago.

"Whatever. I'm going home." I am about to open my car door when he grabs my wrist to stop me. I turn back to him with a scowl. "What now?"

He purses his lips and doesn't release my wrist. "It's my sister's birthday this Friday, and she wants you there. We'll be having a small party."

I ask the most important question. "Will there be food?"

"Of course. It's a party," he says, and I could almost hear a *duh* after that.

"Yeah, okay." I shrug nonchalantly, although I am already feeling excited about party food. "Sure. Alright."

"Great. Looking forward to it. See you tomorrow, Kim." He finally releases my wrist and jogs to his gray Audi that is parked two spaces after where my car is parked.

I climb inside mine and drive straight home.

# Chapter 18

By Thursday morning, the doctors allowed my dad to only have one nurse as a companion, which can only mean that his health is improving. My dad obviously chose the beautiful female nurse. Of course.

I just got home from school, and I look at my dad funny when I see the nurse feeding grapes to him in the living room couch. He merely shrugs as if it's perfectly normal, but there is humor in his eyes.

When my mom died thirteen years ago, my dad drowned himself with work. I rarely saw him then, and I couldn't understand why he'd rather stay late in the office than eat dinner with his daughter—until I was about seven and I realized he was doing it to forget the pain of my mom's demise. He wanted to bury himself with paperwork rather than cry over Mom again.

I have two friends who have step-moms, and I thought my dad would remarry another woman once he has moved on. So, I asked him one day when he'd start dating again. Maybe having another woman in his life would make him happy again. My dad smiled and promised me that he'd never love another woman just as much as he loved my mom. Hence, he'll never date or marry again. I was somewhat relieved when he said that but also sad that I couldn't think of anything that will bring happiness to him again. He's stuck with a dumb blonde of a daughter. I felt sorry for him.

Then on my twelfth birthday, he brought a woman to have dinner with us. Her name was Angel Santiago, a Colombian national. She was really pretty and sweet. I guess seven years were enough for him to move on from Mom. They were dating for six months already when I first met her, and I became aware that she was my mom's best friend, but they swore that they never saw each other more than friends when my mom was still alive. I believed them because I was a witness to my dad's genuine affection for my mother while she was still alive.

I just didn't know if I should be pleased that my dad had finally found a female companion again, or pissed that he waited for months before he told me that they'd been seeing each other for six *freakin* months already.

I could count with my two hands the times he brought her home to have dinner with us, and I was glad he never invited her to spend the night in our house. Although I accepted their relationship, I still felt uncomfortable around her. And after their first anniversary, I asked Dad if he would marry her soon.

He answered, "Maybe next year."

My heart cracked just a little, but I learned to accept it. They broke up two months later when she threatened to kill herself if he wouldn't marry her soon.

As far as I know, she's still perfectly alive and well despite the break-up.

My dad had several girlfriends again even after that psycho, Angel. The last one I could remember was a twenty-seven-year-old model named Hannah, but they broke up last year after their three-month relationship. She slept around, my dad had said.

My dad still flirts with a few women, and I guess I'm fine with it. I have to be fine with it because I know it's only a harmless fun for him. That's why I simply wave hello to the female nurse and go straight to my room to lay myself on the bed like a starfish.

For the past two days and a half, Lance has been acting like he never knew of Ella's real identity when I badly want to have a confirmation already. I feel like I'm in a Korean drama, and the idea of my best friend being the long-lost sister of my new friend is so thrilling.

Jewel is still out of the picture until Friday, since that's scheduled for our music class. I used to look forward to that class. Now, not so much.

All in all, this week is getting hella boring, except for the part that it's our exam week, which I don't really mind. I'm not really trying to get a high score on those tests. What's important is for me to pass, and I rarely fail any subject but math. Once I graduate from high school, I'm going to start my training with our family business while in college, so I don't see any reason why I have to attain *A*s in any class.

So instead of opening a book to study, I close my eyes and sleep—for about ten minutes before my freakin' phone starts to ring. I groan and reach for my bag to fish out my annoying phone.

Damn it.

I should've put this on silent mode earlier.

*Jeremy the Frog calling…*

I really should've put this on silent mode earlier.

"What?" I answer, obviously irritated.

"Were you sleeping?"

I roll my eyes. "What do you want?"

"It's only 3:45 in the afternoon. You shouldn't be sleeping."

Bossy much? "I'm going to hang up if you don't tell me why you are disturbing my sleep."

He chuckles, then becomes serious again. "Jade insists to take us to her friend who owns a fashion business. Be ready. We'll be picking you up in thirty minutes."

I instantly sit up from my position. "What? Today? Don't you think it's too soon?"

Jeremy is silent for a few seconds "Kim, have you asked your dad for the marriage contract already?"

I purse my lips. "Not yet."

He sighs, and I think he's even rolling his eyes. "I told you to ask for it already."

"Sorry. I always forget. What about it?"

114

He clicks his tongue. "We're getting married next week, Kim. On Saturday, I think, two days after your eighteenth birthday."

My birthday is on the thirteenth of December. Today is December 7.

To say I am upset with my dad is an understatement. I'm beyond livid right now.

I take two steps down the stairs and rush in front of my dad. I notice that he is watching his favorite show, *Game of Thrones*. *Good. He'll be missing a lot of scenes*, I tell myself as I block his view from the television.

The nurse must have noticed my annoyed expression because she hesitantly stands up and leaves the room.

Once we're alone, I cry out, "Next week? I'm getting married next week? Dad, why am I not aware of this? I know you're not in good condition right now, but Jeremy and I have been engaged for almost a month, yet you never told me the wedding date! You promised it would be next year in February, but now..."

He attempts to stand up, but I stop him. I know he's still weak and I'm not that cruel.

"I'm sorry, princess," is all he says.

"Dad, why do you keep breaking your promises?" I run my hands over my head. "You told me you won't do something against my will, and the next thing I know, I'm engaged to my math teacher and will be marrying him next week!" I want to punch something or someone. Jeremy is lucky he's not here right now.

Gah! This is so frustrating. I hate crying like this, but the fact that my dad has yet again done something behind my back emotionally drains me.

"Kim..."

I cut him off. "Dad, I've read your letter while you were still in a coma, and I understand that you need the money as soon as possible, but you could've informed me that it will be this soon."

"Please don't hate me." He pinches the bridge of his nose. "I was scared of how you'll react. I'm so sorry, Kim."

I rub my palms over my face. "Daddy, I love you, and I could never completely hate you. But I'm annoyed that you're forcing me into this. You went behind my back and made sure I'll stay engaged to Jeremy, and now I discover that I'm getting married next week? Dad, don't you think this is too much?"

Some might think I'm overreacting. Maybe I am. But spending the first days of my eighteen-year-old life married to that *frog* is really not on my agenda. And we already talked about a February wedding! Why do they keep making decisions without consulting us first?

This time, my dad stands up and holds my hands. I don't stop him. "I know, and I'm really sorry that I'm somewhat…using you to get to your mom's savings, but you have to understand that I'm only doing this for your sake. I want to give you the best of everything, and I need to save the company in order to do that."

"You could've just explained everything to me like a sane adult."

He bows his head. "I didn't know if you'd agree, so I had to—"

I complete the sentence for him. "So you had to *force* me instead just so everything will go your way?" I release my hands from his grip.

"Kim, I'm doing this for you."

I bite my tongue to stop myself from saying more mean things to my dad.

"Where's the marriage contract?" I ask him. "I want to read it."

He hesitates, then nods. "Fine. Stay here. I'll go get it in my room."

"No." I shake my head. "I'm coming with you."

For all I know, he might have a fake one prepared. Somehow, I don't trust my dad as much as I used to.

We climb the stairs and into his office. He walks to his vault and unlocks it, taking out a clean folder with the words *Marriage Contract* printed on top of it, before locking the vault again.

I know this is real because he made sure to keep it safe.

"Here." He hands me the white folder. "Please read it with an open mind."

I ignore his comment. "Jeremy will be picking me up in a few."

His eyebrows furrow. "Where is he taking you?"

A wicked part of me wants him to at least pay for the emotional strain he's giving me. Thus I take advantage of his apprehension. He doesn't need to know we'll just head over to a fashion boutique to buy clothes.

I scoff. "You forced me to be his fiancée, Dad. I think you're aware what engaged couples do." His breath hitches from my remark. "I don't know what time we'll be done. Don't wait up."

"Kim."

I turn my heel to walk out of his room, feeling much worse.

# Chapter 19

"What does BD mean?" I ask them.

Jade and Jeremy are in front, while I am in the back seat. And now we're climbing off Jade's car as I eye the three-story building curiously. Jade is about to answer when a cute guy—no, wait—a *hot* guy approaches us wearing an expensive looking suit and tie. He also has a five o'clock shadow, which adds to his already sexy appearance.

If BD means *baby daddy*, count me in.

He extends his hand in front of me. "Bryan Dalton, owner of Bryan Dalton fashion wear."

I nervously shake his hand. "I...ah, I'm Kim Roberts." Damn, his eyes are smoking gray.

So hot. So sexy.

He smiles, showing one dimple on his left cheek. "Ah, you must be the future Mrs. Lincoln. Jade told me all about you on the phone."

An arm snakes around my waist.

"Yes, she is," Jeremy says as he pulls me to him. I make a dissatisfied face.

Bryan smiles and winks at me. "Ooh...possessive."

My gay radar is beeping. He's giving the gay vibe. I hate that he's giving the gay vibe. Jade chuckles and embraces Bryan. I suddenly want to be her. His arms look so strong.

"I miss you so much, Bree," she exclaims.

"Me too, Jade. Do you know how much I miss watching *Keeping Up with the Kardashians* with you?" Bryan replies, squeezing her back.

Yup. Bryan Dalton is definitely gay. Although I can't really pursue him, seeing as I'm already engaged to this guy who still has his arm possessively around my waist, my heart still sinks a little because deep down, a silly part of me is hoping that the engagement will be called off and Bryan and I will ride into the sunset, have beautiful children, and live happily ever after.

But that dream just shattered.

Jade notices her brother's arm is still around me. "You can stop being alpha male now. You've known Bryan for years and that he swings the other way."

Jeremy hesitantly removes his arm and tucks his hands inside his pockets. "Just in case he's swinging both ways now."

Bryan laughs. "I *only* like men, Jay. Women are complicated." He drapes his arm on Jade's shoulder. "Come on, let's go inside so you can start choosing the wedding clothes I designed."

He leads us inside his building. All the while, I am checking out his behind, inclining my head to see how majestic it is. Bryan's pants are perfectly snug on all the right places.

The inside of the building looks like a corporate one with its glass windows and automatic glass doors. The walls are covered with white paint, and the floors are marbled and almost spotless. A reception desk is located in the middle of the lobby with two gorgeous girls sitting behind it.

One beautiful brunette woman struts toward us, her heels clicking on the marble floor. Her gray top and skirt show all her perfect curves. She's like a Victoria's Secret model.

Is it a requirement to be attractive to work here?

The woman beams at Jeremy. My fiancé smiles back. I roll my eyes at the subtle flirting. I want to kick him for being such a hypocrite.

"This is my assistant, Samantha," Bryan says. "Sam, this is Mr. Jay Lincoln. Kindly bring him to the men's clothing and help him find the perfect suit."

Samantha's smile becomes wider.

"For our wedding," I immediately add.

Samantha simply acknowledges me with a curt nod. "Follow me, Mr. Lincoln." She spins around to lead him to the east wing, Jeremy willingly at her tail.

It still feels a bit weird hearing Jeremy being referred to by his real name. I have known him, for quite some time, as Mr. Jeremy Bradshaw. I guess it takes a little time to get used to.

Jade leans closer to my ear to whisper, "Don't worry, she's not his type. My brother prefers blonde girls." Then she twirls the end of my hair, winking at me.

Bryan snaps his fingers. "And you, my dear, will be coming with me." He takes me by my wrist and pulls me to the elevator, leaving Jade behind.

"What about Jade?" I ask as he pushes the button with the number three on it.

"She knows where to wait," he answers. "I have so many wedding gowns to show you!"

Yey, I'm so excited…not.

We step out of the elevator, and once we enter his office, I take two steps back when numerous faceless mannequins wearing different white gowns welcome us.

"Mother of cows," I whisper to myself. They all look like Slender Man, and I once feared that faceless man when I was a kid, but I still played that game on my iPad.

Bryan looks at me, his eyes laughing. "You alright?"

I purse my lips and stare at the mannequin right in front of me. "Yeah, they're just creepy."

Why do they even have to be completely faceless? They could've at least put a beautiful actress's face on these mannequins so they wouldn't be this disturbing.

He chuckles. "I know. They creep me out sometimes especially when I'm alone. They're like watching my every move while seeping out my soul."

We both slightly shudder.

Bryan excitedly shows me all the wedding gowns that are appropriate for my skin and hair color. I don't even know why we have to wear real wedding outfits. The actual wedding is merely signing a marriage contract with at least two witnesses to verify it. In fact, I was expecting something quicker than those Vegas weddings where couples still have to say their vows and whatnot.

"Don't you think a simple formal dress is enough?" I tell Bryan who is busy rummaging through the closet of gowns. "It's not a real wedding anyway."

He glares at me as if I've just announced I kill puppies in my spare time.

"All weddings are real weddings," he remarks. "And Jade informed me that you will have at least thirty visitors, so you have to be spectacular."

My mouth feels dry. "Thirty? But…"

He pulls out an off-shoulder, white ball gown. "Ah, try this one."

I eye the gown with dislike. "I don't think it's…"

But he shoves the gown in my arms and pushes me in the small dressing room.

~

By 7:30 in the evening, I have probably worn all the gowns in Bryan's office.

He finally approved of one strapless and backless wedding dress with almost four layers of fabric underneath it. But it's beautiful, and it has the perfect shade of white that fairly matches my blue eyes and blonde hair, so I have to praise Bryan for that.

It was still exhausting.

Thankfully, he decided to bring the gown to their private tailor on the second floor to discuss the various changes and adjustments he wants to make to the wedding dress, and that gave me time to rest in his office.

Jeremy also decided to wait in Bryan's office for his perfect suit instead of the lobby.

And now it's been fifteen minutes, and I'm bored out of my mind. Jeremy and I are both sitting on the couch. Unfortunately, he's busy reading an eBook on his tablet while I have nothing else to do. This sucks.

Then I remember the marriage contract I shoved in my backpack a while ago. With a new found enthusiasm, I pull it out and open the folder.

"Is that the marriage contract?" Jeremy asks, cautiously watching me.

I nod. "Yeah. I'm finally going to read it!"

Three sentences from the first paragraph and my mind is ready to shut down…or explode.

I know the words are written in English, but why are they all this complicated? I feel stupider by the second, so I angrily close the folder and put it back inside my bag.

Jeremy looks up from his tablet again. "Done reading it? That was fast."

I shrug, pretending to have read it. "Yeah, it was alright."

He grins. "You couldn't understand anything, could you?"

"Excuse me?" I fake a gasp. "My eyes just feel tired."

"Sure." This guy obviously doesn't believe me, and I don't blame him. He returns to his iPad.

"Hey," I say as my finger pokes his cheek.

"What are you doing?" he asks irritably as he rubs the cheek I just poked.

"I'm bored." I should've brought my iPad with me too. I hate that I don't have games on my phone either.

He scowls. "Go play rock and scissors with a mirror."

"Nah, I'm good," I tell him, crinkling my nose. "C'mon, let's play a game."

He closes his tablet and turns to look at me.

"Okay, let's play a game. You stay there while I do my business here. No talking. No poking. No kicking. No anything. We will not talk to each other until tomorrow. Got it? The game starts now."

"That's not even a game."

He almost smiles. "Yes, it is."

"Oh yeah? Well, what happens when someone breaks the rules?"

"Uh, there will be consequences?"

"Like what?"

"Uh, well. Whoever breaks the rules will have to do a chicken dance?" he proposes, and I roll my eyes at him again.

"Let's play truth or dare." I offer excitedly.

"No."

"Why not? It's a really fun game."

"No, it's not. It's a game for kids…like you."

"Hey!" I protest. "I am not a kid anymore! I'm almost eighteen. Mind the word *teen*!"

"But your brain is of an eight-year-old."

How dare he?

"Oh yeah? Well, can an eight-year-old solve your math questions?"

"No, and neither can you." Touché, my friend, touché.

"Well…" I try to think of things that an eight-year-old can't do that I can.

"You're still a kid. No offense," he says, raising his hands in mockery.

"Well, can an eight-year-old do this?" I challenge then lean down to press my lips over his. I feel his hand clasp over my shoulders as if he's pulling me closer to him.

Our lips don't move. We just stay like this for a few seconds until his hand trails up to my face, and I feel how warm it is. I sense his lips slowly massaging mine while I'm still motionless, staring at his closed eyelids.

Why do people close their eyes when they kiss? Does it make the kiss feel better?

Jeremy continues to lean forward until my back hits the armrest of the couch. My eyes are still looking at his closed ones until I decide to just shut them too. I don't really know how to kiss but instincts start to kick in, and I simply sync my lips with his.

So, this is the Fresh kiss everyone's gushing about.

Well, I guess this is one way to pass the time.

We kiss for who knows how long—until I think that Bryan might see us like this. I pull away before the owner of the couch thinks we're soiling it.

"Ha! An eight-year-old can't do that," I say victoriously, trying to bring back the humor.

He stares at me for a while before shaking his head.

"You're so childish." He returns to his position and opens his tablet again to read an eBook.

"And you liked that kiss." I joke.

I stand up from my seat and go out the door to find Jade. But before the door could finally close, I hear him say something really soft that sounds like a whisper.

"Yes, I did."

# Chapter 20

Jeremy is discussing a new lesson in front of the class, but I'm too distracted by the movement of his mouth to comprehend whatever he's saying. He writes another bunch of numbers and symbols on the board, and I'm still staring at his moving lips.

I can't seem to forget the kiss we shared last night. Now I know why a lot of people enjoy French kissing so much. It makes anyone's stomach flutter with so much *feels*. No, not feelings. Just the feels.

And the fact that he said he actually enjoyed the kiss only makes me even giddier.

Until seething green eyes suddenly catch my attention.

Wait, is he looking at me?

I escape from my trance when I notice his raised eyebrows as if he's expecting an answer. I look at my best friend for help, and she mouths, *"He asked you something!"*

I return my gaze to our math teacher. "Um, can you repeat the question, Mr. Bradshaw?"

He releases a disappointed sigh. "I said please solve the problem on the board."

My eyes focus on the numbers he had written, and as usual, the numbers are dancing and flying again. Well, shoot.

"I...uh, I don't think I can," I admit, a bit embarrassed.

"But you were looking at me, which means you were listening, right? Or were you just daydreaming in class again?"

I chew on my lower lip. "I'm sorry. I was distracted."

He takes a step closer to me. Scowling, he says, "Would you mind sharing with us whatever's distracting you?"

Complete silence hovers in the room, and the whole class has their eyes on me right now.

Alright then.

"I just remembered making out with someone last night." I admit.

Jeremy awkwardly coughs, and I know he's aware of what I'm talking about with the way his ears tint with bright red.

Loud *ooohs* echo in the room.

Lance isn't around this morning because he slept late due to his rehearsals for his upcoming concert in Las Vegas. He said he'll be coming in for his 10:00 AM class. I'm just glad he's not in here right now because he'd definitely pester me for more details.

I suppress myself from grinning as my eyes tell Jeremy, *You wanted to know what's distracting me, right? Well, there you go, Mr. Bradshaw.*

"You are so going to share all the juicy deets later," Ella demands. She has that mixture of shock and happiness on her face while also giving me that knowing look.

"Well, I hope it was good enough to distract you in my class." Jeremy attempts to lace his tone with the usual authority he uses in his class, yet his eyes are gleaming with playfulness.

"Oh, it was amazing."

He presses his lips together, probably to stop himself from smiling. He shakes his head and returns to his spot in front, but I still notice how much he's restraining himself to grin like an idiot. It's like he wants to declare to everyone that he is the one whom I made out with. But of course, he can't do that, so now all the pent-up smugness is going up on his face.

"Alright, class, s-settle down," Jeremy says. "Let's g-go back…" He shuts his eyes close, obviously annoyed that he's actually stuttering. "Let's go back to the lesson."

His cheeks are light pink as he tries to shoot me a coy glare that screams, *How dare you make me feel awkward?*

126

He mindlessly licks his lips multiple times until his math lecture ended.

I mentally pat myself on the back.

~

The students in the music class adore Jewel like she's some kind of singing goddess. I would've loved her too if I didn't know she used to date my fiancé.

Yes, she's beautiful and really charming. Yes, she sings like we're being lullabied, yet I just don't think she's good enough. It's like something is missing, like something is off. But more importantly, where is this hostility coming from?

*Jeez, Kim. Bitter much?*

She doesn't even acknowledge me during the whole class. I'm guessing she's aware that there is something going on between me and her ex. Or she just doesn't want to show favoritism among her students.

Either way, I still don't like her, and I have my reasons.

Lance and Ella are both in the class with me. Jewel asks us to pair up—male and female—for a singing assignment next week. Lance immediately chooses my best friend, and I'm left with "Pick His Nose" Eugene. I feel somewhat betrayed, but I'm still excited about how much they have grown closer.

Maybe Lance will soon tell Ella of our theory as soon as they're both comfortable with each other. I can't wait for Lance to finally be with his sister. But I still hate the fact that I have no choice for a partner since I only have two friends.

Once all the classes are over, Jeremy shoots me a text, telling me to go to the parking lot by 3:30 sharp and make sure no one notices that I'm following his car with mine en route to their place. I check behind my shoulders twice to make sure I am in the clear then change into my midnight-blue sundress inside my car.

This secret affair is hard yet thrilling.

Jade's party is being held in the swimming pool area at the back of their house. I park beside Jeremy's car, and once I climb off, Jade immediately spots me from her conversation with a

127

woman. She's holding a wine glass with a red drink in it as she saunters towards me. The cool December wind slightly blows the end of her knee-length, cream dress, and she tightens her black shoal around her arms.

"Kim!" She presses her cheek on mine. "I'm so glad you came. Let me introduce you to some of my friends." I don't get the chance to protest because she has already gripped my wrist to pull me toward her so-called friends.

A group of five tall girls is standing in a circle, and most of them are wearing cocktail dresses. They turn their attention to us when they notice Jade approaching them. And now I feel like the ugliest person who has ever set foot on this planet once I place my sight on their perfect figures, porcelain skin, and beautiful faces.

They're like Greek goddesses who transformed into humans. And the fact that I'm wearing a simple sundress, while they're in their cocktail dresses, doesn't help boost my confidence at all.

"Girls, this is Kim, my brother's—" Jade pauses then winks at me "—fiancée."

Wait, what?

Did she really just introduce me as Jeremy's fiancée to her friends? Is she not aware that it's supposed to be a secret since I'm his student?

Four girls glare at me while one girl in a simple pink sundress smiles widely.

"OMG, congratulations!" She takes both of my hands. "I'm Chiara, by the way. Gosh, I can't believe our little Jay is getting married!" She laughs. I think I like her now.

Jade is about to say something when the other girl with the shiny silver outfit interrupts. I recognize her.

"Kim," she says with disdain in her tone.

"Hannah," I reply uneasily. She's the same Hannah who used to date my dad.

She fakes a smile. "You look so plain. How come Jay is marrying you?" She crosses her arms over her big boobs. "I dated him once, and I know his type."

"Okay," I mumble under my breath although I really should've seen that coming.

"Hannah, enough," Jade warns her.

Hannah just raises an eyebrow at Jade as if she were challenging the other girl.

"What? It's the truth. You're Jay's sister. You should know his type of girls, and I'm sure he's making a huge mistake for even agreeing to marry this girl," she retorts.

"I said enough, Hannah," Jade tells her again. Her voice is stern this time. She turns to me, and all I could do is swallow the bile that is rising in my throat. "I'm sorry, Kim."

"It's okay. Could you excuse me for a second?"

She hesitates at first but then nods at me.

I really want to get away from those girls. I walk around the pool to search for Jeremy, but he is nowhere to be found. I stand by the buffet table to grab a plate when a hand touches my back.

"Kim, I'm really glad you made it." I hear Mr. Lincoln's voice.

"Good evening, Mr. and Mrs. Lincoln," I say.

Mrs. Lincoln pulls me for a soft hug, and I willingly embrace her back. "Oh c'mon, just call me Carol. I don't like being called Mrs. Lincoln. It makes me feel so old," she happily states as she holds my shoulders in arm's length.

"I don't mind being called Mr. Lincoln. I feel more respected." Mr. Lincoln jokes.

I simply nod. "Uh, have you seen Jere...I mean, Jay around?"

"Yes, he's inside the house. He's in the living room with his childhood friend," Carol answers. I give them one last smile before excusing myself.

Once I step foot inside the said house, I feel like Alice after she ate the cookie with shrinking potion because, damn, this house is huge! It's three times bigger than our own house.

After a few minutes of searching through the maze of halls in this white sandstone mansion, I hear someone shout, "I don't want to hear your stupid reason! Just leave me alone!"

That definitely sounds like Jeremy.

I hide behind the wall, my head slightly peeking through the open arch. I see a man's figure. He's facing away from me, and it looks like he's talking to someone.

"Jay, I only did that because I love you…I love you so much." That has to be Jewel's voice.

She pushes herself up so their faces come closer, but before her lips can even make contact with Jeremy's mouth, I clear my throat, and they both turn their attention to me.

"Kim," Jeremy says as if relieved by my presence.

For the first time, I see Jewel scowl. But she's still beautiful. Damn it.

"Why are you here?" She sneers.

I hesitantly walk towards them. "I…um, just wanted to say hi."

Yeah right.

She sighs. "Look, Kim, we need some privacy, so can you please leave us alone for a moment?"

"No," Jeremy says then immediately pulls me to his side, his arm around my waist.

Jewel glowers at it then raises an eyebrow at Jeremy. "I didn't know it's in you to date a student."

My fiancé scoffs. "And I didn't know it's in you to date your—"

"Stop!" Jewel literally screams. "I'm your fiancée, and that's it!"

"Ex-fiancée, Jewel. Mind the word *ex*!"

Jeremy tightens his arm around my waist, and I see something flash on Jewel's face. Maybe pain or distress, but it's immediately withdrawn after a beat, like she has been expecting him to say that. I really shouldn't have come between them in the first place. They still have some serious issues to fix, and I don't want any part of it.

"We had no choice but to break up," is Jewel's comeback, but the confidence in her voice has now vanished and is replaced by vulnerability.

"Because I had to!" Jeremy shouts, and I want to wriggle my way out of his grasp before the situation becomes worse. "What we had was wrong! I could never love someone like you."

She steps closer to him just as Jeremy digs his fingers deeper into my waist.

"Jay, it hurts," I tell him, but he obviously doesn't hear me or chooses not to.

"No, Jay, you love me. I know you still do." Tears start flowing on her cheeks.

"I'm sorry, Jewel," he replies. I can sense how genuine he says it, like he's really sorry that he could not love her again.

Jeremy removes his arm around me then clutches my wrist to drag me out of the room. Once back outside, he lets go of me, and my skin feels quite cold from the loss of contact.

He takes a lungful of air before he speaks, "I'm sorry you had to witness that."

I swallow the bile in my throat. "Were you really going to marry her?"

Jeremy closes his eyes in annoyance.

"Unfortunately, yes," he soon replies, and then he looks at me as he considers something. "But it's been seven years. We were still young and…naive"

"Naive, how?" I press further.

He shakes his head. "I don't want to talk about it yet. Soon, I guess, but not now."

I still want to know more. "Did you love her?"

He is reluctant for a second. "No, I didn't. But I…cared for her a lot."

Sounds like love to me but whatever.

"Why did you really break up?"

Before he can even open his mouth to say something, a pitchy squeak of a microphone interrupts us. Almost everyone apparently.

"Good evening," someone announces.

All heads turn to the one who's standing on the stage. My eyes immediately widen when I recognize who he is.

"Wayne!" I say happily with a huge grin on my face.

Wayne Brendan Summers is the most awesome big brother of all time. Well, for my best friend anyway, but I still see him like he's my own brother, and he treats me just like his little sister.

He glances at me and instantly flashes his sweetest smile. "So, um, I know I'm not invited here, but I still want to dedicate this song to the birthday girl, Jade. I still want to marry you, love." He sounds like a nervous alien announcing world domination.

"Jerk." Jade throws her glass on the grass and walks away.

Wayne just stands there, a microphone in his hand. His gaze follows Jade's retreating back. He sings a ballad, and I can hear the heartbreak in his voice.

Once he's done, he just leaves the stage and doesn't even bother to say hi to me. I try to understand him and not be offended.

Different bands perform after him, and I think of leaving soon, but then I remember that I don't know the way out of their private subdivision. My memory is not that good, and I have to drive at least three times around a place to remember it. So, I search for Jeremy and find him by the pool with a glass of red wine in hand, obviously bothered by something.

I slowly approach him. "Hey."

He doesn't even look at me. "Your dad called earlier. He said that one of the staff just coughed blood and might be infected with tuberculosis. He wants you to stay the night here until every corner of your house is decontaminated. You can rest first in my room while the guest room is being prepared."

132

He's just standing there, staring at the pool, and not moving at all.

"Um, I don't know where your room is," I tell him.

He quickly faces me, his body tensed. "Kim, I want to kiss you."

"What? Why?" I step back, somewhat afraid of him although I don't know why.

Jeremy chuckles feebly to himself. Looking down, he says, "Never mind. Let's just go."

"Wait." I take a step closer to him and stand on the tip of my shoes so I can at least reach his face. "I didn't say no." I press my lips against his. He presses his hand behind my back to push me closer to him, making me deepen the kiss. Our mouths move sensually as he embraces me.

It's not like our usual kisses that are frantic and done to pass the time. This kiss is slower, gentler, more vulnerable as if he's letting go all of his troubles through this kiss.

And I'd gladly take all those troubles away if it meant seeing this softer side of him, the side where he kisses me like his whole life hinges on my lips and he'll die if he lets go.

He then pulls away slightly, resting his forehead on mine, leaving me winded.

His glistening emerald orbs stare at my sapphire ones. He's not looking at me like I'm the girl who annoys the hell out him.

He gazes at me as if to say, You just made everything better.

Did I really?

"Thank you." He smiles. "Now let's go to my room."

# PART 2: THE WEDDING
## Chapter 21

JEREMY

"Mother of cows!"

I jolt awake.

I almost punch the one who screamed until I realize it's Kim.

"What is wrong with you?" I ask her groggily as I rub my eyes.

"I woke up and found you sleeping beside me." She quickly pulls up the blanket over her chest. "I remember kissing you, but did we do *it*? Did we…"

"We didn't do anything," I say almost angrily. "We kissed in this bed then five seconds later you fell asleep while kissing me."

I try not to be offended by what she did because who falls asleep during kissing?

Obviously, Kim.

"Okay." Then she stays quiet for a few seconds. I prepare myself to sleep again, but she decides to bother me again. "I can't sleep with you in the same bed. I'm not ready to give it up yet."

What the hell is she talking about?

"We're just going to sleep, Kim. Please shut up."

"Fine, stay on your side, and I'll stay on mine."

I smile, amused by her statement. Maybe a little game wouldn't be so bad?

"Sure."

I roll back to face her, and she immediately tenses.

"Why are you looking at me like that?"

"What look?" I innocently ask, smirking mischievously at her.

"That look." She points at my face, and my grin becomes wider.

I crawl over to her side, but she instantaneously backs away, causing her to fall off the bed on her back.

"Ouch!" She grunts after a large thud. Half of her body is on the floor while both her legs are still rested on the edge of the bed.

"You okay?" I look down to check on her.

She glares at me. "Jerk."

I'm not given the chance to react because she unexpectedly pulls me by my shirt, causing me to slide down the bed. I don't know how she managed to move her legs away from the bed, but she did it. So now, we're both on the floor, and I'm on top of her and she's chuckling under me; however, her eyes instantly widen when she realizes our position.

"I think I can fall asleep just right here." I bury my face in her neck.

"Jay!" She struggles to push me away.

"What?" I place my hands on the floor and slightly lift myself up with her still under me. "You're the one who put us in this position." I tease.

Her ocean blue eyes narrow at me in aversion.

She's so adorable.

I play with the hem of her shirt and contemplate whether to risk my life by sliding my hand under it to touch her stomach. But the door unexpectedly slams open.

"Jay, I heard a noise…"

I turn my head to look at the person who just spoke and realize it's my mother.

"Oh, sorry. I didn't see anything."

Then she closes the door, leaving us dumbfounded. I can still hear my mother giggling as she walks away from the door.

135

"Great," Kim says sarcastically. "Now your mom thinks we were doing something."

I push myself up and lend a hand to help her stand up.

"We were about to though," I tell her smugly.

She makes a gagging face. "No, we were not about to."

I laugh. "Fine, you can sleep on my bed alone," I say. "But that's just because you might molest me in my sleep." I joke then head towards the couch.

"Screw you," she says, eyes heated with pure annoyance.

"Don't give me dirty ideas, princess." I wink at her, and she buries herself in the covers.

So damn cute.

~

*Saturday*

"Hey," someone whispers, her breath tickling my ear.

I ignore it and try to go back to my sleep. Why does everyone enjoy waking me up?

"Jay, wake up."

"Go away." I pull the covers over my head.

"You haven't changed a bit," she says softly, a hint of humor in her tone. "Still madly in love with sleep." My eyes flutter open when I recognize who's talking.

"What are you doing here, Jewel?" I say harshly.

"What? No 'Good morning, beautiful?'" She pouts as she places her hand on her chest in a fake hurt. "You used to wake me up every morning with kisses."

"Again, what are you doing here?" I ask irritably.

"I'm waking you up, silly. It's six in the morning, and you know what we always do at six in the morning, right?"

My eyebrows furrow. "What are you talking about?"

"Ugh!" She grumbles impatiently. "We run! Now up you go and get dressed. I missed this place so much."

Why is she acting as if nothing has changed?

136

"Why are you still here? Didn't I tell you last night to leave me alone?" I sit up. She's still kneeling in front of me.

"Aunt Carol told me to spend the night here instead." Jewel tucks a strand behind her ear "Your mom is still fond of me. I guess she still doesn't know that we dated before?"

She's right. I'm a very private person, and I never told my mom that I was dating my childhood best friend. I was a shy boy back then, and I didn't want my mom teasing me.

"Get out, please."

"But, Jay." Her eyes become watery again, but I've had enough of her drama.

"Look." I rub my palm over my face. "You need serious help if you think that I'll come running back to you. What we had was wrong."

She tries to touch my hand but I pull it away.

"Jay, that doesn't mean that what we had wasn't real. Because I know it, Jay. I love you, and I know you still love me too."

She's delusional.

"I thought I loved you. But when I discovered the truth," I purse my lips. "You *disgust* me now." Her head falls, and I know she's crying again.

Damn it. I don't attempt to console her. She brought this to herself. But I still felt bad for what I said to her.

"I'm sorry." She wipes her tears with the back of her hand and sniffs.

My heart wrenches at the sight. Now I feel guiltier. I really want to take back what I said. Not because I still loved her but because I still care for her despite our circumstances.

"Jewel, please, just go." I hold the side of her arms and help her stand up. Her head is still hanging low, so I put her hair behind her back and tilt her chin up. "You really need to talk to someone about this. This is not normal anymore."

137

Her hazel brown eyes stare longingly at my green ones. And I should've seen it coming when she pulls my head down to kiss me. Kim is still in the bed across the room.

Without hesitation, I push Jewel off me. "What is wrong with you!"

She grimaces at my sudden outburst. "I just want to feel your lips on mine again."

This girl is obviously sick in the head.

I grab her arm and pull her towards the door. "Leave!"

That gentleman status be damned. I push her out, and I'm about to close the door when she stops it with her palm. "Are you serious with Kim? She's your student!"

I don't think twice. "I like her. A lot. And maybe I'll fall in love with her soon."

Her body slumps at my answer. She knows me too well that what I've just said is true. She doesn't need to know that we're forced into this relationship. All she needs to understand is that I've definitely moved on from her and that I have real feelings for someone else. Unlike what I used to think I felt for her. That was a misconception.

I slam the door on her face and head towards Kim who's still curled up like a fetus under the blanket, still wearing the blue sundress she wore last night. Who would've thought she's a heavy sleeper?

I slowly lay on the bed and spoon her. "You're the only girl I've really liked, Kim."

And somehow, that scares me.

# Chapter 22

After brushing my teeth and changing into the white shirt and black shorts I saw hanging on the chair, I quickly head straight to the room where I hear loud bickering. It's coming from the dining area. And I'm not going to lie, I take a few wrong turns before I finally reach my destination, and I'm glad these loud voices have led me to the right place.

The first thing I see is Jade, her arm raised with a slice of bacon on her hand as if she's about to throw it to Jeremy who is right in front of her. Her eyes shift to mine, and she immediately lowers her hand.

"Oh, good morning, Kim." She greets me. Then everyone in the room turns to me.

"Good morning, too." I beam at her.

"Good morning. Have a seat." Mr. Lincoln gestures towards the chair beside Jeremy.

I slowly take the seat next to him, expecting a "good morning" as well, but he doesn't even bother to acknowledge me. As if we didn't share a great kiss last night. Or maybe it's just me overthinking it. I try not to feel miffed and start the greeting instead.

"Good morning, Jeremy," I say cheekily, forcing a smile.

He just glances at me and nods, obviously in a bad mood. What happened to him? I thought we were already on good terms last night.

139

"I'm sorry if you had to witness that, but Jay kept kicking my leg under the table!" Jade exclaims, her hands waving in the air in frustration.

"Well, stop teasing me." Jeremy narrows his eyes at his sister.

"Am not!"

"Both of you, enough. Have some manners." Carol demands in a stern voice. They both roll their eyes and continue eating their meal. "Feel free to choose whatever you like, sweetie."

I take only one bacon, and Jeremy obviously disapproves because he puts more food on my plate. I glare at him when I realize I have three pancakes, two slices of bacon, and a lamb chop in front of me.

"Don't act so demure, now. I know you love these," he says as he cuts a piece of pancake and feeds it to me with a fork. I eat it, but my eyes are throwing daggers at him the whole time.

He's so confusing. One minute he acts like he doesn't give a damn, then the next thing I know, he's spoon-feeding me.

I notice Mrs. Lincoln smiling at us, so I gently push Jeremy's hand away.

"So, did you have fun last night?" Jade suddenly asks.

"Oh, yes. My body still feels a little tired," I say, remembering how much I enjoyed the party, especially the part where different bands performed on the stage.

But my smile slowly fades when I notice their shocked reaction.

What? Did I say something wrong?

"She's not referring to the party," Jeremy utters. I look at him in confusion.

Jade softly chuckles. "What I meant to say was: did you have fun with my brother last night? Mom told me that she saw you two doing something."

I almost choke on my own saliva after her statement.

"How many times do I have to tell you that we didn't do anything last night!" Jeremy snaps then turns to his mother. "Mom, was it really necessary to tell her that?"

"Of course. She's your sister. She must be aware of her future niece or nephew," she answers, chuckling.

Jeremy makes an impatient grumble and shakes his head. "This is ridiculous."

"No, it's not. It was really sweet." Jade gushes.

"Shut up, Jade."

All the while, their father is quietly eating his omelet.

"He's right. Nothing happened last night. We just fell off the bed," I finally say, getting the attention of everyone.

"But why did you fall off the bed? It must be because you were doing something, am I right?" Jade continues to taunt, wiggling her eyebrows playfully.

"Um, no. We were just, um…teasing each other."

"Oh! I forgot to tell you both that you're visiting your new house today." Mr. Lincoln suggests, making my eyes widen in surprise.

"What? That's not part of our agreement. You only told me to marry her. You never told me that I have to live with her, too." Jeremy argues.

"Jeremy, that's also part of our agreement. We all know that when a couple gets married, they leave their parents' house and live on their own." His father explains calmly.

"But we're not a real couple." I meekly protest.

No way in hell I would leave my dad and live with this jerk.

"Our decision is final. Don't worry, Kim. We already talked about this with your dad," Mr. Lincoln adds. I hear Jeremy groan in exasperation.

"You already forced me to marry this girl who is my student, might I add, and now you're expecting me to live with her too? That will only make our situation more difficult! I'm saying no," he says furiously before walking out of the room.

Why is he such in a bad mood today?

141

After Jeremy's small episode, we just decide to continue our meal while talking about different matters. We share a few laughs and chuckles. We exchange different facts about each other...Well, they're the ones who were doing the asking.

"I really like you, Kim. You're so much like your mother," Carol says, and she must have sensed the sudden tension because she tries to explain herself more. "We were really close before. What happened to her was unfortunate. I know it's late, but I'm sorry for your loss."

"It's fine. It was a long time ago." I smile at her.

For a second, something flashes on her face, and I somehow distinguish it.

Guilt and regret.

Because even though no one is acknowledging it right this second, we all know that one of their family killed her. And they all had a part in not giving her the proper justice she deserved. Despite how long time ago it was, injustice is injustice. Perhaps that's why they're willing to help our company—to cover up what they've done—and my father has no choice but to accept it. Which brings me to another possible reason.

"When my dad was in the hospital..."

She cuts me off. "Oh yes, I heard that too. Is he doing well now?"

I slowly nod. "Yes. He's improving, but...when he was in a coma, his lawyer came and gave me a letter from him. It contains why he wants me to marry your son."

Her husband shifts uncomfortably. "Go on." He beckons with a hand.

Carol touches my hand. "Go on, dear."

Now I feel more reluctant. What if my dad's reason is different from theirs? What if I screw up their agreement because of my intrusive mind?

I shake my head. "I...uh...it's nothing. He just wants to comply with your request."

"You're not a very good liar, Kim," Mr. Lincoln states, not too harsh but not too friendly either. His wife glares at him and hits his arm.

"Daryl!" She admonishes. Wait, his first name is Daryl?

I'm going to marry their son in a few days, and I've only known of this guy's name now?

*Way to go, Kim. Way to go.*

"It has something to do with my mom."

Carol beams brightly. "And a trust fund, I presume?"

"Yes." I purse my lips. "You're also aware of that?"

Daryl grins. "Why'd you think we want you to marry our son?"

Somewhere in my brain, a short circuit is happening. "But..." I'm so speechless right now. "But why would my Mom want me to marry Jeremy in the first place? I know you're all friends, but why him?"

Daryl merely shrugs. "We're not so sure either. All we know is that once you marry our son, we will have twenty-five percent of that trust fund. That's the agreement with your dad. That's how we're helping your company."

By practically selling their son.

Because money is money with these people, and it doesn't matter if they're giving away their son as long as they'll profit from it. I think I'm going to be sick.

Carol gently squeezes my hand. "A union of two great families will also be good for the business. You understand that, right?"

I barely nod.

~

Sitting on this very comfortable couch makes me want to lie down and sleep again. I'm currently watching a show called *Phineas and Ferb* where two kids with their friends enjoy their summer for eternity.

"Good morning, Kim."

I look up and see Jewel standing beside me, a towel in her hand. She's wearing a sporty outfit with Nike rubber shoes. I assume she took a run around the neighborhood. Her long ebony hair is still in place despite the fact that she's all sweaty and exhausted.

If I were in her place, I would be like the female version of Albert Einstein—minus the genius mind, my hair sticking out in every possible direction.

"Uh, good morning, too." I greet her back.

She moves forward, and I scoot to my right side to give her a place to sit on.

"I'm really sorry for what happened last night." She bites her lip as she gazes straight into my eyes. "You weren't supposed to see my *bitch* side."

"It's okay…I don't rea—"

She places her hand over mine.

"No, it's not. Jay and I are done. And I'm really sorry for acting the way I did. When I saw how protective he is over you, I felt jealous, so, the first thing that came into my mind was to bring up our past. It was a bitchy move. I'm sorry."

"As I said, it's okay. No need to apologize, Miss Jewel. It's no big deal."

It's not like I became a green-eyed ogre when she told me that she was his fiancée before.

Did I? Nope. Not one bit.

*Sure, Kim, sure.*

"So, can we be friends?" she asks, smiling.

I am about to answer her when Jeremy's voice interrupts me.

"Kim, stay away from that liar." He pulls me away from her.

"What's your problem?" I ask him as he brings me back to his room.

"I don't like you hanging out with her," he mutters. "Just stay away from, Jewel, please."

144

I slide my wrist from his grasp so I can squeeze his hand. "Okay."

# Chapter 23

"Jay, come here!" Jade hollers from downstairs.

I groan, my head falling back in annoyance.

What does she want now?

"I'm busy!" I call back as I continue checking my students' assignments in Calculus.

It's really exhausting to be a teacher. We sleep late at night to review the next lessons for tomorrow then wake up early in the morning to meet my ungrateful students. Can't they just simply appreciate our efforts by being obedient and quiet in class?

It's infuriating. But for whatever reason, I still enjoy this profession, knowing that everything that comes out of my mouth is being absorbed by my students which they will soon use in their future.

Kim is obviously an exception, and it's infuriating that the girl I like isn't even putting much effort in my class.

"Jay, if you don't come down here, I'm going to drag you myself."

I immediately set the papers down when I realize Jade's threat.

I know how authoritative my sister is. She won't drag me by the arm; she'll drag me by my feet.

I groan. "Fine! I'm coming!"

I reach down to the bottom drawer of my desk and file away the folders before standing and rolling my stool forward so that it is under my desk.

Annoying giggles and laughs make me aware that Jade's friends are here for the night again. Call it a hunch, but I have a feeling that my sister wants me to keep them from being bored.

Jade notices me descending the stairs. "Took you long enough." She gestures to her friends. "I want you to make them comfortable while I bake some cookies, okay?" My hunch never fails me.

"Why can't you just ask our cook to bake for them?"

We have dozens of kitchen helpers. I really don't see the reason why she has to bake them herself.

"Because they like my cookies better. Am I right, girls?"

"Uh-huh." They all bob their heads like those bobbing toys I put on the dashboard of my car.

"See? Be good to them, Jay." Then she's off to the kitchen.

Great.

"So, um, what do you want to watch?" I ask as I rummage through our stack of DVDs.

A girl named Louise giggles. "We'd like to see you dance."

They all laugh at her small joke.

Ha-ha. Not funny.

"We have some really awesome movies here." I suggest while checking all the DVDs we have under the TV rack.

"Nah, we want *you* to dance for us." Hannah insists.

I turn to face them, and they are all giggling. How could my sister possibly be friends with these girls? My sister deserves better than them.

"Oh, I know, just sing for us!"

I'm not an entertainer for Pete's sake.

"We also have tons of musicals."

They just roll their eyes at me.

Isabelle stands up from her seat and approaches me, resting her hand over my shoulder.

"Your sister told you to entertain us, right?" she says, batting her fake lashes.

"But that doesn't mean that I have to be a male stripper just to keep you entertained. She just wants me to make a conversation with you to prevent you from being bored." I boldly state.

"Oh c'mon. Don't be such a buzzkill. We just want to hear you sing," Hannah says.

"Yeah, because singing in front of you is normal." I turn away from them and head back to my room.

I can't believe my sister can stand their attitudes. And besides, it's almost midnight! Why are they still here? And why would my sister bake cookies at this hour? Girls are so weird sometimes.

I lie on my bed flat, staring mindlessly on the ceiling. I'm really desperate for sleep now, but I still have to check all of my students' assignments so they can go back on the items they need to improve on once I give the papers back to them. But my eyes are really feeling a little heavy.

Oh well, I guess a short nap won't be so bad. I take my phone and set the alarm at exactly 12:30 AM. A forty-five-minute nap would really be satisfying for my restless body.

As I let myself doze off, I feel the lower part of the bed dip. At first, I think it's just in my head until I feel someone's arm grazing my stomach.

My eyes immediately flutter open, and I turn my gaze to whoever that someone is.

"Hannah, what are you doing here?" I swat her hand away and carry myself to seat up. She just smiles at me wickedly, her head resting over her bent arm.

"Come on, Jay, I know you want me."

Wow, I knew she was a little crazy, but I didn't know she's delusional too.

I stand up and point my finger towards the door. "Get out of my room now."

She carries herself up from the bed and walks toward me. She places her hand over my arm, but I immediately swat it away. "Jay, baby, I thought you like me."

"No. I don't. Jade only asked me to take you out on one date." And obviously, it was a big mistake. She kept blabbering about herself and her dead puppy the whole time on our date.

"But you wouldn't agree if you didn't like me, right?"

"Nope," I instantly answer. "I just wanted to prove to my sister that I wasn't gay."

After my break-up with Jewel, I was so heartbroken that I rarely went out of my dorm during my freshman year in college. My sister went to the same university I did. And just because I didn't hang out with sorority girls like most men do in college, rumors about me being gay had started to circulate in the campus. This rumor, of course, reached my older sister, Jade, who was a graduating student at that time.

Although, to this day, I still can't see their logic and why they thought I was gay. I mean, college is meant for studying, not for sleeping around. What kind of a role model would I be to my future students if I wouldn't focus on my college studies?

But Jade was having none of it, so she forced me—yes, forced—to take one of her friends, Hannah, on a lunch date. It was dreadful, to summarize it. I really shouldn't have accepted that five hundred bucks that my sister bribed me with if I knew that Hannah would turn out to be this crazy.

I'm surprised when Hannah suddenly pushes me back on the bed and hovers on top of me. Both her legs are one either side of my thighs. Her eyes are full of lust and desire, her hands pressed over my chest.

"I want you, Jay." I can smell the strong scent of wine from her breath.

"Hannah, please. Get up." I grip her wrist and slowly lift them up from my chest.

"What if I don't want to?"

149

"I know that deep down there, you're a nice girl. So, please stand up and leave."

She still smiles despite my hard grip on her wrist. "Oh, I'm a nice girl who will do bad, bad things to you, baby boy."

Why do I always get myself involved with psychotic women? First, Jewel and now, Hannah. I swear that Kim is not this wild. She's silly, but I'm pretty sure she's not this crazy.

I sigh and try to push her further away from me. "Hannah, I don't want to hurt you."

She pouts. "Kiss me, then I'll leave."

This girl must be really delusional if she thinks I'd really do that.

Jade told me that she had already introduced Kim as my fiancée to her friends, but why are they still acting like this? Especially Hannah. Her actions only show how depraved she is since even after knowing that I'm already engaged, she still throws herself at me.

My phone unexpectedly rings.

Hannah quickly grabs it and presses the 'accept' button.

I try to seize it back from her, but she runs inside the bathroom with it. I hit my palms against the door. "Hannah, give it back!"

"Oh hello, Kim," she answers.

I immediately tense up when I hear my fiancée's name. "Hannah, please! Give my phone back!"

"This is Hannah. Jay is not available right now because we're currently busy making babies. Just call him later, alright?" What the hell is wrong with this woman? "Okay. Bye."

The door opens after a few seconds, revealing a smiling witch.

"What was that for?" I shout, my whole body raging.

"She told me you're dead," she says, smirking evilly at me.

"Give me that." I snatch my phone from her grasp.

Kim and I are not married yet, and what Hannah told her might make her think I'm a cheater. I can't have her thinking that I won't be loyal to her. No matter what the circumstances are, even with how our engagement has started, I'm already keen on that girl despite her childishness because, at least, she's honest.

I search for Kim's name in my contact list and just when I am about to press the call button, I hear Jade's most terrifying voice downstairs that will haunt me for the rest of my life.

*Please tell me that she didn't call my sister about Hannah.*

"Jay! You are so dead!"

I quickly run to my door to lock it. But before I can even shut it completely, I am taken aback when Jade suddenly slams the door open, causing me to sit flat on the floor.

She narrows her eyes at me. "Where's Hannah?"

"I'm here!" Hannah cheerfully exclaims.

Jade glowers at her.

"It's not what you think!" I tell my sister as I stand up.

"Oh yeah? Then why is Hannah half naked?"

My eyes immediately widen in shock.

I turn my gaze to Hannah, and I'm surprised that she's only wearing her bra and shorts, her white blouse placed on the floor.

"When did you take off your clothes?" I ask her.

She giggles. "You're the one who took it off, silly boy."

"No, I did not."

"Hannah, get out now!" my sister says.

I see Hannah roll her eyes and shake her head as if she can't believe that Jade is such a killjoy. She takes her shirt from the floor and walks out of the room.

"I know you still want me, Jay!" Hannah says on her way out.

"Shut up," I shout back. If only I could also add *whore* to that, but I'm a gentleman.

"She's such a bitch," Jade says. Couldn't agree more to that.

"Jade, I swear that we didn't do anything."

"I know. I was just annoyed at you."

151

"Why? I didn't do anything to her. She was the one who attacked me."

"But Kim still thinks that you're cheating on her. I love you as much as I love that sweet girl, and I don't want her to look at you differently."

"Did you at least try to defend me?" I ask.

"Nope. That's your punishment for not kicking Hannah out." She chuckles.

"Oh please, I was just trying to be a gentleman."

"Yeah right." Jade rolls her eyes. "I baked some cookies. Wanna join?"

"No, thanks." I shake my head. "I've had enough of your psychotic friends for one night."

She pats my head like I'm a little boy. "They can be nice sometimes, though."

Yeah, sometimes. On very rare occasions, like when a puppy dies and they would all cry.

I close the door behind her, locking it for assurance. Who knows who might come in here again? I dial Kim's number, and she immediately picks up. Thank goodness!

"Kim!" I excitedly greet.

"What's your problem?"

"I just want to explain myself," I tell her. "I swear I didn't do anything with Hannah."

A long pause.

"Okay, I believe you. What sane woman would even say 'busy making babies' anyway? I just texted Jade to make sure, and she texted back a few seconds ago that everything's alright."

Finally, I relaxed.

"Good. So why did you call earlier? Did you miss me already? You just got home last night. Don't worry, it's alright to miss me." I tease her.

Kim scoffs. "*Please*, get over yourself." I'm sure she's rolling her eyes at me right now.

I press my lips together to suppress a smile. "Alright, what's so important that you decided to call me earlier? At this hour?"

She sighs heavily. "So, I guess you haven't heard of the terrifying news yet."

My eyebrows furrow. "What news?"

Someone knocks on my door. It's as if people enjoy disturbing me tonight.

"Jay, are you in there?" That's my dad's voice.

"I'll call you later. My dad's at the door," I tell Kim and hang up.

I turn the knob and open the door, revealing my smiling father. "I have good news for you."

Oh no. If he says it's good news, it actually means bad news for me. We've been having this conversation for years. This must be the news Kim was talking about.

"What's up?" I ask.

He grins wider before answering, "You're getting married this Wednesday night. On Kim's eighteenth birthday."

# Chapter 24

KIM

Most women look forward to their wedding day. They anticipate wearing their beautiful white gowns, walking down the aisle covered with flowers, seeing all their happy guests, and being finally united with the love of their lives.

But I beg to differ.

Because I had no choice but to agree to my dad's demand.

He showed me a red line on his laptop that's going downward. Our numbers are dropping, and this only means that our business is doing terrible and he really needs that money to prevent us from plummeting to our ruin. I'm the only key. I'm his only hope.

So, I guess I'm getting married earlier than what was agreed on. And I'm not looking forward to it. Not one bit.

When Monday morning comes and I begrudgingly go to my first class, which is Math, Jeremy eyes me curiously as if he's expecting a reaction from last night's news. Even when he is discussing the new lesson to the class, I can still feel his intense gaze on me.

Does he want me to feel angry? Depressed? Elated?

I'm upset, to say the least, but a few days early isn't really going to change anything. We're getting married whether we liked it or not. Displeasing, yes, but it's not like we have a choice anyway. I've learned to accept that as long as I'm being fed and roofed by my dad's money, I'm shackled and should be ready to submit to his every whim.

And the bad news doesn't end there.

"After this Christmas vacation, my granddad is taking me to London." Ella sighs, squeezing the peanut butter sandwich in her hands. "I'll be homeschooled there and go to college after. I don't know when I'll be back."

The lunch table remains quiet. Ella and I are sitting beside each other while Lance is in front of us. We can't really say anything because she has already explained everything. Her parents wanted her to stay in London with her grandfather because their main business is there and they want to train her how to run it in the future. We won't be seeing her again after Christmas, and it royally sucks.

"But you'll stay in touch, right?" Lance asks.

Ella looks at him as if he's insane. "Duh? Why would I stop communicating with *the* Lance Knight?"

I agree. "Don't worry, man, she won't forget you that easily."

Lance smiles, and I can sense he's holding something back. Of course, he is. My best friend is leaving the country, yet he still hasn't confirmed whether she is his long-lost sister.

Lance may be from England, but his biggest market is the US. That's why his manager wants him to stay. Moreover, his dad also wants their family to stay here for good. Given the situation, he really can't follow her to the UK. Not anytime soon, anyway.

But I really want some form of closure to this Ella and Lance's Korean-like drama. Lance is obviously in a dilemma, but it's not my place to tell Ella no matter how giddy I am to find out the truth. So, I just have to wait until he speaks up—which, apparently, is now.

Lance leans forward to touch Ella's hand who's still holding the sandwich.

"Is your name Aiah? Or maybe just your middle name?"

Ella looks confused. "Um, no. I'm just Daniella Summers."

He shakes his head. "Are you sure?"

"I'm pretty sure I know my full name." Ella laughs.

Lance pushes further. "But your mother is Jeanne Bricks."

"Yeah, she uses that as her pen name. But my name's not Aiah."

"It doesn't make any sense."

I'm watching them like a ping-pong ball match, and this is getting really interesting. My best friend releases her grip from the sandwich and chooses to hold Lance's hand.

"What doesn't make any sense?" she asks.

He squeezes her hand. "You don't really remember?"

"Remember what?"

I hold my breath. Is he really going to say it now? In a lunch table? In the cafeteria? Full of high school students who may be eavesdropping because who wouldn't want to hear celebrity gossip?

Lance blows a lungful of air and shakes his head disappointedly.

"Nothing. It's nothing." He pushes himself backward, stands up from his seat, and heads out the cafeteria without even bothering to say goodbye or 'see you later.'

Ella becomes more confused. "What's gotten into him?"

"I think he likes you," I suddenly blurt out. I don't think telling her she's his sister would make this better anyway.

"No way. He likes you." She points a finger at me. "Lance told me that he's been planning to ask you as his girlfriend, but I couldn't tell him that you're already engaged. Anyway, I know when a guy likes me. And the way Lance looks at you is the same way Kyle looks at me."

Wait, hold up. Did I hear her correctly?

"Kyle? As in my semi ex-crush, Kyle?"

"Story for another time." She pushes me off the table. "Now, follow Lance and see what's wrong with that hottie."

She doesn't have to say it twice. I need to tell Lance that he should just inform her the truth about Aiah so he'll have his peace of mind. The sooner he tells her, the sooner we will all get this over with.

156

I exit the cafeteria as fast as I can, hoping to catch Lance, but I can't see him anywhere. I'm sure he couldn't have gotten out the building that fast.

And just my luck, a classroom door is open. As I step closer, I can hear voices coming from the room, one of which I immediately recognize as Lance's.

"It's been like three weeks, and you still haven't gotten any information about Ella!"

I peek from the small gap and see Lance talking to someone. My position is so limited that I can't really determine who he's talking to. But I've been in this school long enough to recognize the voices of some of the teachers, especially the one who really stands out.

Like Mr. Gregory Campbell.

"I apologize, Lance, but Jeanne Bricks is a powerful woman, and she obviously made sure that Aiah has no link to her."

Lance and Mr. Campbell? Why are they talking about Ella or Aiah?

My friend pinches the bridge of his nose. "Greg, I'm paying a thousand bucks for every information you can get, and yet you're still stuck on that damn Jeanne Bricks!"

Mr. Campbell stutters. "I...I'm really trying my best here."

"I know being a private investigator while being a teacher is hard. But please, man, do your job and find more information on Ella Summers and her real connection to Aiah because it's been three damn weeks and we still got nothing!"

I feel a warm hand clutch my wrist. I whip my head and come face to face with Jeremy.

"What are you doing here, Kim?"

I glance back to Lance. Suddenly, he and Mr. Campbell are now staring at me, dumbfounded.

"Ms. Roberts, how long have you been standing there?" Mr. Campbell asks.

"Enough to know you're a private investigator."

Jeremy is obviously not aware of this. "A what?"

Lance glares at Mr. Campbell. "We'll talk later." He walks out of the room and heads south, taking me with him by my arm, Jeremy trailing behind us.

He stops in front of another empty classroom.

"Lance, what's going on?" I ask incredulously. "Mr. Campbell is your private investigator? How? I mean, didn't you save me from him in the parking lot the first time we met?"

Jeremy crosses his arms over his chest. "Speak up, Mr. Knight."

Lance sighs heavily. "Yeah, Gregory is my private investigator. Being a teacher is just his sideline so when his family and friends ask him about his job, he'll have something to say because you can't really announce to everyone that you're a paid stalker, right?"

I'm still a little confused. "Okay?"

"Gregory is not the nicest man you'd meet, but he's known to be great at his job. Or so I thought. He even dated Hailey just to get more information out of her because we thought that she was Aiah. But now the game has changed."

"Because my best friend is now your new subject."

He shrugs. "Yeah. But he still got nothing. What a waste."

"Wait, I don't get it. What's going on?" Jeremy looks so confused.

Lance shakes his head, but I still answer. I know it's his story to tell, but I don't think keeping something from your future husband is a good thing.

"Lance's dad is your uncle who killed my mom thirteen years ago. His dad—your uncle—actually has a daughter named Aiah from his first wife who was adopted by his wife's friend. No one knows what happened to Aiah. So, Lance hired Mr. Campbell to search for her. At first, they thought Hailey was her. That's why this guy fooled around with that slut for some information. Anyway, Aiah has heterochromia, just like Ella, and now we think my best friend is Lance's long-lost half-sister."

158

My fiancé gawks at me. I think his mind just exploded from all that information.

"You're…" Lance stammers. "You're that woman's daughter?"

I shift my attention to Lance. I know which woman she's referring to. I slowly nod.

Jeremy rubs his chin with his thumb as he stares at Lance. "And you're my cousin."

Lance gapes at Jeremy. "I thought your name is Bradshaw, not Lincoln?"

"I only use that name to avoid attention. But I'm Jeremy Lincoln, son of Daryl and Carol Lincoln, owner of the Lincoln Corporation."

Lance puts his head between his hands and paces around. "Wow, okay. I think my head hurts." I totally understand him. He then looks up to me. "Why didn't you tell me when we were at the coffee shop?" His breath quickens. "My dad killed your mom, Kim." He runs his hands through his brown hair. "Shit, I'm so sorry. I'm so sorry."

He's stressing about this too much.

"I didn't know how to tell you that time, but I'm telling you now, it's alright," I assure him. "It's not your fault, Lance. I don't blame you, I swear."

No matter how much it hurts that Lance's father is actually the one who accidentally killed my mom, I can never hate my friend for that. He has nothing to do with the accident and the obvious injustice, so I shouldn't hold it against him.

"I need to sit down. I'm sitting down now. Okay, I'm seated. I think I need a minute or two." Lance sits on the tiled floor, and all I can think about is how dirty the school floor is, but I remain quiet instead.

The number of germs on the floor is definitely least of our problems.

Several minutes of silence pass by, and Lance is still contemplating about his life on the germ-infested tiled floor while

Jeremy is staring mindlessly on the wall, hands on both hips as if in deep thought. I'm just playing with the tips of my hair, waiting for one of them to speak.

"What if it's just a coincidence, then?" Jeremy suddenly suggests.

"What coincidence?" Lance and I ask simultaneously.

He turns his gaze to Lance. "About Ella being your sister, Aiah."

"That's why I have Gregory to investigate further," Lance answers. "But it's been three weeks since I told him about my theory, and all he got is nothing."

"Alright, let's say Ella is really Aiah. What happens next?"

"I don't know." Lance runs his hand through his hair. "But I guess I won't do anything. Ella's obviously happy with her life. I just want to make sure that Aiah is safe and alive." He blows a lungful of air. "You have no idea how dreadful it is that I'm a partaker of what happened to her and her brother because if I haven't been born, my dad wouldn't have left them. If Aiah is really alive, then I'd be at peace."

Be at peace?

"You're not gonna die, are you?" I ask. "Like, you don't have some life-threatening illness, right?" I don't think I'll be ready for that.

Lance chuckles and shakes his head. "No, my life is not that dramatic. I just want to know if Aiah is alive so I can focus on my music better."

The bells rings, signaling the start of our afternoon classes.

"I have a class to teach. I'll talk to you later," Jeremy tells me as he fixes his tie.

He leans down and plants a kiss on my lips—in front of Lance. It happens so fast. I don't even get the chance to react quickly. Then he casually walks away, leaving us to go to his next lecture, as if what he did was perfectly normal.

What in the hell is wrong with him?

"Um, did he just...did our math teacher just kiss you?" Lance probes disbelievingly.

I nervously glance at him. "Maybe?"

His hands form into a fist at his sides. "I thought there's nothing going on between the two of you?"

"Um..."

How do I explain that we're only forced into this relationship?

But that jerk kissed me! In front of his student! So, convincing Lance that Jeremy and I are not at all happy in this agreement is quite impossible.

His jaw tightens. "So, you're the girl my cousin is marrying then?"

Why is he, all of a sudden, acting like a jealous boyfriend?

I slowly nod. "Yes."

"I don't feel like coming to class today." He storms out, leaving a heated vibe.

*He likes you.* I remember Ella telling me.

But I made it perfectly clear that we're just friends. He can't act like I'm his property all of a sudden. That's just foolish. Or is it?

He's going to find out about it at the wedding anyway. I don't have to be guilty, right?

My phone vibrates inside my bag, so I fish it out and notice a text from Jeremy.

Jeremy: *Did I just kiss u in front of Lance?*
Me: *Yes, u did dumbass.*
Jeremy: *Crap. This is what wedding jitters do to me.*

And now we're screwed. Stupid wedding jitters.

# Chapter 25

KIM
*December 13, 2017*

It's my birthday, and I should be celebrating.

But no. Instead, I'm sulking in the Lincoln guest room as Bryan finishes the final touches on my face.

I have just turned eighteen, and I'm already getting married. To my math teacher, might I add. I want to cry, but it'll definitely ruin the mascara Bryan just put on me, and I'd hate to see him disappointed. He's been a really nice and sweet guy, and I don't have the heart to ruin his work of art.

Yet I can still say that our parents are complete dorks. I'll start with how they prepared our mini wedding for today. Carol told me that even if this is just a simple contract signing, she still wants to see her future daughter-in-law walk down the aisle while her son waits for me at the altar. One tiny problem though, their house doesn't have an aisle for me to walk on and they don't have an altar for Jeremy to stand and wait by.

My father, unfortunately, thought of a plan to improvise. They arranged rows of chairs in the garden, leaving a small gap in between for me to walk on. And for the altar, they just used a high table and covered it with white linen.

So now, here I am, holding a bouquet of flowers, walking down the "aisle" with my dad beside me, and our closest family members and friends as our guests. Lance is here too, with his dad who, by the way, accidentally killed my mom in a car crash.

Can this day be any more uncomfortable?

"Woooh! Go, *Kiremy*!" Ella shouts, making my cheeks burn in humiliation. I glare at her.

*I am going to kill you.*

I glance to my left and notice a grinning Jade with a very beautiful Chiara sitting next to her. When I finally reach the so-called altar, my dad kisses my cheeks and looks up to Jeremy with a smile. "She's your problem now." He jokes.

Jeremy takes my hand then beckons me towards the high table where the marriage contract is placed. Jeremy's dad, who is, shockingly, also a marriage officiant, beams at us.

"We are all gathered here to witness the wedding ceremony of my son and his fiancée."

Um, duh?

Unless we're here to celebrate the president's birthday, then let's go.

He turns to face Jeremy. "Are you ready, son?" he asks in a hushed tone that only the three of us can hear.

"Not really," he answers in a flat voice. I totally agree with him.

Mr. Lincoln narrows his eyes at him then turns his attention to me. "What about you? Please say you are."

"My father didn't raise me a liar, Mr. Lincoln," I tell him with a slight smile. Jeremy suddenly turns to look at me, and I see a small hint of amusement on his lips.

Daryl sighs, and I know he's thinking that we're really impossible. We just face each other and hold each other's hand to get this over with.

"Alright. Do you, Jeremy Lincoln, take Kim Adriana Roberts to be your lawfully wedded wife, your constant friend, your faithful partner, and your love from this day forward; in sickness and in health, in good times and in bad, and in joy and as well as sorrow? Do you promise to love her unconditionally, to support her in her goals and to honor and respect her, to laugh and cry with her, and to cherish her as long as you both shall live?"

Wow, that was a long one.

163

Jeremy purses his lips and looks at his father again. "Well…"

"Jeremy!" His father scolds, and I look at the crowd, and some of them are keeping themselves from laughing since they probably know that we really hate each other's guts.

Jeremy just rolls his eyes and turns to face me again. "Fine. I do."

"Good. Now, do you, Kim Adriana Roberts, take Jeremy Lincoln to be your lawfully wedded husband, your constant friend, your faithful partner, and your love from this day forward; in sickness and in health, in good times and in bad, and in joy and as well as sorrow? Do you promise to love him unconditionally, to support him in his goals and to honor and respect him, to laugh and cry with him, and to cherish him as long as you both shall live?"

I've always thought that saying the words *I do* in front of your husband-to-be is the most romantic scene in the world. Now, I change my mind.

"I do," I mumble. But I think it came out more like *adoh*.

"What was that, Kim?" Daryl presses.

I sigh heavily. "I do."

"Good. Now you may sign the papers." He hands us the pen, and we both sign the bottom paper with our signature. "Happy Birthday, Kim," he adds.

I'm officially eighteen *and* married.

We also exchange the rings that Carol bought for us. I didn't even get to choose my wedding ring.

My wedding sucks.

"Now kiss!" Ella shouts, and I glare at her.

Jeremy lifts my veil, and something flashes in his eyes. "I'm sorry."

"For what?"

"For ignoring you since yesterday. I was having wedding jitters."

He was. The last interaction we had was that kiss and that text last Monday afternoon. Then after that, he acted like he didn't know me at all. Tuesday passed and he never gave me a glance. I started to worry that he was going to leave the country and cancel the wedding.

As much as I hate being married right now, my dad needs that money.

"It's alri—"

But I don't finish my sentence when his lips press against mine. When we pull apart, he just gives me a small smile.

"Yey! Now make some babies!"

Note to self: Choke my best friend to death later.

Jeremy and I adamantly refuse to do the cliché couple walk, so the ceremony simply ends after that kiss. I try to search for my dad to ask him what time we'll be going back home, but despite the small number of guests, he's still nowhere to be found.

Luckily, I notice Daryl talking to a man around his age, probably another businessman.

"Mr. Lincoln, sorry to interrupt, but have you seen my dad?" I ask him.

"Yeah." He points their house. "He's inside."

"Thank you."

He smiles. "And Kim, just call me Daryl."

I nod and immediately rush to find my dad. I stop when I see him talking to the last person I expected him to converse with today.

"Dad." I slowly approach him.

Both of them turn their attention to me. "Kimmy!" my dad exclaims. I give him a questioning look, hoping he'll get the signal. Sadly, he doesn't. "Richard, this is my princess, Kimberly. Kim, this is Richard Lincoln." He gestures to the dark blonde man he's talking to.

"Yeah, I know." I nearly roll my eyes. "He's the one who killed Mom, right? Nice to meet you *Dick* Lincoln."

"Kimberly Adriana!" Dad's eyes widen at my remark.

"It's true." I nonchalantly shrug.

Why is he acting like this man in front of us didn't cause him severe pain and loss? Did he suddenly have amnesia or something?

"Your daughter is quite feisty." Richard chuckles, making me grimace. "Don't worry, I always go by the name Dick Lincoln. It's much quicker to say."

Dad faces him and forces a smile. "Can't wait for you to come to my office tomorrow."

"What?" I huff. "Why are you even talking to him, Sad?" I know I'm being extremely rude right now, but what in the world is going on here?

The repulsive man offers his hand before me. "I'll be one of the new investors of Golden Shovel Properties. I guess you didn't know that your father and I have been trying not to let our pasts hinder us from doing far greater things here in the US."

I scoff. "Figures."

My dad is willing to forget whatever this man did to us for the sake of money.

He retreats his hand that I didn't shake and beams at me, showing his perfectly white teeth. "I heard you are friends with my son, Lance?"

"That's none of your business."

My father's jaw clenches. "I didn't raise you to be disrespectful, Kimberly."

Richard laughs and pats my dad's shoulder. "Adrian, don't be so harsh on her."

Since when did they call each other by their first names?

This time, I roll my eyes at how absurd this situation is. How could my dad do this to Mom? This douche, Richard, killed my mother and probably bribed the entire justice system. He used his money to escape from the consequences of his actions, and now they're suddenly friends just because he's going to invest in our company?

"I hate you." I whirl around to leave the murderer and the greedy.

# Chapter 26

JEREMY

During our reception, all I can think of is how I can look at Kim without her or anyone noticing it. She really looks elegant in her wedding gown. She's only wearing light makeup, so her natural beauty still shines through. I can honestly say that she's more beautiful than ever. Every time I stare at her or even just take a glimpse of her, someone teases me about it. Then Kim would turn to me and blush, which of course, makes her a lot more adorable.

I continue eating my medium-rare steak when a very familiar voice calls my name. I look up and see Jewel as if she's not quite sure if I'm really me.

"Jewel, what are you doing here?" I ask her as I put my fork down. I stand up from my seat to greet her. I'm still a gentleman even though I dislike her.

"Your mom invited me," she replies. She takes a step closer and kisses my cheek. My mother still has no idea about my real relationship with Jewel. "I can't believe you're already married," she says as her hand rests on my left shoulder.

"I can't believe it either," I say in all honesty. But I'm not regretting one bit.

She smiles at me. "You're still the same."

What is this woman talking about?

I clear my throat before speaking, "Anyway, I hope you have a good time. I need to find my wife," I tell her before stepping aside to give myself some space. Just as I am about to walk away from her, I feel her grip around my arm.

"Can we talk? Please?"

I turn around to study her face, and I can see that she's really desperate to talk to me.

"Fine. Talk." I cross my arms over chest, lifting my chin up.

"Can we talk in someplace more private?"

"No. If you want to talk to me, then do it here. Not some private place where you can throw yourself at me."

"But Jay—"

"You have two minutes before I leave you alone, Jewel. Now say what you need to say."

She closes her eyes and takes a deep breath. "I'm still in love with you."

Unbelievable.

I shake my head in plain annoyance. "And you're telling me this because?"

She looks up to me with pleading eyes. "Because I want you back...I want *us* back."

My arms automatically fall to my sides.

How could she say that after what she did to me? After what I discovered about her.

"Whatever relationship we had before, it's gone, Jewel, and there's no way in hell I'm going to get back with you."

I'm not going to let her feed me with her lies again.

She purses her lips. "But, Jay, I know you still love me. I know it. You still do!"

Good thing the music is loud enough to drown our conversation.

"What part of 'I never loved you' do you not understand? And how many times do I have to tell you that I will never fall in love with you?"

"Not enough for me to believe it," she says, tears gleaming in her eyes.

I sigh.

This girl is impossible.

"What do I have to do for you to believe me?" I ask. "I'm married now, Jewel. Isn't that enough for you to believe that I don't have any feelings for you?"

"No, it's not. I know that you just married each other because of your parents' agreement. You want me to believe that you really like her, but I'm too smart for that. We still have mutual friends, Jay." She smiles cheekily. "I just can't give up my man to some random girl, right?"

"I really do like Kim," I say seriously. "And I'm not your man."

She frowns. "But you were. A lot of people can attest to how we both loved each other."

"Because you lied to them too. You lied to everyone," I retort. "You knew all along, but you never said anything about it because you wanted to keep me despite our situation."

"I did what I had to do to keep you because I love you!" she shouts, and I'm sure that the music isn't enough to keep our guests from overhearing our conversation this time.

Everyone turns in our direction, eyeing us curiously.

"What's going on here?" My dad interjects, walking towards us. When his eyes land on Jewel, he grimaces. "What are you doing here, Jewel?"

"Carol invited me. And I'm still family, right?"

I really want to throttle this woman. "Jewel, I swear…"

But Kim immediately interrupts before I can even say foul words to this wench.

"Am I missing something here?" she says as she saunters in my direction, her heels hanging on her hands. I look down and see that she's already barefoot.

"It's nothing. Jewel is just leaving," I tell her, my eyes on Jewel.

Kim turns to Jewel. "Oh, you're here."

"Yeah, I thought it was your funeral, so I had to come," Jewel says.

"Jewel!" my father and I say at the same time.

Kim's eyes flicker with an emotion I can't explain. Maybe it's distress or loathing, but she instantly hides it with a disdainful smile.

"Sorry to disappoint you, but I'm still alive. Although if you keep touching my husband, it might just be a funeral. For you."

Jewel softly chuckles. "Do you really think I'd be threatened by that? The world doesn't need a petty piece of trash such as yourself."

I grab her wrist to throw her out. How dare she talk to my wife like that.

I am about to kick her out when Kim suddenly speaks, "I prefer to be called a pretty piece of trash." She smirks. "Ass butt."

What does that even mean?

"What?" Jewel asks confusedly as she looks at me. I'm pretty much confused, too.

"Jewel, please leave now before I call the security." My dad warns her.

She glares at him before pulling away from my grasp and storming out. We watch her stomp her way out of the garden.

"Well, that was one hell of a show," Kim says, breaking the silence. Our guests go back to their own conversations. I'm glad they don't press for more information. Well, except for Kim, of course.

"Jay, what was that about?"

"Just leave it alone, Kim. It's none of your business," I say as I run my hand through my hair in frustration.

She sighs. "I'm sorry for talking to Jewel like that. I didn't mean to offend her in any way. But she was so mean and I had to defend myself. I don't know why she was acting like that because the last time I saw her, she was really nice to me. Did I do something wrong?"

"No, you didn't." I smile at her and clasp her bare shoulder. "It's okay. She deserves it."

She smiles back, but it instantly disappears.

171

"I know this isn't the right timing, but I really need to know if there is still something going on between you two."

"There's none, Kim. Don't stress yourself about it."

She narrows her eyes at me. "Why can't you tell me what was that about? We're married now. Even if it's only in name and not for real, we're still married. You could at least tell me what is going on with you and the girl who claims to be still in love with my husband. Not that I'm jealous or anything, but I still need to know so that when people ask me, I'm not clueless. If she's still your girlfriend, then I'm fine with that, but please tell me. I don't want to be a laughingstock and—"

I lean closer and give her a soft kiss that lasts a little longer than what I've planned. As much as I hate a nagging woman, I really find her amusing.

"Jewel and I are done," I assure her with a smile.

She blinks a couple times as if she can't believe I just cut her off with a kiss.

"Why did you break up then?" She stares at me with persuasive eyes.

Oh well, I guess I just have to tell her before she starts rambling again.

"Jewel is my half-sister."

# Chapter 27

"No way!" I gasp.

I was expecting him to say something different like they broke up because she cheated on him, or that Jewel had to leave for Korea. I didn't expect her to be his half-sister.

Because, please, what kind of sister looks at her brother with lust and passion? That's just disgusting. Not to mention it's incest.

"Um, yes way?"

"But…how?"

"Can we not talk about this here?"

I raise an eyebrow at him. He's kidding, right?

"Oh no! You can't just drop a bomb like that on me! You need to tell me about this now!"

He runs his hand through his hair, making him look sexier. "We'll talk about this soon, just, not now. Please? Let's just enjoy our wedding day."

Damn. I hate it when he does that. His hair becomes unruly, and I find it really hot.

"Alright. Just promise me that you'll tell me about her later," I say.

He smiles. "I promise."

Jeremy takes my hand and leads me towards our guests who have been eager to talk to us since they arrived here. He introduces me to some of his relatives and closest family friends. And just like Jade's friends, some are nice, and some are…not.

173

Most girls gawk at him while he's talking as if he's some kind of Greek god. It's not completely their fault though because my husband really looks like a son of Aphrodite.

Sometimes, I swear he looks better than me, and it's really upsetting.

After the small gathering, everyone goes home, except, of course, my best friend.

Ella decides to invade my privacy by entering my room—I mean the Lincoln's special room for me—without any warning while I'm removing my bra. I swear this girl is going to be that death of me.

I quickly cover my chest. "Ella! Ever heard of knocking?"

She gives me a comical look. "Kim! Ever heard of locking the door?"

I glare at her and nod. "Touché."

She giggles as she lays herself down on the bed. "You're lucky that it wasn't your husband or else you're going to spend your honeymoon too early."

"Shut up." I hiss as I fish out another pair from the closet because, apparently, Jeremy's mom decided to shop for clothes for me. I still don't know why.

"Oh, come on! It's not like he's never going to see you anytime soon, right?"

I glower at her while mentally strangling her with my bare hands.

"I'm not going to do it with him anytime soon." I dress in a white T-shirt with a big *LOVE* printed on it. "I'm too young for that," I add as I wear the pair of blue cotton shorts. Wow, this closet has everything.

She sits up and gives me a quizzical look. "Bish, you're freakin' eighteen! Heck, sixteen-year-old kids have more action than you do."

I take a clean towel and go inside the bathroom without closing the door. I soak the towel with water and wipe it on my face. "It's still weird. And you're one to talk. You're a virgin too," I tell her as I rub the towel over my eyelids. I'm really not used to wearing makeup.

"But it's because I'm saving myself for marriage," she answers. "You, my dear, are already married."

I exit the bathroom and hang the damp towel over a chair. "Whatever. I'm still a teenager. I feel like it's not the right time yet."

"Oh well, I'm sure sooner or later you'll finally bang him," she declares. My face heats up, and I give her a defiant look. "Because just look at him! He's so hot, I'm gonna die!" She plops on the bed and squeaks as she rolls over.

Sometimes I wonder if my best friend was raised by a family of pigs.

"You're unbelievable." I shake my head in amusement. When I hear a knock from the door, I look at my rolling friend. "That's knocking right there, Ella," I tell her as if I'm a teacher in a kindergarten class.

She stops rolling and sits up. "Just open it already. Maybe that's your very irresistible husband!"

As soon as I open the door, my friend squeaks again.

"Hey," Jeremy says in a low voice. He smiles at me, but then it immediately turns into a confused frown when he notices Ella breathing heavily on the bed. "Um, is she okay?"

"No. Do you know a psychiatric hospital around here?" I joke.

"Why? Are you already going crazy about me?"

My eyes widen. "What?" This guy is unbelievable. "No! I was talking about Ella!"

He just smirks at me. "Sure."

I close the door behind me so he can't see Ella. "What are you doing here?"

"Our parents are calling for us. They want us both in Dad's office."

~

175

Marc Eaton is sitting beside my dad on the couch while the Lincoln couple is in front of them. My dad beams at me once we enter the office.

"So…" Jeremy starts as he sits on the love seat next to his parents. There is no other space other than beside him, so I take my place right next to my husband.

We all sit around the coffee table in front of us.

"Congratulations to both of you." Marc greets us. "I was there in the background, watching your wedding."

I don't think he's here to only congratulate us. I just wish he'd go straight to the point so we can go leave and have a good night's sleep.

"Thanks," Jeremy says, tapping his hands on his thighs. "So, what did you call us for?"

My dad pushes a folder towards us, and Jeremy reluctantly takes it.

"Both of you should sign that, then we'll send it to Kim's mom's attorney with your attached marriage contract and certificate so we can finally open the trust fund," Carol explains.

Without further deliberation, Jeremy takes the pen from his mother, puts his signature at the bottom of the page, and passes it to me. I can feel his annoyance at the situation. I just don't know why.

I do the same, and Marc reaches forward to take it back. Both our parents also sign on the paper, and finally the attorney. Then he closes the folder and puts it inside his suitcase.

"You should be able to access the trust fund by Friday morning," Marc informs us, and we all just nod.

"Is that all?" Jeremy asks. "Can we leave now?"

"Yes, you can leave, son. Good night," Daryl replies coldly.

Jeremy stands up, pulling me by my arm to exit his dad's office. He continues to drag me until we reach the door of his room. He releases his clutch on my wrist and groans as he runs his hand through his hair, facing away from me.

What's the matter with him?

"Are you alright?"

He shakes his head. "No."

"What's wrong then?"

He spins to face me. "You."

I take a step back, feeling offended. "Me?"

As far as I know, I did nothing wrong today. Did I?

"I hate that I'm married to you right now."

Hurt grips my chest as if its trying not fall in an abyss.

He could've at least said it a little nicer.

"It's not like I had a choice, too," I tell him. "You can have some side-chicks if you want. I don't really care."

His jaws tick. "That's not what I meant."

I wave my hands in frustration. "Then what!"

He takes a step forward and puts my head between his hands. "I hate that I'm married to you because of a stupid trust fund when I want to marry you just because I like you."

Big-headed teacher says what?

He aggressively takes my lips with his and tugs me inside his room.

"You taste like strawberries," Jeremy mumbles against my lips as he pushes me down his bed.

One minute I was hurt by his words, and now we're making out? Zero to one hundred real quick.

My back hits the comforter, and he hovers over me. His lips travel down on my neck but I slowly push him away from me.

*Too soon, buddy.*

"I'm not ready yet," I confess. "And what in the world did you just say?"

"You taste like strawberries."

I roll my eyes. "No…that you *like* me?"

A wide grin spreads across his face. "Yeah. I like you. I've always liked you, Kim."

Whoah.

I sit up and completely shove him off me. "I call B.S."

"Why?"

Did he really just ask that?

"Because!" I exclaim. "You've always been mean to me, and if you really did like me, you won't act like an arrogant wacko, humiliating me in class almost every day!"

"Because you're my student and it's still your responsibility to listen to my lectures and learn."

He places his hands behind my neck, pushing my head closer to his and kissing me again.

He's insatiable.

I pinch his waist, which causes him to pull away. He glowers at me as he massages the skin I just pinched. Sorry, not sorry.

"We're not done talking yet."

He groans. "What do you want to talk about? I've always been attracted to you since the first day of class, but you're my student, so I didn't do anything. It's not rocket science, Kim."

I narrow my eyes at him. "I still feel like you're lying."

He makes an annoyed face. "Remember in your diary, when you said I glanced at you? I didn't just glance, Kim. I gazed as many times as I could." He takes a strand of my blonde hair. "You have this golden hair that rightly frames your charming face. Your eyes are so deep blue as if I might sink and drown. I was so amazed by your smile that I almost stuttered while introducing myself on that first day." He squeezes my hand. "But I also knew that you're my student and I shouldn't be interested in you. But I am. For several months, I tried to fight my attraction to you but miserably failed. Despite how bad you are in Math, I still like you."

"But I'm not the only blue-eyed blondie in your class," I state the obvious. "What makes me so different from the rest of them then?"

Okay, I'm definitely fishing for compliments.

"You're the only one who doesn't cry." He gives my lips another quick kiss. My eyebrows knit in confusion, so he explains further. "For two years that I've been working as a high school teacher, there's quite a number of students who fail my subject, and all of them do their waterworks on me just so I would tweak their grades. And then you came along and started bribing me for a passing score. You never cried whenever you see an F on your paper. Instead, you annoy the hell out of me with your quirky remarks, and for some weird reason, I find it...endearing."

This time, I willingly kiss him.

Unexpectedly, he lifts his head.

He rests his forehead against mine. "I hate being scared, Kim. I hate it so much."

I give him another swift kiss. "What are you scared of?"

"I'm scared to break down my walls just to be hurt again."

My hands gently caress his cheek. "Jay..."

He then rolls off me, and now he's facing the ceiling. I watch his chest rise and fall as he looks for the right words.

"Jewel's adoptive parents were a close family friend. She was only a year younger than me. We instantly became close friends, since they only lived a few blocks away from our house. She was really pretty and charming."

I lie on my side so I can see him. "Thanks for boosting my confidence."

He faintly chuckles and shakes his head. "She was cute. I can't deny the fact that I did like her. But that's just it. I didn't completely fall in love." He clears his throat. "Then when I turned sixteen, I decided to ask her to be my girlfriend, but we pretended that we were just friends in front of our parents. We never told them about our relationship because I hated being teased about it. My mom still thinks I'm a baby."

A smile creeps on my lips. "Yeah, she still does."

"I proposed to her on our second anniversary as a couple. Of course, I asked her adoptive dad first, and he gave me his blessing." A ghost of sadness passes over his face. "When she said yes, I was so excited to tell my dad about our engagement. I thought he was going to be just as excited for us, except he wasn't. He was furious, to say the least."

179

I place my hand over his. "So, you mean, your dad knew already that you were siblings?"

He nods and swallows the lump in his throat. "When I brought Jewel home to tell my dad about our engagement, the distress on his face couldn't be painted. He thought we were only friends, so he let us be. Then he pointed at Jewel for being a disgusting slut—his words, not mine. He said she knew since she was fifteen that I was her half-brother, so he couldn't understand why Jewel would allow me to even propose to her in the first place.

"I was so confused that I slid off my hand from Jewel's hold and looked at her with so much disbelief and pain. She was sorry for not telling me sooner about our real relation, but her feelings for me were true. She said she really did love me and promised we won't have children if I'm worried they'd have health complications. That just made me sick even more."

"That's really messed up." I can't help but make a repulsed face.

"I refused to believe everything that was happening, but after a while, Jewel started sobbing and begging me not to break the engagement off just because she's my sister. I could still recall the guilt in her eyes and how much I wanted to kiss those tears away, but I restrained myself. She lied to me and made me look like a fool."

"Do you know her real parents?"

"No. All I know is that my dad cheated on my mom. Jewel is my dad's illegitimate daughter. He kept it from us for as long as he could. I hate my dad for what he did."

"I'm so sorry." I cup his cheek with my hand.

"The first time I met her, I was instantly drawn to her. We were so alike. I thought it was some romantic spark, but it wasn't. The instant connection was due to the fact that she was family—my sister." He blows out a breath. "Remember when you asked why I chose to be a teacher and I said because my sister hates it? I was talking about her. Jewel does hate this profession. She thinks being a teacher is boring and useless, so I proved her wrong. And now I learned to love what she hates the most."

It's like the missing piece of the puzzle has just been found. "So, you never went back together after that?"

He nods. "Yes. But she still tells some of our friends that we recently just broke up to get their pity. I tried to forget her completely, but it's so hard when she's the first girl I thought I loved."

"Is that why you tried to push me away? Do you still have feelings for her?"

"No." He shakes his head and touches my hand on his cheek. "I pushed you away because I'm scared that I'll find out something about you that will make me lose you. Just like what happened between me and Jewel. I tried to hate you because how could I lose you if you were never mine in the first place, right? You don't know how much I denied my feelings for you. I tried so hard, but you kept pulling me towards you without even knowing it. So, I just stopped denying and let my stupid self fall for you. And that scared me the most. It still does.

I am beyond speechless. How can this man say these romantic words to me? Can he not remember how much I'm a nuisance in his life?

"Jeremy, I—" But he cuts me off by pressing his lips to mine.

He pulls after a while, and his green eyes gaze through my blue ones with so much adoration. "I like you, Kim. Simple as that."

# Chapter 28

Jeremy: *Lets have lunch together in my office @ 12. If someone asks you why you're there, tell them I need your help with a project.*

I read his text again for the third time as I wait for him in his office. It's already ten minutes after twelve, yet I'm still alone here with my cheeseburger and apple juice. I left my best friend so I can have lunch with my husband, but he's nowhere to be found. I'm so going to strangle that guy.

I've also been staring at his gray tuxedo hanging at the back of the chair behind his desk. It looks so tempting, so I finally situate myself on the stool and grab his tuxedo and bring it under my nose.

Just a quick sniff to pass the time. Nothing's wrong with that.

It smells like a mixture of eucalyptus and oakmoss, an intoxicating herbaceous scent. I bury my face on his tuxedo. I probably look like a drug addict sniffing heroin from its fabric, but I don't really care. It's just me, my husband's tuxedo, and my cheeseburger on the desk.

Maybe if I stuff this in my bag, he won't notice?

"What are you doing?"

"Nothing!" I instinctively throw his tux on the floor in shock.

Jeremy is standing by the door with a curious expression as if he's somewhat worried about my mental health. He's still wearing the same clothes he wore this morning in our math class: crisp white shirt, rolled-up sleeves with two undone buttons, and black slacks.

He looks so hot.

"Why were you late? I've been bored out of my mind here." I change the topic.

His expression changes into an apologetic look. "Sorry, we had a short meeting with the head of the math department."

He places his laptop on the desk, and I stand up so he can settle himself. Once he's seated, he grabs the tuxedo and folds it. I'm just glad he doesn't ask further why I was so engrossed with it a while ago, or I'll be mortified.

I'm about to return to my usual spot when he unexpectedly grabs me by my waist to pull me on his lap.

He kisses my left cheek. "I missed you."

"You just saw me this morning." I try to wriggle away from his arms, but he tightens his hold on me. "Jeremy, how can we eat lunch if you're hugging me like this?"

He reaches his other arm across the desk to grab the cheeseburger and gives it to me. He opens his laptop and opens a document that looks like a lesson plan. "I still have to pass this to our department chair before 1:00 PM."

"You're not going to eat?"

He shakes his head. "Later."

I unwrap the cheeseburger and offer it to him. "You have to eat."

He raises an eyebrow and gives me a funny look. "Since when did you become concerned?"

"Since you invited me for lunch today but it turns out you're not going to eat." I push the bread on his parted lips, and he takes a small bite with a smile.

For about five minutes, we share my burger as I watch him type on his laptop with one hand. My math teacher is making our lesson plan for next week while I—his student—am sitting on his lap with his right arm tightly wrapped on my waist. Never in my whole did I ever imagine I'll be in this situation. But I'm also not complaining.

He suddenly stops from typing. It doesn't take long before he moves my hair to the other side and plants a swift kiss on my cheek.

I push his head away. "I thought you need to finish this before 1:00 PM?"

"I'm too stressed out. I need to relax a bit," he says through kisses.

"And this relaxes you?" I bite my lower lip as I sense him smiling on my skin.

He cups my jaws so I can face him. "You relax me."

Jeremy returns his gaze on his laptop and rests his chin on my shoulder. The light from his laptop illuminates his face, and I can clearly see how long his eyelashes are and how perfectly sculpted his nose is.

I give him quick kisses on the cheek whenever I notice he's thinking to somehow ease his mind, and he would return it with longer kisses. I'm surprised he actually finishes the lesson plan he's doing.

We hear the bell ring an hour later. He hesitantly releases me from his grip. "Go to class, my beautiful wife."

I leave his office, probably grinning like an idiot as I make my way to my next class. Lance is already sitting on his usual seat, and I'm not even worried if he's still mad at me. I'm that happy today.

"Hey." My friend greets once I'm seated. "So, I have something to tell you and—" He's cut off when Mr. Campbell enters the room. Lance sighs heavily. "I'll tell you later."

"Okay."

Ella later comes in and notices my weird smile. "Someone's a happy wife today."

I bite my lower lip. "Shut up."

Mr. Campbell starts discussing, and I look out into the window when lightning catches my eyes. My elated mood somehow deflates when I notice the clouds turning dark. The weatherman said it would be a bright shiny day.

184

I'm too preoccupied with the sudden change of weather that I don't notice the school secretary entering the room.

"May I please excuse Miss Kimberly Roberts? It's a family emergency," she tells Mr. Campbell.

Confusion and fear overwhelm me. What's going on?

My history teacher nods at me, and I slowly stand up from my seat, unsure of the situation. I release the pen in my hand to leave it on my desk, but it slides down to the floor.

I'll just pick that up later.

I follow the secretary to the guidance counselor's office, chewing on my bottom lip in dread. Once we're inside, she beckons me to take a seat on the comfy looking couch.

"I'm sorry to excuse you out from class, Ms. Roberts." Miss Shaina starts.

"Uh, it's alright. Why am I here?"

She sighs. "The hospital just called us. Your dad had a heart attack while driving..."

My knees start to tremble. "And? Is my dad okay? Please, tell me he's alright." I don't think I can handle another two weeks of him being in a coma.

She shakes her head, and I think I just stopped breathing. "We're really sorry, Ms. Roberts, but your father has passed away."

"No..." I can't breathe. Please, gods, no.

"We can drive you to the hospital if you want."

I look down on my hands, and they're shaking.

"I hate you," was the last thing I told my dad, and I refused to talk to him after that.

I repeatedly punch my chest to stop the excruciating pain inside, but it still damn hurts.

*Dad, I'm so sorry.*

This is just a bad dream. A really, really bad dream.

*Dad, I don't hate you.*

No. This is not happening.

I gasp for air. Miss Shaina moves immediately to my side and gently rubs my back, but I still can't breathe. She puts my head on her chest as I cry my heart out.

I want my mom, but she's also not here.

Now they're both gone.

It feels like my whole world is falling apart and all I am left with is sheer anguish. Piece by piece, I'm shattering, and I can't do anything but cry.

*I love you, Dad. I'm so sorry.*

~

My mom died a day before my birthday. Now, my dad died a day after my birthday.

It's like the universe wanted to surround my birthday with horrible memories. I was born on the thirteenth anyway, so I guess I shouldn't really be surprised.

Now, it's been two days, and I find myself curled in my husband's bed as he envelops me in his arms, kissing the top of my head during an overcast Sunday afternoon.

Everything happened so fast, and I feel so disoriented. They just buried him this morning, and it still feels so surreal. My dad is gone, and I'm all alone.

Maybe this is all just a bad dream, a painful nightmare. But it's been two days, he's still gone, and I'm still crying my eyes out. I guess I need to accept this horrible reality no matter how quickly it happened.

I hear a knock from the door, but I don't budge from my position. It opens, and Jeremy lifts his head to see who it is.

"Kim has to eat." I hear Carol say. "She hasn't eaten for two days."

"I ate a banana yesterday," I whisper to Jeremy. That still counts as food.

Jeremy tips my chin up. "My mom's right. You have to eat."

"I said I ate a banana yesterday."

"That's not enough."

I close my eyes and bury my head in the crook of his neck. "I don't feel like eating."

He merely sighs and faces his mom. "I'll talk to her."

The door closes.

"I just want to sleep. Please don't force me to eat."

He plants a soft kiss on my forehead "Okay. Let's sleep."

~

I wake up with my head resting on Jeremy's chest. He's still sleeping, so I slowly wiggle my way out of his arm. I look at the alarm clock on the side table and notice that it's already six in the evening.

I haven't eaten properly for two days, but my stomach isn't rumbling yet. I guess this is what depression does to a person.

The Lincoln family has been very accommodating. I've been staying at their house since I received the horrifying news. I still can't bring myself to go back to our house.

Jeremy and I haven't also gone back to school. He has never left my side since we've gone to the hospital to arrange the documents for my dad. I've been sleeping in his bed for two days and only gone to the shower once, but it was only because I wanted to be alone and cry.

I open the door and exit his room. Jade's room is across his. Although she has her own place, she chose to stay here for a few days, probably to be here for me. I contemplate on knocking on her door until she opens it and finds me staring nervously.

"I wanted to knock, but I thought you might be busy," I say, almost like a whisper. "I didn't want to disturb you."

She smiles. "I was just about to grab a snack downstairs. Do you want to eat with me?"

Hesitantly, I nod. "Okay."

We both go down and enter their kitchen. She opens the refrigerator and hands me a carton of chocolate milk. She closes it with a box of cookies in her hands. We silently eat on the marbled center island.

She then starts to speak. "I heard you know Wayne."

187

I'm so glad she chooses a different topic instead of bringing up my dad. Because as much as I love and miss him, it's still painful to talk about him.

"She's my best friend's brother."

She nods. "Anyway, we're back together now."

"You and Wayne?" I didn't see that coming.

"Yeah, we finally talked, and he explained everything." She shrugs "He said he didn't really date my friend. He only used her so he can find out more about Jewel's biological mother since her adoptive parents are my friend's real parents."

"Did you ask him to?"

She shakes her head. "No. Wayne did it on his own. If he knew it would cause us to break up, he wouldn't have dared to intervene. But he said he just wanted to help since I informed him of my dad's affair."

"And did he find out who Jewel's mother is?" I probe.

She thinks about it further. "Some girl named Angel Santiago."

I almost drop the cookie in my hand. "Angel Santiago?"

"Yeah, you know her?"

"She was my mom's best friend who later dated my dad after my mom died."

Her mouth falls open.

What a freakin' small world it is.

"So, she didn't just bang my dad, but she also did yours." Well, if she puts it that way.

"Jade, language!" We both glance at Jeremy who just joined us in the kitchen, looking all sleepy and sexy. He then turns to me and says, "You're eating," with a wide smile.

As much as I hate my life right now, I still don't want to die of starvation.

I offer the cookie to him. "You want some?"

He shakes his head and leaves a kiss on my forehead before opening the fridge.

"You two are so cute." Jade gushes.

I don't want to admit that what he just did made my heart flutter slightly, so I just make a disgusted face and shiver in fake repulsion.

"I saw that, Kim," Jeremy says playfully. "I'll try not to be offended."

All three of us eat cupcakes and cookies while discussing how much of a slut Jewel's mother is. According to Wayne, she's now back in her hometown in Colombia, jumping from one rich guy after another.

Carol later enters the kitchen with a box in her hands. We all look at her with curiosity.

"Someone sent this an hour ago, Kim," she says. "It's from your mom."

~

The box contains a CD, a letter, and a picture of my mom holding me. I almost cry again right on the spot, but I restrain myself.

According to the letter that was written by my mom's lawyer, it's her wedding gift to me once my marriage to Jeremy is verified. My mom had nightmares that told her she was not going to live long enough, so she secured me a trust fund that can only be opened once I achieve my dreams. I have no idea what that means. Marrying my math teacher is hardly my dream at all. Have my first kid, yes. But being tied to this guy? Not so much.

Jeremy and I go back to his room to play the CD. The home video starts with a little girl sitting on a familiar boy's lap in a playground.

"That's me!" Jeremy says as he points at the little boy in the video. "I remember this."

The little girl is obviously me. I was, I think, about four years old. In the video, Jeremy is building a sand castle in the large sandbox while I am sitting quietly on his lap, watching him build the castle with his hands.

Damn, Jeremy was such a handsome eleven-year-old kid.

*"They're so adorable."* I hear someone suddenly say from the background, and almost immediately I recognize the voice as my mom's.

*"It's the first time they've met, and they're already best friends!"* another voice says. From the sound of it, there's no doubt it is Carol.

The camera zooms in. *"Addy, say hi to Mommy!"*

Addy. That was my mom's nickname for me since my second name is the same as hers, Adriana. Then when she died, I told my dad not call me Addy because it reminds me of my mom. He knew it then how hurt I was and started calling me by my first name, Kim.

I watch the four-year-old Kim look up and wave. *"Hi, Mommy! Jay-jay is making a castle!"* My voice is so tiny and almost inaudible in the video.

Eleven-year-old Jeremy kisses the top of little Kim's head. *"So cute!"*

The video continues with the two women gushing how the two of us are so adorable.

Once the sandcastle is done, I see my mom focusing the camera on me. *"Addy, is this your castle?"*

The little girl nods. *"Yes! And Jay-jay is my prince!"*

*"Do you want to marry Jay-jay when you grow up?"* Carol asks.

*"And live in the castle with him?"* my mom adds.

Oh my gosh! What's wrong with our mothers? We were just kids, and they're already asking us those kinds of questions?

Jay-jay laughs. *"Mom! Shut up."*

*"Oh c'mon, we're just playing here."*

The camera shifts to the castle, and I hear myself say, *"Yes. I want to marry him."*

I literally face-palm myself as the twenty-five-year-old Jeremy chuckles beside me. I was such a weird kid.

*"Are you sure? Once you marry him, it's gonna be forever, sweetie."*

The camera focuses on me again. *"I want to marry Jay-jay many times so he can make me castles many times!"*

Carol giggles. *"And how many times do you want to marry Jay-jay?"*

I really want to reach out into the video so I can slap both of them. I was only four years old! How dare they ask me that!

Little Kim taps her chin as if to think, then suddenly exclaims, *"A hundred!"*

Jay-jay squeezes the little girl on his lap, laughing. *"You want a hundred weddings?"*

The innocent little Kim eagerly nods; I'm surprised her head doesn't fall off. *"Yes! Mommy, please make sure I marry Jay-jay a hundred many, many, many times. Pretty please?"*

The video ends, and I stare at the screen in utter disbelief. My mom based her condition about the trust fund on a four-year-old kid's request?

"Well, that was weird," Jeremy says.

We were just kids, and our mothers were already asking us questions about marriage. Something was seriously wrong with them, especially with my mother who freakin' made a trust fund that can only be accessed once I'm married to Jeremy just because I told her fourteen years ago!

Now I know what her lawyer meant by "once I achieved my dreams" in the letter because apparently, my mother thought it's my "dream" to marry this guy. She really did make sure that I'm going to marry Jeremy.

I think I'm going to have a headache.

I cover my face with my hands. "My mom is so embarrassing."

Jeremy snickers as he tries to remove my hands so he can look at me.

"Hey, you should thank her because now you're married to this sexy beast."

I glare at him. "Need I remind you that we signed a contract that inhibits us from separating? All because my mom listened to my four-year-old self."

My mom is really something.

He gently presses his lips on mine. "And I'm really glad we did."

# Chapter 29

KIM

It's been three days since my dad died, and I'm still staying in the Lincoln household. Going home would only remind me that I'm completely parentless and left with a big mansion and a company to take over. It's still overwhelming to think about.

At least when I'm at the Lincoln's, I can pretend that I'm simply staying over at some friend's house while my dad is in his office at home, too busy with his paperwork to notice that his daughter has been having a slumber party for several days.

I don't know how long I can tell myself that.

I'm just glad Jeremy's parents have allowed me to stay in his room. I'd probably overthink and cry myself to sleep if I were alone in the guestroom.

Jeremy's soothing embraces have been putting me to sleep almost every night, and I can't ask for anything better than a simple, comforting kiss on my forehead, especially during times like these.

I'm mindlessly scrolling through my Instagram profile in my husband's bed when the door opens and his head pokes with an irritated expression.

"Your boyfriend wants to talk to you," Jeremy says bitterly.

I gape at him confusedly. "I don't have a boyfriend."

Jeremy enters the room with a scowl. "Lance is here."

"He's not my boyfriend."

"Well, he's a boy and he's your friend, so that means he's your boyfriend," he blankly states before taking my hand and leading me out his bedroom.

Once we reach the living room, I immediately see Lance sitting on the couch with a glass of orange juice in his hands. He stands up when he notices us.

"Hey." He greets me nervously.

"Hey." I give him a quick smile.

"I...uh...I'm sorry about your dad. Are you okay?"

I shake my head. "Not really. But I'm almost there."

Jeremy squeezes my hand, and Lance's attention instantly shifts to our linked hands.

Pulling me closer to his side, Jeremy asks, "What are you doing here, Mr. Knight?" I refrain from rolling my eyes. This guy is acting all alpha male again. It's stupid, really.

Lance purses his lips. "I just want to apologize for not—" But my husband cuts him off.

"Apology not accepted. Now leave." He commands.

"Jay, let him finish." I scold him, and he glares at me as if he can't believe I'm defending Lance.

Lance takes a step closer. "Kim, I'm really sorry. I shouldn't have acted like some jealous boyfriend. I'm sorry if I didn't even talk to you on your own wedding day. I feel so stupid."

"It's alright."

"No, it's not. Just because I liked you, doesn't mean I have to act like you're mine or something." He pauses. "I was hurt, yes. But I've thought about it and realized I was such an ass for acting like that."

I pull my hand from Jeremy's grip and walk towards my friend to pull him into a tight embrace. I sense my husband burning a hole at the back of my head, but I don't care. I missed Lance so much. "Apology accepted," I tell him.

He doesn't return my hug and slowly holds me in arm's length. "I...uh, have something more to tell you."

"Can't you just leave already?" Jeremy interrupts. I glare at him, giving him my sternest look. He senses my annoyance and rolls his eyes. "I'll be in my room."

Once Jeremy has left, I ask Lance, "What is it?"

He removes his hands from my arms and takes a step backward as if he's scared of me. "I hope you won't hate me for this but..." He clears his throat. "I kind of told the principal about you and Jeremy?"

And now I know why he stepped a little farther from me.

"You did what?" I practically shout.

He raises both hands in defeat. "I swear it was before your wedding!"

I cross my arms over my chest, arching an eyebrow, prodding him to continue.

He takes another step backward and starts explaining. "The minute I discovered about you and Jeremy, I sent an email to our school board and told them about your relationship. Then, uh..." He scratches the back of his neck. "Right after your wedding, my dad told me that everything was merely arranged by your parents for the betterment of both your companies."

"Why are you just telling me this now?"

"I meant to tell you the next day, on our lunch break to be exact, and then in our history class. But with everything that happened to your dad, then my concert in Las Vegas yesterday, I just...um, forgot. I only thought of it again when I received a text this morning that my message has recently just been read and they will act on it as soon as possible."

"So, you forgot to inform me that Jeremy's job and reputation are in jeopardy while my dream of graduating high school is practically over?"

He clears his throat then blurts out, "And I just recently confirmed that Ella is my sister!" As much as I'm happy to hear that news, I still feel like he only said it to change the subject.

I narrow my eyes at him. "How?"

"Ella and I talked during your wedding reception, and she bit her tongue while eating." Typical Ella. "She touched the blood then wiped it off on the table napkin. Long story short: I stole it and brought it for testing. The DNA results just came back yesterday, and it turns out we really are related."

I slowly nod. "That's great then."

He shrugs. "Yeah, I guess. But I don't have the heart to tell her yet. She obviously looks contented with her new life. If I told her about her past, about her abusive mother who killed her older brother, I don't know how she'll take it. She obviously forced herself to forget about it for a reason, and I won't bring it up just because I miss my sister."

"Oh."

"Knowing that my sister is alive is good enough for me."

# Chapter 30

When we buried Kim's dad last Sunday morning, I knew she couldn't go back to their family residence just yet, so I figured, why not prepare the house our parents bought for us instead? I used to dislike the idea of living with her, probably because I know we're not both ready to step to that level yet. I know she wouldn't like the idea of leaving her dad either at that time.

But things changed. Once we sealed our marriage with a kiss, I wanted us to be official. And I'm certain that living together is the best solution to remove the idea in Kim's mind that she's alone.

So, by Tuesday morning, I decided to bring her to our house.

The house already has appliances and furniture. Our wedding photos are all framed up on the walls, together with the other paintings made by famous artists. All that is missing is a picture of us and three playful children that I remember my wife wished in her diary.

*Wife.* That's such a beautiful word.

"So, what do you think of the house?" I ask her when we reach the kitchen area.

"It's beautiful." Her eyes wander around the room. "How long has these things been here?"

"Since Monday morning. I helped them set it all up." I try to suppress my grin.

She looks at me suspiciously. "I know that look. You're hiding something."

I shrug. "Maybe. Maybe not."

"Oh c'mon!"

I chuckle. "Go upstairs and see it for yourself. First door on the right."

She hurriedly goes upstairs before I can even blink.

Smiling, I follow my excited wife and see her standing by the door, obviously enthralled by the sight before her eyes. The office room is already furnished with a wooden desk and a black stool. Two cushioned chairs stand on either side of the desk. A long grey leather couch is parallel to them. In the middle of the room is a glass table with artificial sunflowers.

Kim looks amazed at the gigantic map of the world on the wall behind the desk. Selected countries have a red mark on it. There's no doubt that anyone would already have an idea what my plan is.

I stand beside her proudly, both my hands tucked inside my pockets. I glance down at my wife, and her mouth is still hanging open, her eyes glistening with equal amazement and confusion.

"What's this?" she asks, obviously bewildered.

"I'm sure you already know what that is."

"You want to expand your family's business around the world?"

I groan, my head falling back in frustration. "Just so you know, Kim, our company is operating worldwide already, so there's no need to expand it further unless someone can prove that there's life on Mars."

"Well, what's this?"

I take a lungful of air and breathe out to prepare myself.

"Kim, I love you, and I want to travel the world with you," I tell her, my hands shaking in nervousness. The sweat from my palms is possibly even dripping on the marble floor.

Her eyes search mine for clarification. "Jay…"

I walk closer to her and touch the map plastered on the wall, but my eyes remain glued on her confused face. "I want to explore all these countries with the first girl I've ever loved."

She swallows a lump in her throat, then averts her eyes from me. That quick action just made me feel like an avalanche had buried me, and now my chest hurts.

Why did she look away? I thought she would be over the moon for this. What's happening?

"I'm sorry," I hear her whisper, and I think I just died from those words.

"Kim…" I'm surprised I even have the energy to speak.

She shakes her head and almost whispers, "Jay, I don't—" But I hold up my palms to stop her. I think I already know what she's about to say, and I need to be seated so I won't bask in embarrassment when I fall on my knees in sadness.

I run my hands through my hair as I make my way towards the grey couch and sigh. Once I'm seated, I stretch my arm forward to beckon her to come closer. With her lips pressed together, she does, and I place her between my legs as she looks down at me with sadness in her beguiling ocean-blue eyes.

I snake my arms around her waist. "It's okay if you don't love me." *Gods, she's so beautiful.* "I just want you to know that I'm in love with you and I'd understand if you don't feel the same."

She rests her hands on my shoulders as she closes her eyes, and a tear slowly trickles on her left cheek. "Jay, I'm really sorry."

Damn it. She's crying.

"Sssh. Come here, love." I pull my wife closer to me and help her straddle my lap. Now both her legs are on either side my waist as I embrace her tightly to comfort her. "It's okay."

She shakes her head and wipes the single tear with the back of her hand as she pushes back to look at me. "My dad just died, Jay. My best friend will be starting a new life in London. My mom's birthday is next month. The school board is requesting a meeting tomorrow." She exhales heavily. "I have so much in mind right now, and you just proclaimed your love for me out of the blue.

Everything's too overwhelming. I'm so sorry." She looks down on her chest and puts both her hands between us.

I give her a quick reassuring kiss. "It's alright."

"No, it's not." She gazes at me again. "But trust me, Jay. I really, really care for you, but I don't know if it's enough to be called love. Right now, all I'm feeling is grief, and I'm sorry if, right now, I can't say that I love you too. I don't even know how you can love someone like me. I'm a mess."

I lift her chin and look at her straight in the eyes. It wounds me to see her like this especially when I'm the reason why she's upset right now. I love this girl. I love this girl so much that it pains me to know that she doesn't have any idea if she can feel the same way for me.

But who am I to feel outraged? I can't control her feelings. No one can force someone to love another person, and I'd be the most foolish human being if I hated her just because she doesn't know when or if she can love me back.

"I told you I love you not because I was expecting the same words from you. I was hoping, yes, but I didn't say it so you could say it back. I love you simply because I do. You may be a mess, but my heart chose you. Not anyone else." I make sure that she's staring directly in my eyes. "I realized I love you when the thought of not seeing your sweet smile again scares the hell out of me, and I don't even care if you're smiling because of me or not." I rub my thumb over her knuckles. "All I want from you is to let me love you, Kim. And knowing that you care for me is more than anything I could ever fathom."

"You're so cheesy. It's sickening." She teases me with a small smile.

I kiss her gently on her soft lips then pull away to whisper, "I don't care if it takes you years to love me back. Just let me love you, Kim. That's all I'm asking."

Hesitantly, she nods. "Okay."

"And don't hang out much with Lance. He still has the hots for you." I joke, and she rolls her eyes at my poor attempt at humor. "I'm serious, though."

"He's not even a threat in this relationship." She leans forward, and I kiss my wife with so much passion that I'm willing to be out of breath as long as I die with my lips joined with the one girl I've ever loved. But then I remember that I still have more plans for her like traveling the world, having babies, teaching them how to dream and achieve their goals. I guess death should be out of the picture until we've achieved all of those.

Our kisses become more fervent. I grip her waist, somewhat afraid that all of this is just an illusion and she'll vanish into thin air. But that fear is quickly dispelled when she pulls back slightly, showing me her amazing smile—a smile full of contentment and love. Even though she hasn't realized it yet, I know she already feels something for me just with the way she smiles.

"So, you really want us to travel the world?" she suddenly asks.

Part of me is scared that she wouldn't like the idea of exploring the world with me, but when I notice how her eyes twinkle with admiration at the thought of it, I am convinced that she likes it just as much as I do.

I nod. "Only with you, Kim."

She bites her lower lip then grins. "When will we start?"

"Since you're not coming to school until next year and Christmas break starts this Saturday anyway…" I clear my throat. "Maybe we can start preparing everything tomorrow?"

Her face falls. "But we have a meeting with the school board tomorrow."

Damn it. Almost forgot about that.

Stupid Lance.

# Chapter 31

KIM

I've never been in any school board meeting before.

The room is enclosed in a wall of one-sided mirrors. We can see the hallways from inside, but anyone outside can only see their reflection. I try to remember if I once forgot that this was the school board meeting room and simply fixed my hair in front of their judging eyes. I sure hope I've never done that because right this second, a sophomore—I presumed because of the designated patch on her uniform—is currently putting lipstick in front of the one-sided mirror, completely oblivious of our stares as we waited for the owner of this school.

Whoever designed this place clearly doesn't care about the students' reputation.

They soundproofed this room so no one would dare eavesdrop. During our freshman year orientation, it was explained that the room was designed this way so the faculty inside would know if trouble is happening in the school hallways.

Obviously, most students forgot about it or just don't care.

The glass door opens, revealing Mr. Leonard Weatherford, the current school president whose family solely owns the institution. The sophomore's eyes widen when she realizes a meeting is being held right this second. She scurries off immediately, and I really feel bad for her.

Leonard takes a seat, and now he's across from us in the long wooden table.

Light illuminates the streaks of gray hair in his brown locks. I've only seen him twice in my four years of staying in this school, and I can't help but wonder if he's a vampire. Gray strands may be visible on his head, but his face refuses to echo his age. I heard he's already in his early fifties, but looking at his appearance will make anyone believe he's just hitting thirty.

And the fact that Mr. Leonard Weatherford looks like a mature male model doesn't hurt my eyes either.

"I've been notified that the both of you have currently embarked in a student-teacher relationship." His voice is stern and grave. "I will not be uttering any names of who reported it, but I am hoping you would give me inclusive answers regarding this matter. Am I clear here?"

Jeremy and I both nod.

"Alright. First of all, we all know that having the said affair is strictly prohibited by the law and by the school rules. Am I correct?"

"Yes," I answer softly. He turns her eyes toward Jeremy.

"Mr. Bradshaw?" I'm not sure if he's only using Jeremy's pretend surname for formality's sake or he doesn't really know his real identity.

My husband shifts from his seat uncomfortably. "Yes."

"And if we ever confirm such foulness, the teacher will surely be removed from their job and may be confined in prison, whilst the student will, without a doubt, be expelled unless under exceptional cases, i.e. if the student was forced by the said educator," the principal, Mrs. Agatha, sternly states.

"We understand," we both reply.

"As the owner of this institution, it is my job to ensure that my students here are secured and guarded; thus, the consequences may or may not be harsh for whichever student is caught having sexual intercourse with a teacher. The teacher, of course, will be severely punished."

I almost stand up from my seat. "But we never had se—"

Jeremy suddenly nudges me. "We understand, Mr. Weatherford."

I cross my legs and refrain from rolling my eyes. "Yes, we understand."

"So, is it true then? That both of you are having some sort of illicit affair?" the guidance counselor, Ms. Shaina, inquires. Her voice is so calm and reassuring. It's no wonder why the school hired her as our guidance counselor.

"Yes," Jeremy simply answers.

"Why, may I ask, Mr. Lincoln?" Mrs. Agatha presses further. She, on the other hand, has a very pitchy tone that makes you recoil in irritation or distress. I've heard she's a nice lady to behaved students while very strict to the wayward ones.

Jeremy is about to reply when I interrupt. "Our parents forced us to marry each other. They thought that getting us married will benefit both of our companies." I don't have to mention the trust fund to them. They might be interested in its amount and demand a share or something just to let us off.

Mrs. Agatha looks at me intently. "Correct me if I'm wrong, Ms. Roberts, but from what I've heard, your family owns the Golden Shovel Properties, one of the biggest land developers in the world. So, if what you said is, in fact, true, why haven't I heard of it, your engagement and such, seeing as your company is, perhaps, always under the public eye?"

"It's because we kept it hidden to steer clear of dramas like these," I reply nonchalantly.

"What about you, Mr. Lincoln? Do you agree in this made up secret wedding story?" she asks. The disbelief in her tone is evident, and I just want to choke her with my bare hands.

"She's not making it up. We really are married, Mrs. Agatha. We are willing to provide enough papers and evidence to prove that we are indeed wedded."

"Do you have those evidence with you?" Ms. Shaina asks.

Jeremy takes the manila folder from his lap and hands it to Mrs. Agatha.

"Here," my husband says with a rough voice. Knowing him, there's no doubt that he's as nervous as I am.

The principal then hands it to Mr. Leonard, and he studies it carefully. The deafening silence is so uncomfortable that I just have to repeatedly tap my fingers against the desk to entertain myself. I feel Jeremy's glare on me, but I don't care. I'm bored as hell here.

"You've been married for a week now?" he asks eventually.

"Yes," we answer together.

"And you never told anyone?"

"Only a few trusted family and friends," he answers.

"I see." He closes the folder and turns his attention back to us. "Unfortunately, this still doesn't change the fact that you two are in fact in a relationship, forced or not."

"Our parents obliged us!" I boldly state. I couldn't help but raise my voice. "What were we supposed to do? Oppose our parents' command? We never asked for this. We were just dragged into this shit hole of an agreement we never asked for! And I just turned eighteen when we got married so it's not really illegal in this state."

"Language, Ms. Roberts!" Mrs. Agatha warns.

"Kim, calm down." Jeremy holds my hand under the table, and I instantly feel calm from his touch. This guy really has an effect on me. It's kind of scary now.

"Ms. Roberts, I'll have you know that the decision hasn't been made yet concerning both your expulsions, therefore, if you still want to stay in this school, then I suggest you two control yourselves unless you're really eager to be kicked out, then the door is always open for you to leave." Ms. Shaina warns, but the way she says it so serenely, it doesn't sound like a threat at all.

"I'm sorry," I mumble.

"Very well." The owner of the school scoots forward on his seat and continues. "I expect the both of you to answer me in full honesty in my next question. Am I clear?"

"Yes."

"Have you had any sexual intercourse before or during your marriage?"

Jeremy shakes his head. "No, we haven't."

"Why so?" Ms. Fionia, the school head advisor, asks.

205

"Because we're both trying to keep this relationship as professional as we can, given that I'm still her present math teacher." Oh really? I bow my head to hide my smile. I didn't know making out multiple times is a professional thing between students and teachers.

"So, you never had any intimate interactions?" Mrs. Agatha asks us curiously.

I hear the click of Jeremy's tongue against his inner cheek "No, Mrs. Agatha." The irritation in his voice is now more noticeable.

"What about kisses on the lips?" Mr. Leonard questions.

"Don't you think you're asking too much of our private life already?" I annoyingly spat.

"We're just clearing things here, Ms. Roberts," Ms. Fionia says with a firm tone.

"You told us to answer all your questions honestly, and we willingly did. We even gave you a proof to confirm that we really are married and were just forced by our parents. And now you're asking us about our life as a wedded couple? Yes, we kissed a couple of times, but that's just it. We never got past that. Now, any more questions? If none, please make the decision already so we can end this meeting."

Wow, who knew I can be this bold?

All of them fall silent.

"Very well then," Mrs. Agatha says with a raised eyebrow. "But let me ask one last question first before we proceed."

"Fine," I mumble, twiddling my thumbs under the desk in anticipation.

"Are you both willing to file a divorce if ever we asked you to?"

I suddenly feel Jeremy's hand tighten around mine. We know our marriage contract encompasses the unattainability of divorce unless we give up more than half of our inheritance.

But even without the contract, we'd still both say, "No."

~

206

The panel came to a unanimous decision to remove Jeremy from his job as a high school teacher. Although he's allowed to come back after two years, it's still annoying that the school board members didn't keep an open mind about our situation. It's not like we wanted to be married in the first place. They should've at least considered that and let my husband keep his job.

Once we step out of the glass room, Jeremy sees my grim expression.

"Hey, what's wrong?" he asks while we walk through the hallways. It's ten in the morning and students are in their respective classes, so the risk of being seen together is not high.

I cross my arms over my chest. "They didn't have to fire you."

He chuckles. "They had to, Kim."

"No, they don't."

I notice him tuck his hands in his pockets. "Look at it this way: you're failing math, and as your husband, there's a great chance that I'll tweak your grades just to pass you. They're just eliminating the risks of dishonesty."

I face him with a scowl and practically whisper, "But Ella's mom donated a large amount of money to the school just so she could pass physics."

"Yeah, I heard that too from the other teachers." He nods. "But the difference here is that Ella's mom didn't exactly demand a passing grade for her daughter after she made the donation. It was a subtle bribery, and it's still up to the teacher if he will let Ella pass or not. In our case, I have a hold on your grades while having a romantic relationship with you."

"But you're not a dishonest man. I know you won't do that. You take so much pride in what you do."

He looks down and laughs. "Yeah, you're not wrong on that. But the board still won't take any chances." He takes my hand and gently squeezes it. "Don't worry. I'm still training to be the next CEO of Lincoln Corporation, so no need to be bothered about our finances." He jokes.

I roll my eyes at him. "And I'm the heiress of Golden Shovel Properties. My grandma will be training me to manage the business while I'm in college. You're not the only rich one in this relationship."

He grins widely. "Our children will never be hungry. That's for sure."

"And we'll also help other kids together, right?"

My husband kisses my hand and gazes at me tenderly. "And you wonder why I love you."

Damn it. I'm blushing again. "I'll just use the girls' room before we leave."

He nods. "Sure. I'll be in my office packing my things too."

We both look around to make sure no one is in the vicinity, then we share a quick kiss and go on our separate ways. Once I step inside the bathroom, I notice Hailey first before I see the cracked mirror. Her head is bowed with her hair covering the sides of her face. My eyes trail down to her bleeding hands resting on the marbled counter.

Did she just punch the mirror?

She immediately whips her head to me and grants me a deathly glare.

"What are you looking at, bitch?" Her eyes are swollen as if she's been crying for hours. I try not to gawk at her smudged makeup and how she looks like a dying cat.

"I…um, are you alright?"

*Of course, she isn't, Kim. Can you be any dumber?*

I'm expecting her to give an angry remark of how stupid I am or cuss at me to leave. But never in my whole life did I ever imagine her to start crying in front of me as she holds on to the counter for support. It's the kind of cry that is full of anguish and hopelessness. I know because that's how my dad cried when he heard of my mom's death. And that's probably how I cried too when I lost him. That's how people cry when they feel all alone.

If this were another girl, I won't hesitate to comfort her with a hug. But this is Hailey West—the one girl I've always hated ever since she started dating Kyle in freshman year while also seeing other men. I hated her for having the one guy I've always dreamed of yet she's taking him for granted. I've always thought she doesn't deserve such an awesome guy like Kyle.

But my conscience can't take it anymore and I force myself to approach her. I slowly take her bleeding hand, and surprisingly, she allows me to put it under the faucet. I let the water wash the blood from her knuckles.

I'm surprised when she suddenly speaks, "My mom just died, and I hate myself for being happy." She sniffs. "My mom finally died of lung cancer this morning, and I know I should just be upset that she's gone, but I'm so sad and so happy at the same time, Kim. And I hate myself for being this happy."

I gently rub off the small pieces of glass stuck on her skin, and she winces from the pain. "I'm sure you have a reason why you hate your mom." Or maybe Hailey is just a really mean person with no compassion at all.

"Even in her final days, she still kept reminding me how much I ruined her life since she was sixteen. She never failed to remind me that I'm a worthless piece of shit who screwed her up."

If someone told me that I'll one day feel sorry for Hailey West, I'd probably laugh at their faces. Yet here I am now, fighting off the urge to embrace her.

"Do you have any idea how frustrating it is that I have to use one guy after another just to support myself while my mom drowned herself with weed and heroin? It's crazy, Kim, but it's not like I have a choice."

I turn my head to see her face. "But...I mean, you're studying in an expensive private school."

She scoffs. "I'm here because of a scholarship, Kim."

"Oh."

Why haven't I heard that before? Now, I feel awkward, so I simply take her other hand and place it under the water as well.

"Kyle's parents helped me get that scholarship." She explains. "They said a smart girl like me shouldn't be trapped in a public school." She scoffs. "Anyway, as long as I don't have a grade lower than A-minus, I'll be able to stay here."

"Is that why you dated Kyle?"

She slowly nods. "Yeah. My mom worked for them for a while, and Kyle said he's always liked me. I felt obligated to date him after what his parents did for me. I guess we were in love for a while. But I pushed him off many times because of my dirty habits, and now he's in love with someone else." And that would be my best friend. "I don't blame him, though."

"Then why do you keep cheating on him? I understand that you needed the money, but can't you just ask your boyfriend?"

She rolls her eyes as if I'm hopelessly stupid. "Kyle gave me gifts, but it's not like I can sell them. Despite what others think, he's still special to me. So, I have side-guys who give me expensive gifts, then I'll sell those for a few hundred bucks. I know it's unethical, but I need to survive in this screwed-up world. I have to ride in other men's cars while my boyfriend is in football practice because my mom will surely slash me with a knife if I come home late again."

I remember Lance telling me that he once saw a long scar on Hailey's chest the first time they met. And now I feel bad for judging her. For nearly four years, I saw her as a wicked wench who jumps from one guy after another just to satisfy her lust. But Hailey obviously has some skeletons in her closet, and now I feel guilty for even defining her as someone she's not.

Hailey West is not a leech.

Hailey West is actually a strong woman who risked being called a slut by us just so she can survive. It's probably not the best option, but who am I to know better than her? She has her own demons, and she's dealing with it her own way.

Once her hands are now clean from blood and some shards from the broken mirror, she slowly pulls it from the water while I turn off the faucet. She takes out a small towel from her bag, and I help her wrap her right hand, which has the most cuts.

"You're going to visit the clinic, right? To get that stitched up or something?" I remind her.

"Duh. I'm not stupid." Well, she did punch the mirror with her bare hands, and that's pretty stupid in my book.

Hailey wipes off her smudged mascara in front of the cracked mirror with her left hand. She then arranges the stuff in her bag, checks her face in the mirror again before walking to the door as if nothing happened.

"We're not friends, Kim," she says before opening the door. "I just told you that because my friends obviously don't care about shit except about the Kardashians."

"Not friends. Got it." I wink at her. "And I won't tell a soul."

And for the first time since I've met her, Hailey West genuinely smiles at me.

# Chapter 32

"Where's my black bag?" I ask Jeremy, my hands on my hips.

"Which one? You have four black bags," he answers while opening the box marked with *Kim's Celebrity Posters*.

"The big one with EXO sewed on it."

He peers at me. "Oh, that EXO thing?"

"Yeah."

"It's still in the van," he answers and goes back opening the other boxes.

After the meeting with the school's board members this morning, Jeremy and I suddenly decided to pack all our stuff and finally live together in our new house. Perhaps because that school meeting proved our mutual feelings for each other and we thought it would be best to start really living the married life.

But now, I'm starting to question our hasty decision.

I groan. "Why did you leave it there?"

He drops the scissors on the floor and scowls at me. "Because I've been carrying a lot of your stuff for the past hour. Can't I at least have a break?"

"Fine." I leave him in the living room and saunter towards the kitchen to fix the supplies.

We already ordered boxes of grocery items through the phone. At first, I was ecstatic to see the boxes when it arrived, but now, I regret buying a thousand dollars' worth of grocery goods.

Our refrigerator is already full, but I still haven't placed half of the items yet. I'm such an irresponsible wife.

"Jay!" I call out.

"What!"

"We don't have any space left for the other groceries!"

"Didn't I say not to exceed five hundred dollars?"

"I thought you were telling me that because we don't have enough money when obviously, we're loaded."

"I told you not exceed five hundred dollars because we don't have enough space in the fridge, but obviously, you didn't listen!" he shouts back.

"Well, I'm sorry!"

I hear him growl. "Fine, I'll order another fridge."

"But it'll be waste of money!"

I see him stride through the kitchen arch with a pout on his face. "Then what do you suggest we do with all these frozen meats you ordered?"

"I don't know," I mumble.

"I'm going to call the appliance store and ask them to deliver the same fridge I ordered," he says grumpily before grabbing a bottle of Coke.

He opens the cap and takes a sip in a very sexy way I didn't even know was possible. I watch him drink the soda smoothly, and I can't help but wish I was the bottle. The way he squeezes the bottle and how his lips move every time he takes a gulp is so hot it makes me want to jump on him.

Wait...since when did I start thinking like this?

Oh my gosh! I'm becoming a pervert!

I swallow my own saliva and compose myself. "Okay. I'll be upstairs, uh, cleaning our room." I walk past him and hurriedly run upstairs.

When I reached the master's bedroom, I lie on the bed, my face on the mattress and breathe heavily. I stay like this for at least five minutes until I hear my husband's voice.

"You left your phone downstairs."

I instantly roll myself to look at him. Jeremy is standing by the door, holding my phone in his hand. His face is worried as he approaches me, handing me the phone. I take it and check the screen.

"My dad's lawyer called?" I ask. "What did he say?"

"He said he wants to talk about your dad."

"I thought he's already handling whatever my dad left so I wouldn't be bothered anymore."

"He already did. He'll be discussing that with you once you're ready."

"Do I really need to?"

"Yeah." He sits beside me. "You're Mr. Roberts's only daughter and the heiress of your company, so I'm sure whatever you two will be discussing will surely be important."

"Stop calling him, Mr. Roberts. It's too formal. Just call him Adrian."

He smiles. "Don't you think it's a little weird that your parents' names are almost the same? Adrianna and Adrian...it's just a little unusual."

"No. I think it's romantic because they share the same initials. It's like they really were meant to be," I say with a smile, but that smile instantly fades after a few seconds.

He scoots closer to me and touches my hand. "It's going to be alright, okay?"

"No. It won't be. It will never be alright. My mom got hit by your uncle's car while my dad had a heart attack." I clench my hands and try my hardest not to cry. I've shed so many tears already. I don't know if I can cry anymore without breaking down.

He slowly wraps his arm around my shoulder and pulls me closer to him. "Hey, we're supposed to be celebrating. The school agreed not to expel you."

I turn to face him. "But you lost your job. Even though you're allowed to return after two years, I can still recall how you got mad at your mom when she told you to give up your job for me."

"Well, that was before I fell in love with you. It's different now." He touches my cheek with his warm palm. "I don't really need that job, Kim. It's just something I love to do so I won't be stressed while I train to be the next CEO. And between love and convenience, I'd always choose love, Kim. Always *love* with you."

We share a fleeting kiss. I slowly put my palms on his chest and say, "I'm really tired, but I won't sleep until my pillows are all in here."

"Fine. I'll go get your things now." He leaves the room with a smile that is the same as mine.

I see his black backpack by the loveseat and decide to unpack it since he's been busy doing all the heavy stuff. I carefully remove all his shirts and place them all on the bed so I can arrange them all in the closet.

The bag is already empty except for one thing.

I cautiously take the small foil packet and study it closely by rubbing it between my two fingers.

My eyes travel to the words below the two letters and instantly feel my face burn red. "Ah!" I immediately throw the packet across the room, as far away from me as possible, like it has some sort of deadly virus.

Jeremy comes running through the door and notices my shocked expression.

"What happened?"

I shake my head. Too quickly, I shout, "Nothing!"

If my heart is capable of jumping out of my chest, it would've had beaten Usain Bolt with how fast it's thumping right now. It's beating so loud, I'm afraid Jeremy would hear it.

He takes a step closer and puts the pillows on the bed. "You sure?"

Jeremy's eyes wander around the room, and I think he notices something on the floor—probably the one I've just thrown—that made his body freeze as if he's having a stroke.

My throat hurts with how much it's clogged with. "I'll just, uh, check the groceries."

He gulps down then quickly nods.

"Yeah, um…y-you do that." His eyes don't leave that thing on the floor.

I dash downstairs to avoid the awkwardness.

# Chapter 33

Bobby pins. Bobby pins everywhere.

I've only been living with Kim for two days. Two freakin' days yet she has already managed to practically cover the house with pins. And strands of hair!

The first bobby pin I found was yesterday morning on the couch. I thought it simply fell off her hair, so I simply put it back on her makeup box. The second one was on the kitchen counter, but I also let it pass, thinking she must have used it to open something Zeus knows what. The third crime was discovered on my side of the bed when I felt three thin metals poking my back, and that's when I started to wonder if my wife is an illegal bobby pin dealer.

But finding about five bobby pins in the toiletry holder while I'm taking a shower is just plain creepy. Where is she even getting these from? We unpacked our stuff days ago, and I didn't even see her with a sack of bobby pins.

And the strands of hair. Baby Zeus, Rhea, and Kronos, why is it everywhere?

I'm surprised my wife isn't bald yet with the amount of hair I'm looking at the shower floor right now while I'm soaping my chest. My brain is wedged on the thought of how often a girl's hair falls and grows. As a twenty-five-year-old professional, I ought to be thinking about politics, world crisis, and finances; yet here I am, speculating a woman's endless hair growth. I think I'm going crazy.

I step out of the shower and wrap the towel around my waist with the decision in mind that I'm just going to clean the bathroom tomorrow evening. Kim and I decided to not have maids in the house until we have kids. She said she wants us to live like a normal couple first. But I'm pretty sure being a normal couple means at least taking turns in the kitchen, yet for two days, I've always been the one cooking for her. She's lucky I love her.

I'm expecting my wife to be sound asleep since it's already eleven in the evening, but nope. I find her blowing a balloon as she sits on the edge of our bed.

"Kim?" I clear my throat. "Love, what are you doing?"

She stops whatever she's doing and looks up to me. "Practicing my blowing skills."

I think my brain just short-circuited. "You're what?"

She lifts up the balloon and looks at it curiously. "I think I'm getting the hang of it."

*Jeremy, you love your wife, so don't say something stupid that will surely hurt her.*

*Think before you speak unless you want to be decapitated.*

Okay. Good pep talk with myself. I think I'm ready now to converse with my wife again.

"Alright then." My feet cautiously take several steps to her. "And who told you about this?" I ask as I gently take the plastic from her hands.

"Ella told me to practice my blowing skills with something so I'll be more prepared before our trip to Paris."

Why is her best friend giving her tips? What is going on here?

I release the air from the balloon. "And did she also tell you to practice it with this?"

"Nah," she says with a wink. "I just figured it all by myself. Cool, huh?"

I stare at her as if she's gone completely insane. She stares at me with her innocent blue eyes, brows arching, and evidently oblivious on how much she's mistaken.

"Love," I tell her as I tip her chin up. "Right now, you need to sleep. Okay?"

218

She purses her lips. "I'm just trying to be aware of it."

I want to tell her that if she really wants to know something, she needs to do her research properly. Sadly, I don't have the heart to scold her, so instead, I lean down to plant my lips on hers, kissing her gently, only to back away immediately when I feel her hands inching towards my abdomen.

Red instantly creep up her cheeks. "Sorry. Stupid hands." Then she slaps the hand that just touched my towel with the other. "I'm going to sleep now. Sorry."

She positions herself on her side of the bed and heaves the blanket up to her neck. I change to a pair of boxer shorts and a thin white shirt before snuggling to my wife.

"It's alright." I spoon her closer and whisper, "You're just curious. But not ready."

"When I saw that thing the other day, I panicked," I hear her say. "Probably because I know I'm not ready yet, but I also don't want to disappoint you."

I smile as I hug her tighter. "Don't stress yourself over this."

She places her hand on top of mine that is currently resting on her stomach. "But what if I will? You might think differently of me."

I can't help but snicker at what she just said. "Kim, we're both inexperienced. The only difference we probably have is that I've read countless books about it."

The words *and I'm not stupid* are itching to come out of my mouth, but I stop myself. I don't want to risk being smothered to death with a pillow. Or with her bare hands.

She pulls my arm towards her lips and gives it a tender graze. "Good night, Jay."

"Good night, Kim." I kiss her shoulder. "Rest well. We're going to Paris tomorrow."

# Chapter 34

KIM
*Paris, France*

"You like it?" my husband asks as I continue to gawk at the large chandelier. It's so freakishly huge; I have a feeling it will plummet down and crash on the floor anytime soon.

My eyes wander to the kitchen area, and I swear I can see my reflection through the glass counters. I open another classy wooden door with a golden knob, and my eyes instantly land on a black and white king-sized bed. My jaw drops open.

"It's so beautiful," I mutter to myself as I look around the penthouse we have just entered in.

"A beautiful room for a beautiful girl."

I turn my head to face him and smile. "I like it."

"Great." He saunters towards the bed and places down the bag he is holding. "So, you want to rest first before exploring the beautiful city of Paris?"

I sit down beside him and yawn. "Yeah, I'm feeling a little jetlag. An hour nap won't hurt, I guess."

"Alright. I'll just take a shower, okay?" He places his warm hand on either side of my cheeks and plants a swift kiss on my forehead. "Don't do anything stupid."

I glower at him but still nod. "Yes, sir."

He smirks smugly. "You have no idea how sexy that sounded like."

"Shut up."

He kisses the top of my head before pushing himself up. "I love you."

"I...I really like this room," I mumble. His smile fades for a moment, yet he still manages to hide his disappointment with another boyish grin.

"I'm glad you liked it then." He gives me one last peck on the lips before striding out the room and closing the door behind him.

I fall back on the bed and cover my face with a pillow. Why can't I tell him I love him? He already admitted it, so why can't I? It's just three words, right? I never failed to remind my dad that I love him, so why can't I say it back to my own husband?

Maybe because I still don't? Maybe because I still can't get over the fact that he's related to the person who took my mom away from me?

I press the pillow harder on my face and groan. I'm starting to hate myself right now.

I'm hurting Jeremy. I know I am.

I care for him, like, so freakin' much. I just don't know if it's enough to be called love.

How could I even know that I love him if I haven't even been in love in the first place? How could people tell they have feelings for someone when they're just new to it as well? Do they just simply feel like saying it? Does something weird happen to tell you you're already in love?

I used to play with the word *love* when I was younger, thinking that if someone is hot, I already love him just like I believed I loved Kyle. But after Jeremy's confession, I know that what I felt for Kyle is nothing compared to what Jeremy feels for me. What I felt for my childhood crush is a mere infatuation while Jeremy loves me with his whole heart.

So, I can't just blurt it out. I have to be sure of my feelings first. I just don't know how.

I remove the pillow off my face and stand up from the bed. I saunter towards my luggage and take out a pair of shorts and a shirt. Just as I am about to pull up my dress, the door opens, and I

221

immediately pull it back down. Jeremy's head pops in with a curious look.

"Don't you know how to knock?" I reprimand him.

He chuckles. "You should've locked it if you didn't really want me to get inside."

"What do you want?"

"I was just wondering if you want to order champagne or anything."

"Nah, I'm good."

"How about strawberries?"

"Nope."

He sighs. "Alright. I'm gonna go for a shower now."

"Okay," I say. He sighs as he slowly closes the door. I quickly change into my fresh clothes and go back to bed.

I'm in between sleep and consciousness when I hear him come back to the room. The sound of the shower later comes from the bathroom, and the sound of water sprinkling on the tiled floor is akin to a lullaby.

It doesn't take long before sleep engulfs me.

# Chapter 35

Sometimes my wife's innocence is seriously disappointing. Yes, I like her being naive and all, but can't she just take a hint that I'm trying to be a little romantic here?

Doesn't she watch romantic movies or read books at all? Champagne and strawberries are like the best aphrodisiacs.

I take my towel and walk inside the bathroom. A long cold shower would do me good. I'm already twenty-five years old yet still a virgin. Almost every year, my sister would ask me if I gave it up yet, and I always give her the same answer: no.

She thinks I'm being weird just because I'm one of the richest eligible bachelors in the US.

I still don't see why men have to get laid to be called a real man, and if a woman is not a virgin on her wedding night, her morals are questioned. Everyone has their own stance regarding intimacy, and people should just start respecting each other's choices.

I've had two girlfriends after Jewel. One girl only lasted two months while the other didn't even last for a week. Both of them wanted me in bed, and I just couldn't do it. I wasn't in love with them. So, when I broke it off, both girls called me gay after the break-up. I simply brushed it off and walked away.

I want to be with a girl not because of our carnal desires but because of our deep affection for each other. I don't care if women question my sexuality because of my standards. I'm not into the no-strings-attached kind of thing, so sleeping with anyone is out of the picture until I'm certain that I'm deeply in love.

And now, I am.

After my refreshing shower, I go inside our room and find Kim sleeping agitatedly in our bed. Her eyebrows furrow as if she's irritated about something while her hair covers the pillow like a fan. Suddenly, I remember those parts in the movies where the guy stares at the girl of his dreams while she sleeps.

Yeah, not going to happen here. She looks like a deadbeat banshee right now, so maybe later when she's all enlivened and calm because gazing at her while she's looking like this wouldn't be as romantic as I imagine it.

I have already changed into a new pair of clothes when I hear my phone buzz. Who could possibly be calling me right now when everyone perfectly knows that Kim and I are on our honeymoon?

I don't bother checking the caller ID and irritably answer it. "What?"

"Did I disturb you and your wife, Jay?"

My breath hitches, and I slowly look at the screen. "Jewel." Great, just great.

"Let me guess, you didn't check the ID caller again."

I leave the room and proceed to the chaise longue. "What do you want?"

"I heard you're in Paris right now."

"That's none of your business."

"Guess what. I'm at the hotel's elevator right this moment."

My jaw clenches. "You're lying."

"You know I don't lie about my whereabouts, Jay, especially when I'm so near to you."

"Fine, what's the name of the hotel and what room are we in right now?"

"Le Meurice. You're renting a penthouse."

And as if on cue, I hear a knock on the door. You've got to be kidding me.

I place the phone close to my mouth "Jewel, I swear, if…"

"Aren't you going to invite me in? I'm not a vampire, so don't fret."

"Go away, Jewel."

"I'm not leaving until I see you."

"What do you want from me?"

"You'll know once you open the door."

"You must be delusional. I'm calling security if you don't leave right now." I furiously press the end button before dialing the hotel's number. What kind of safety measures do they have if they let random strangers walk freely in their hotel?

"Just open the door, Jay. I just want to talk to you," Jewel mutters behind the door.

"Go away if you don't want to get hurt," I shout back.

"Five minutes. I'm just asking for five minutes."

"So, are you saying that you flew here from California just to have a five-minute talk with me?" I bellow.

I hear a soft chuckle before she speaks. "You're so full of yourself. I'm here because my best friend got married yesterday. And then I heard that you're here too. I just want to see my…*brother*. That's all."

"Don't you even call me that. You make me sick."

"I thought you hated me because I don't acknowledge our real relationship, and now, you're saying otherwise. You're so confusing, to be honest."

I walk to the door, clutching on the doorknob. "Just go away, Jewel, before I call security."

"Even if you do, they won't arrest me because I'm staying in this hotel as well. Small world isn't it?" She laughs condescendingly.

"Just go, Jewel."

"Fine. If you don't want to show yourself, let's at least talk here."

225

"Fine. What do you want?"

"I'll ask a question first."

"What?"

"Do you still have feelings for me? Even just a little bit?"

I hold the knob tighter. "Jewel..." She knows I don't have anymore.

"Just answer the question."

"Why do you want to know?"

"Maybe because I saw how happy my friend was at her wedding, how in love she and her husband looked like. I don't know...I guess I was a little jealous. I envied her husband's love for her."

"You're a beautiful woman, and I'm sure you have thousands of admirers," I whisper through the gap, my forehead pressed over the wooden door.

"No one knows that for sure. So, I'm asking you now, do you still care for me?"

"Jewel, I thought I loved you before, but..."

"Just answer the damn question, and I'll leave!" she says almost as if she's crying. "Just answer the question, and I promise...I promise to see a therapist soon." She already knows that she has a problem. Why can't she just drop it already?

I close my eyes and take a deep breath. "Jewel, I love Kim so much."

"I'm not asking if you love me. I'm asking if I still mean something to you, if there's a small part of you that still cares for me."

"Yes." Because no matter what happens, no matter how screwed up our relationship was, she's still the first girl I almost loved.

"Jay." My heart almost drops to the ground when I hear Kim's voice behind me.

I spin around and see her standing dumbfounded by the bedroom door, her eyes full of confusion and lament.

"Kim, I thought you were asleep."

226

"Yeah, until I heard someone shouting outside."

"How…how much did you hear?"

"Enough to know you lied to me."

# Chapter 36

"Kim, please open the damn door." He beseeches, but I ignore him and continue brushing my hair. I've just finished a thirty-minute shower, and I still haven't opened the door for my sweet and adorable husband.

His keys are on the side table, so there isn't really a way for him to go inside unless he risks the humiliation of coming to the desk lobby and tell them that his wife locked him out.

"Please, we talked about this. We've been through this already."

I roll my eyes. "Nope, I'm pretty sure we haven't talked about this one."

"I care for Jewel, but I don't love her. I never will."

"That's still the same thing!"

"No, it's not! Jewel became a big piece of my life and part of me still cares for her, but it's nothing compared to the love I feel for you. Why do we always fight like this? Why do we keep arguing about things that shouldn't really be problems in the first place?"

I throw the hairbrush at the door. "Don't you dare lecture me right now!"

"Please, Kim. I love you so much, and I'm really sorry if I upset you. I never lied to you about my true feelings and never will, so please open the door and we'll work through this."

"You still love her. You can't love two persons at the same time."

Just when I thought that I finally have someone who really loves me, I find my husband talking to his ex-fiancée through the

228

door, telling her that she still means something to him. They're related for Pete's sake! This is so messed up.

I could understand that Jeremy fell in love with her before he found out they're actually siblings. But he already knows it now yet he still cares for her? That's just plain sickening.

"Kim, please. I love you, not Jewel. Only you."

I stare at my knotted fingers on my lap. "I don't know what to believe anymore, Jay."

I am expecting him to give another apology or persuade me more, but a loud thump is the only thing I hear as if he has punched the door.

Then silence.

I wait for him to give another apology, but a couple of minutes have passed and he's still not saying anything. Is he gone? Did he leave? Did he muster the courage to go to the lobby to request for the keys?

"You know what?" he suddenly speaks. "I'm so tired of this. I'm so tired of you! You're always acting like a spoiled brat. You never listen to me. You think you're always right when you never were! You always crave to get what you want! You're a selfish brat, and I will forever regret that I agreed to marry you. I'm tired of all this drama, Kim, and I'm really glad we're having this talk because you made me realize how much of a fool I am to even love you in the first place."

I clamp my mouth with my hand and almost choke on my sobs. No. He's just saying that. He doesn't mean all of that. He's not just going to leave me, right?

Right?

He loves me. He told me he loves me. He can't just end us like this, right?

Am I really a selfish brat?

*Yes. Yes, you are.*

"Hope you'll have a nice life," he says. "I'm really sorry, but I'm just so tired of all this drama."

"Wait!" I immediately run towards the door and swing it open, only to see him standing before me, smiling with a bowl of red petals in his hands.

"You're so gullible, love." He chuckles.

My mouth falls agape. "What the—"

"These should be on our bed, but you ruined my plan." He shakes his head in amusement. "Oh well." He then pours the bowl of flowers on top of me, showering me with red rose petals.

I'm still lost. What in the world is happening right now?

But I'm not given a chance to ask because he immediately captures my lips, cupping my cheeks as he pushes me back to our room.

I slightly pull away. "What's—"

"I love you so much. Let's just talk about this, please?"

"Um...okay."

"Why are you blushing?"

Stupid yankee dankee doodle sack of fat face. Why do I always blush? It's embarrassing.

He kicks the wooden door behind him, locking it for good measure.

# Chapter 37

Jeremy
*Sunday morning*

"How's Ella?" I ask her as I stir my cup of coffee with a spoon. I delight in the scent of it before lifting it up from its place, then walk to the sofa and sit beside my wife who is currently busy reading a book entitled *The Selection*.

"The last time I talked to her, she's with her aunt in Georgia. She said she still hasn't gotten over the fact that her real mom was a psychotic killer, while her current mom, whom she's always known and love, isn't even her real mother."

Last night, I showed Kim how much I love her through my kisses. We didn't really do anything more than that. I want our first time to be special for both of us. And she's only 18, still too sweet and innocent for any of that.

Then while I was peppering her face with kisses, her best friend called her, crying and panicking over the phone. I let them talk in private, and later Kim told me what it was all about.

Apparently, Ella invited Lance for dinner at their house, and when she asked her parents for baby photos, they failed to give them anything. Ella thought they were joking because she remembers seeing her baby photos when she was a kid. Lance couldn't bear to keep it a secret anymore and told her everything, in front of her adoptive parents who confirmed it.

"She can't hide from Jeanne forever."

"I told her just that, but she said she needs time to think about all the stuff that came crashing down to her." She draws her attention from the book to me. "Finding out you're adopted is really not the best feeling in the world."

"I know it's not much of a crisis, but she's not used to these kinds of situations. Ella's a happy-go-lucky girl. I think the last problem that she faced was when she got an A-minus in her math class in sixth grade. She was too afraid to show her grade to her parents. Now, this is the first time she encountered a real-life dilemma."

"There's always a first time for everything." I point out. "She's only eighteen. She'd face more crap in life when she gets older. Trust me on that."

She gazes at me curiously. "Why? Have you stumbled upon a big setback before apart from suddenly getting wedded to me?"

"First of all, getting married to you is the best thing that has ever happened to me, and I'm sure there would be more to add on the list every time I'm with you. Second, yes, I've had problems in the past as well, but I faced them staunchly and some I brushed off."

"For example: Jewel," she says nonchalantly.

I nod reluctantly. "The worst of them all is acquainting myself with Jewel, and perhaps I'm still working on keeping her at a distance, but I'm not that affected with her anymore. We all have problems. Some might be big while some might be small, but they're still problems, and having them only proves you're human. No one is really weak. We just have our own limits."

She sighs and purses her lips. "Do you think Ella will get over hers?"

"She will. I don't know when, but she will." I sip my coffee. "She's been living in her happy bubble for a while now. I think it's time for her to live in the real world."

"She is living in the real world. She's not in Narnia," she states, chuckling. "Her closets are full of clothes and other junk. Narnia wouldn't even fit a leaf in there."

I want to elaborate more about Narnia but decide against it. "Do you want to tour the town now?"

232

She blinks a couple of times then nods slowly. "Okay."

~

A waiter places our meal in front of us, glancing nervously at my wife that has a creepy dubious expression plastered on her face as if she's going to kill anyone who dares to step on her line of attack.

The poor lad turns his gaze to me and gives me a questioning look about her countenance. I just smile at him and offer a reassuring nod, telling him with my eyes that she's perfectly normal...sort of. He tensely nods back and steps backward to leave us alone.

I can't really blame his reaction though.

"So, you mean to tell me that your dad has been trying to rekindle the friendship between our families for years?" Kim raises incredulously.

"I'm surprised you only knew about it today."

"Why am I the last to know about this?"

I shrug. "I thought you already knew."

"Well, I don't." She pauses. "So, let me get this straight, even without the twenty-five percent share from the trust fund, your dad is still more than happy to marry you off to me?"

"Yeah." I take my fork from the table and decide to eat dessert. "Our parents were practically best friends, so when your dad severed ties with us because of the accident, it really hurt our business and their feelings. My dad really wanted Lincoln Corp and Golden Shovels to be sister companies again, but your dad adamantly refused for years. Until your dad finally asked mine to help save your business and my dad was like, *Sure, take my son. He's all yours. We don't care. Please let's work together again.*"

She sighs deeply. "I don't blame my dad for refusing to talk to yours, though. Your family did cause us severe pain when your uncle accidentally killed my mom and got a reduced sentence."

I try to reach her hand, and she willingly lets me touch it. "I'm sorry for what my uncle did. I was young when the accident happened, but I assure you that my parents had nothing to do with

233

my uncle screwing up the justice system. I know my parents, and they won't do something to hurt yours. But I know where you're coming from. I bear the same last name as the one who caused you so much pain, and I apologize for what the Lincoln family did to yours. I really am."

My wife offers a small smile. "Hey, it's been more than a decade now. I guess it's time for me to move on from our horrible family history and just look forward to…"

"The family we're going to make together?" I continue for her, squeezing her hand.

"Yeah, uh, that." She presses her lips together, and pink paints her cheeks again.

So damn cute.

I chuckle. "Anyway, I remember that video of us on the beach was our first and final meeting when we were kids. And now I know why I was so drawn to you on the first day of class; your ocean-blue eyes were so familiar."

Her eyebrows furrow in mock annoyance. "You always compliment my eyes. Stop."

I smirk. "Never. I'll never stop complimenting every part of you until you accept that you're breathtakingly beautiful."

She looks down on our entwined hands. "But it's still uncomfortable when someone tells it to me."

No matter how much she tries to deny it, I'm aware that my wife knows she's not ugly, but she also thinks her beauty is not breathtaking either. She has this idea that she's mediocre despite how many times I've told her how gorgeous she is with or without make-up. I remember studying something about the type of mindset she has in our psychology class back in college.

Most people whose parents don't give much time to them, tend to suffer from an inferiority complex wherein they have this inkling that they always lack something, that they're always not enough, that they're always lesser than the other person, that someone will constantly be better than them.

I hope they'll find someone who'll prove them wrong. Because I will spend my whole life trying to prove to this woman that she is exceedingly the best thing that's ever been mine.

"I guess I just have to tell you every day how amazing you are until you finally accept it."

She laughs. "You have my permission then."

We eat our meal in comfortable silence. I later ask for the waiter and pay the bill. He looks more comfortable now that Kim's expression isn't as grim as a while ago.

We take off and visit different famous tourist spots. I'm saving the best for last of course.

# Chapter 38

KIM

No words can describe how incredible this city is. Paris is amazing. End of story. I'm not going to waste my time thinking of poetic and deep words to illustrate how beautiful Paris is. That will only fry up my brain cells even more.

"Did you know that the Eiffel Tower consists of 1,665 steps?" Jeremy suddenly asks.

"Nope. Don't know. Don't care," I answer. I sense him rolling his eyes at my response.

"You wanna go up?"

"By taking 1,665 steps? Um, no thanks. I'm good down here."

He laughs and shakes his head. "No, by taking the elevator, of course. I'm not that cruel. I know how much of a lazy ass you are."

"Shut up." I playfully slap him on the arm. "Alright, let's go." I take his hand, and he pulls me towards to what looks like a cart or something.

A middle-aged guy is guarding the elevator. He sees our wedding rings and smiles genuinely at us.

"Honeymoon?" he asks.

We both nod. "Just got married," Jeremy answers proudly, lifting our intertwined hands midair before kissing the wedding band around my finger.

"You're a fortunate man, *monsieur*. She's *magnifique*."

"Couldn't agree more to that." Jeremy winks at me, and I can't help but blush again.

When we reach the highest part a tourist could get to, we walk out of the elevator and walk inside a small restaurant filled with lights...and flowers?

Wow. Who knew there's a restaurant in here? Probably everyone but me, I guess.

The moment we step inside, romantic music starts to play, and I'm startled when three men with banjos—I think—come over me. One guy hands me a bouquet of roses while the other two each give me a white rose.

I feel Jeremy's hand slip away from mine as he saunters to the middle part of the restaurant. There aren't any customers inside except the crews and the musicians. And us.

"Hi," he nervously says, his arms behind his back.

I beam widely. "Hey."

"So, do you like it?"

I merely nod, suppressing the urge to smile even wider.

"Good. So, um..." He stutters. "I'm not really good with this kind of stuff, but I'd still try so please bear with me, alright?"

I giggle. "I will."

Wait, did I just giggle like a thirteen-year-old girl? Ugh.

"Okay, so, you already know my plan where we will travel the world as part of our honeymoon and, well...there's still more to the surprise."

I gaze at him confusedly. "There's still more?"

"Yeah." He nods. "I want to repeat our marriage vows on each country we will visit. I literally want the whole world to know that I am married to the most amazing woman I've ever met in my entire life. I want everyone to know that I am in love with you, and only you."

"Jay..." I'm totally speechless right now. I think I know what he's going to say next.

"Our story started because you wanted a hundred weddings when you were four." He clears his throat. "So, we'll be doing just that. A hundred weddings in a hundred countries."

I chew on my lower lip and feel hot tears slowly flowing down my cheeks. I wipe my eyes with the back of my hand. How can he say these things so smoothly?

And just like that, I realize now how people know when they're in love. It's like describing a city like Paris. Words aren't enough to portray how breathtaking it is. So, you just let your eyes wander around and feel the contentment inside you.

What I'm feeling right now is exactly in the vein of that. I feel at ease and calm while I'm looking at him. I don't see the conceited teacher who failed me in every exam anymore, the arrogant jerk who treated me like I'm some kind of lost cause.

I now see the guy who is jealous of my friend Lance. I now see the vulnerable man who's afraid to fall in love. I now see the loving and caring husband who he has always been.

Jeremy has been so patient with me, and I'd be a fool if that doesn't make me adore him even more. He is a man who loves me despite how immature I sometimes might be.

And I guess that's how love really works. You may know your lover's mistakes and negatives but still find them beautiful. I stare at him in awe and wonder how my life was before Jeremy Bradshaw Lincoln came along because I realize that I'm much happier with him by my side. It's not that my life was terrible before him, but I can honestly say that it has become simply better. This speech of his triggered my brain cells, telling me that I'm really head over heels for this man.

And I have finally decided to love him today and for the rest of our lives.

"I love you, Jeremy Lincoln. So much," I immediately blurt out before I can chicken out.

A wide smile breaks onto his face. He quickly paces towards me and pulls me into a tight hug. I bury my face on his chest and let myself relax on his familiar scent.

He kisses my nose then gazes at me adoringly. "Say that again, please."

I give him a soft kiss. Smiling, I say, "I love you."

238

We share another fleeting kiss before he unexpectedly kneels down and takes out a beautiful blue diamond ring from his pocket—blue like my eyes.

"Will you marry me, *again?*"

# Epilogue

CHLOE

"Mommy! Mommy!"

My head instantly turns, and my eyes land on the ten-year-old girl running towards me, her strawberry blonde hair bouncing up and down her shoulders. She's smiling widely. Beside her is her three-year-old brother who has his hands tightly clutched to hers. He looks just as excited as his sister but at the same time quite worn-out from all the running.

"Don't run, sweetheart." I remove my feet from the pool and stand.

They slow down when they're almost in front of me.

"Daddy's calling for you," she says between pants. "He said we need to go."

"Mommy!" The small boy stretches his arms to me, implying he wants to be carried. I scoop him up and kiss his chubby cheeks, inhaling his baby scent.

"Alright, let's go." I take her hand while carrying my son with my other.

We circle the house and reach the front porch where my beautiful husband, Daniel, is waiting patiently, the car parked outside.

"Ready?" He greets. I nod and give him a quick peck on the lips to keep it PG for the kids.

I strap the three-year-old grinning boy in his baby seat while my husband secures our daughter beside her brother. He plants a swift kiss on her nose and ruffles her hair. I can't help but smile. They look so adorable.

"I'm excited to be with Grandma and Grandpa again!" my daughter, Jasmine, happily exclaims.

"I'm sure they're excited to be with you, too." I enter the vehicle as Daniel starts the engine.

Together, we leave to see my parents.

"Mommy, tell me more about Grandma and Grandpa," Jasmine asks while my husband U-turns on a curb. We're only a few kilometers away before we reach our destination.

"Apart from they're the craziest people you'd ever meet?" I tease.

She grins. "I want to know more about them. I was only eight the last time I saw them, and we rarely visited them in California."

A sad smile appears on my face, but I immediately dismiss it.

"Well, they loved each other very much."

"Grandpa said he was Grandma's teacher before. I told my teacher about it, and she said it's bad. Is it true, Mommy? Were they bad people?" she asks curiously.

"No, sweetie. They're not bad people. Their story is a little complicated. You won't understand yet, but I assure you that Grandma and Grandpa weren't bad people."

"Hmm 'kay." She smiles again. "But Mommy, is it true that they married again and again and again and again around the world?"

I beam at her, remembering my parents' weddings in a hundred different countries. My dad wanted to make sure that everyone knows about them, so they repeated their vows on every available and safe country they could get to.

It was the most romantic thing I have ever seen.

I nod. "Yes, they wanted the whole world to know that they love each other."

"Did Daddy do that too?"

"Nope. I made my own history for your mom," Daniel smugly states. I roll my eyes at him.

"Really?" Our daughter's eyes twinkle with both amusement and interest.

I scoff playfully. "But not romantic enough to beat my dad."

He shrugs. "Well, yeah. I mean, would you have agreed to marry me if I beat the history of the first man you loved the most, also known as your dad?"

I chuckle. "Touché."

"I want to travel the world too, Mommy!"

"Me twooh!" her brother joins in.

"Daddy and I are still a bit busy, but I promise we'll visit every landmark where Grandma and Grandpa remarried." Cheers erupt from both of them exactly as the car comes to a complete stop.

"We're here," my husband announces.

We release the two kids from their seatbelts, and they hurriedly scurry away from us, running towards them.

"Be careful!" my husband and I both call out.

We walk hand in hand until we reach their spot.

"Hello, Grandpa! Hello, Grandma!" My daughter merrily greets. She places the bouquet of white flowers between their tombstone. "Did you miss me?"

"Ganma, ganpa," my youngest son, Jeremy, says and sits on the verdant grass.

"Hey, Dad," I say wearily. "Hey, Mom."

They've been gone for two years now. Today is my mom's second death anniversary and sixty-first birthday; hence why Daniel and I decided to visit California once again despite our busy schedules. I'm just glad our sixteen-year-old son agreed to be left in Europe. At least someone is there to supervise the place.

My mom died because of a heart attack. Apparently, it runs in the family. Aunt Ella was so devastated of her best friend's death that she cried and didn't eat for two days until her husband, Uncle Kyle, talked her through it. Aunt Ella's brother, Lance, was also

242

heartbroken by my mom's sudden death that he didn't talk to anyone for a week, except to his wife, Hailey.

One month later, my dad followed Mom to the grave because of depression. His body simply shut down from the overwhelming sadness from my mom's sudden passing. Aunt Jewel and her husband, Marc Eaton, never left my dad's coffin during his wake.

Although my siblings and I were consumed with grief for being left by both parents subsequently, we still thought it's for the best that they finally have their rest.

Maybe they'll meet and love each other again in another life.

Their marriage wasn't merely a walk in a park. I've heard them fight more times than I can count. Dad slept on the living room couch at least once a year, and mom's eyes were probably so tired from glaring at my dad that she chose to just close them forever.

But they made sure they never separated despite their heated arguments. My parents proved that only death would part them. They kept their marriage vows until their last breath. And I'm glad they did because I wouldn't be proudly stating these things if they ended up separated.

I sit down beside my son and kiss the top of his brown hair. "Look, you have Grandpa's name." I point at Dad's name imprinted on the stone.

"Jay-re-my!" my son says proudly, leaning forward to touch the phrase plastered on the stone.

> *JEREMY BRADSHAW LINCOLN*
> *THE LUCKY GROOM OF AN AMAZING BRIDE*

I've seen that statement a lot of times already, but I still can't help but smile every time I look at it. I remember him telling me to put it on there a few years before he died. Mom heard him and asked me to do the same. And they also let me promise to never make their funeral fancy and expensive. They want an ordinary and down-to-earth (no pun intended) burial.

I sense my husband and my daughter sit beside me, my husband's arm brushing mine. I turn to look at them and smile. I reckon when my twin siblings and I got jealous of our parents' romantic adventure. They told us that one day, we'll have our own love story to live.

I glance at my husband, Daniel, and know they're both right.

"I miss them both, Daddy," Jasmine whispers.

"Everyone does, sweetie."

Jasmine smiles and pulls out two notebooks from her pink backpack—my mom's diary and my dad's journal.

"I'm so happy they had their happy ending," she says as she stares at the notebook I've been reading to her for the past nights.

She then leans forward and does what her brother did earlier. Her small fingers gently touch the phrase printed on my mother's gravestone, making a smile curve on my lips.

> *KIMBERLY ADRIANA LINCOLN*
> *THE AMAZING BRIDE OF A HUNDRED*
> *WEDDINGS*

This is their daughter, Chloe, saying thank you for reading their rollercoaster of a story.

# BOOK YOU MIGHT ENJOY

## THE BEST PART OF HELLO
### Hollie Armstrong

Some people just can't stand each other. Kayla and Evan are definitely one of those people.

It's annoying enough that they are plane partners and have to sit next to each other through the entire flight to Italy for their senior class trip, but things go from bad to worse when their plane makes an emergency stop. Their lives unexpectedly change as soon as Kayla follows Evan into a dark corridor, and right after, things just escalate from worse to tragic.

"I won't begin to suggest that I know what you're feeling, but I know what it feels like to love someone who doesn't love you back."

To add icing to Kayla's wretched cake, she finds out that that Ben, her perfect boyfriend, isn't so perfect after all and has been hiding a basket full of dirty secrets from her. Dead set on getting back at him, she turns to the only person she thinks who is just as hurt as her and crazy enough to sign up and play along with her plan—Evan.

"Be my fake boyfriend, Evan Winters. I promise never to love you, care for you or…well…you get the idea."

But they're just pretending. Except when one of them is suddenly isn't…

A freak storm, stolen chickens, a language barrier, and a big adventure. The senior trip of their life. But will they ever be the same people once they go back?

Find out in this unexpected romantic comedy that has Kayla and Evan butting heads as they meet interesting people, end up in jail, learn valuable lessons, and experience heartaches and new beginnings—together.

# BOOK YOU MIGHT ENJOY

Of all the men she could have pissed off, it had to be him.

## MEETING MR. MOGUL
## Mel Ryle

"Just because you're the boss does not mean you can just treat me however you want!"

With those words, Andy Peterson made an enemy out of William Maxwell, a billionaire who is the epitome of leading men in romance stories for many—ridiculously enough. If it were up to her, she wouldn't have to deal with him at all. Unfortunately, he is one of the most powerful men in the city, which means he can crush her like a bug if he wants to.

And just when things are about to take a turn for the worse, she gets help from the most unlikely source. Alexandra Maxwell, William's older sister, was so impressed with her feistiness and seeming immunity to the billionaire douche's charms that she hired Andy as an assistant.

Although the job seems too good to pass up, the problem is she would have to work with that SOB. Will Mr. Mogul continue to make her life a living hell? Or will their explosive chemistry lead to something else entirely?

Grab this romantic comedy that is the first in the Mogul Series!

# ACKNOWLEDGEMENTS

First of all, the highest praise to my Lord Jesus because this book wouldn't have been possible without His guidance.

I would also like to extend my gratitude to the following people:

My sister, Jeanneth, thank you for bringing me all the snacks I wanted while I was writing this book.

To my girl best friend, Kim Lacanienta, whose name I used in this story, and Corinne Martinez, my reading buddy. I probably wouldn't have survived high school without you two!

To my guy best friend, Anthony, who told me all about their American traditions.

My bestie, Hans Abergos, who excitedly promoted this book in our uni.

Ella, Julien, Kaycee and Jeanne, thank you for fangirling with me over this book and constantly sharing it online.

The Supangan cousins, Leonard, Leanne, Louisse, Sam, Shaina, Sofia, Chiara, Marc, and Fionia, thank you for always making me laugh whenever I don't feel like smiling anymore. You guys are my inspiration.

To Sandra, Blessilee, Cheska, Ezekiel, Christian and Matt—thank you for being my eating-buddies!

To my English teachers & professors, especially Sir Michael, thank you for making me appreciate the literary world more. I really hope I didn't disappoint you all haha

To everyone at Typewriter Pub especially my ever-awesome agent, AJ Dane, and amazing editors, Precious and Klare, thank you for seeing the potential of this book and for helping me whip it into a published novel.

And to YOU, my beloved reader. Thank you so much for choosing this story.

# AUTHOR'S NOTE

Thank you so much for reading *A Hundred Weddings*! I can't express how grateful I am for reading something that was once just a thought inside my head.

Please feel free to send me an email. Just know that my publisher filters these emails. Good news is always welcome.
jessica_schreave@awesomeauthors.org

Sign up for my blog for updates and freebies!
jessica-schreave.awesomeauthors.org

One last thing: I'd love to hear your thoughts on the book. Please leave a review on Amazon or Goodreads because I just love reading your comments and getting to know you!


Can't wait to hear from you!

*Jessica Schreave*

# ABOUT THE AUTHOR

Jessica Schreave is a young author who is still clawing her way out of college. She adores little kids so much and aims to build her own daycare center one day. She also loves reading books of various genres while eating chocolates. Jessica is currently living with supportive yet strict parents and a visual artist sister in Santa Rosa.